MISTER NIGHTMARE

OTHER WORKS BY ARIEL RAE

Blood Hunted Series
Blood Hunted #1
Blood Trail #2
Mister Nightmare #2.5
Blood Queen #3

Drag Her Down Duet
Drag Her Down #1
To The Fires Below #2

MISTER NIGHTMARE

ARIEL RAE

SPACE FOX
BOOKS LLC

This book is a work of fiction.

Cover design by Rachel A. Desilets

ISBN-13: 979-8-9888483-5-6

Space Fox Books, LLC
Paperback Second Edition: 2024
spacefoxbooks.com

Sure, tiger, do whatever you want. Build your own world.
But save enough space for a nightmare.

JULES

The music stopped, and the disgruntled, drunk patrons let out a collective groan. For the last few hours, my head had pounded and hadn't stopped, despite the medication Finian kept on hand for his employees. He seemed cross when he passed me the pill, like he wanted to say something further about my request, but his mouth clamped shut soon after. He had been unusually quiet since.

I appreciated my job and my boss, because plenty of humans didn't have the same protection I did. Though, that protection came from forcing myself to keep up a continuously cheery attitude around drunk humans and Fae who tried way too hard to get me to submit to their whims and fancies. Raskos kept us on a low dose of Faerie wine throughout our shifts, so Fae couldn't compel us. Raskos didn't allow compulsion in his club, but he didn't take chances with his employees. While his court might not have been the most luxurious, it held stability.

In the five years since his club opened, he had only lost one employee, which was a good record. Plenty of other employers fared much worse. I was grateful, even if my headache was making me anything but.

This, however, was my favorite part of the day. The lights blared to life, and the music crumbled into oblivion. It left the patrons dazed and confused, but they funneled toward the exits, sometimes with the help of the burly doorman Finian kept employed. Once everyone was out of the building, the doors slid shut and the locks clicked into place.

As soon as the club was empty, I could breathe for the first time this evening. With only the closing tasks left, I felt a burst of energy, and without the pounding music, the ache in my head waned.

I walked around the floor, grabbed the empty glasses as fast as possible, shoved them into the dishwasher, and got the bar cleaned for the next round of patrons.

Once the bar was tidy and the glasses gleamed, I turned toward Finian's office. We received a final dose of Faerie wine for the night. It was for our safety net. While most Fae didn't try things within Finian's court, he didn't want to remove all caution. The patrons of the club knew we were off limits, but Finian knew better than to trust every Fae. He had all sorts of people who came to his club—good and bad.

Honestly, he was more thoughtful than most men I had dated, and I was grateful to have stumbled upon his club three years ago. My life had been a chaotic mess before finding a job here. Sure, there were people who had it worse—but I could never keep a steady job. Soon after I received one, a Fae would grow curt with me and dismiss me without reason. I never knew if I would be employed the next day.

One time, a Fae told me he never wanted to see me again, effective immediately. When I took a step closer to him, he shrank back, shrieking for me to leave. There was no telling what went through a Fae's mind, but I wanted a job. I wasn't the Fae Slayer or another kind of monster. I was just me. Boring and human— nothing in the scope of the Fae's lives.

Squinting, I noticed one last glass on the other side of the large, empty dance floor. Most people didn't use the booths near the entrance, because it wasn't easy to cross the floor with drinks in hand and not spill them everywhere. Though sometimes humans would try to bring their Fae lovers drinks to keep them satisfied.

I told Finian he should invest in shatterproof glass, as he'd probably save a lot of money if he didn't have to keep replacing the damn things.

On my way across the room, I froze after I got halfway. There was a man in the club. I glanced around, because even my coworker Katie had disappeared from the room. The doorman was missing, too. Katie not being here for closing duties was nothing new, as she often had several private moments with some Fae or another toward the end of the night.

"Can I help you?" I asked as I approached the table.

"Perhaps." The man kicked out the chair across from where he sat. He lounged back in the cushioned booth. His hair was a perfect silver, falling just shy of his ears with a part off to the side. He had piercing gray eyes that lanced through me. His jaw pulsed, bringing attention to his angular cheekbones and chiseled chin. "Why don't you take a seat?" His voice cascaded over my skin and for the first time in my life, I realized why Finian was so worried about his employees being compelled by the Fae. This man's voice sank into my skin, surrounding me with a lullaby that promised everything under the sun.

And I found myself wanting it.

I sank into the chair across from him as I watched him warily.

"What's your name?"

"Jules."

"Jules. Do you have a last name?"

"Senado."

"Interesting."

"What is?"

"Not something I expected to hear. Having a surname is interesting."

I blinked at that, as all the Fae I had ever met had a surname, and humans had one as a given. "Who are you?"

He arched an eyebrow. "I would think with the close eye Finian keeps on you, he would have warned you to stay away from me."

I shook my head, finding myself leaning forward. Snapping out of it, I stood up and offered my hand. "I'll take your glass. We're closed."

He smiled, pressing the cup into my palm. He put his other hand on top of mine, keeping us locked together. "I am Nightmare, but you can call me Night."

"What kind of name is that?"

"One I deserve." His eyes flashed bright blue before settling back to silver. "You can ask Finian about me, as I'm sure he would love to hear that we met. I'll see you around, Jules. I plan on staying in town."

I blinked, but he was already gone. Disappeared into nothing. The Fae could move fast, but nowhere near impossible to track. I didn't hear a door so much as close. It was like he... teleported. But that was impossible, right?

Dazed, I stumbled back to the bar and tossed the glass into the washer, slamming it shut. I walked into Finian's office where he was readily counting out coin.

"Jules," he said, moss eyes brightening as he caught sight of me. The smile cresting his lips warmed the room. "Close the door. Come in."

"Did everyone else go home?"

He waved a hand as if it didn't bother him either way. "I gave everyone their final dose, so it doesn't matter what they do now. You made quite a lot tonight. I was counting out your tips, if you don't mind waiting." His long, delicate fingers gestured to the seat across from him.

I ran my hand over my opposite arm, wondering how to mention what had just happened to him. Finian frowned upon patrons staying after last call, and I didn't want to get someone banned from the club when they did nothing offensive. "There was a man in the club after we closed."

"Did you get one of the guys to kick him out?"

"No, I mean... He left, but he sounded like he knew you."

Finian stopped counting and dropped the coin on the table. His eyes rose to meet mine. "Who did they say they were?"

"Night?"

He blinked, and at first, I thought he might not have heard me, so I opened my mouth to speak again, but he shook his head. "He didn't do anything, did he? Did he try to..." Finian gestured to his head.

"No, I don't think so. I felt... Well, I felt strange, and I don't think I've felt like that around another Fae before, but he handed me his glass and left."

"Did he touch you?"

"What?"

Finian stood up, hands slamming down on the table and scattering some coin out from under him. "Did he touch you?" His face became a darker shade, colored with red.

"Not like that. I took his glass."

"I didn't mean like *that*." He breathed out sharply and pressed his fingers to the bridge of his nose.

"I've never seen you like this. What's wrong?"

"Nightmare is a Dream Walker. He's not Fae." The last words escaped his lips as if they pained him.

"What?"

Finian sighed and crossed to the other side of the table in a flash. He grabbed my hands in between his, running his thumb over my knuckles. "I would like you to stay here tonight."

We had talked about this before—the other two times he had asked me out. It was to dinner, as a date, but I wanted to keep our relationship professional. He was my boss, after all. While I found him attractive, desperately so, I needed this job.

"Finian, I—"

"Jules, he feeds off dreams—nightmares. He touched you so he could get into your head. What he ends up seeing, what he makes you witness... It can be very traumatic and horrible. I'd like it if you stayed here tonight, so I can be there in case..." He dropped my hands and opened the space between us. "I understand if you don't want to. It was forward of me to ask."

I swallowed, feeling a hollow pit in my stomach. I was tired, and while I wanted to go home and sleep in my bed, I trusted Finian not to try anything if Night decided to *feed* off me. What a horrible image that brought about.

What would it be like to be someone's food?

"How bad are these nightmares?"

Finian's face remained drawn. "It's not something I would wish on my worst enemy."

I could sense his fear. Whatever Night could do was dangerous enough to set Finian on edge. I swallowed, not knowing if I should cross this line with him, but it also felt like being alone wouldn't be the smartest decision. "You have a guest room, right?" Because if I had to stay in the same room as him, I would risk being by myself.

Finian smiled and pushed his hair behind his ears. The brown locks had come loose from his topknot and rolled in waves down to his shoulders. "Yes, I have a guest room. And I'll be here for whatever you need, even if I'm asleep. Okay?"

I nodded, feeling better knowing we would have space between us. "I need to go home and get some clothes."

"I have some clothes in the dresser. If none of them are to your liking, I'll walk with you. It's safer that way. And a toothbrush, if you want it. New."

"You seem awfully prepared."

"I'd rather be prepared than be left wanting. So, you'll stay?" The way he said it was so full of hope, as if he would wait for the rest of his life to hear my answer.

"Show me the wardrobe, and we'll see if I have to head home for supplies."

Finian gestured for me to follow him. His apartment was off the backside of the club, up another set of stairs. As for the few other courts I had seen, most Lords and Ladies had a massive mansion to their name. Not Finian. He lived above the club, and his apartment spanned the entire top floor of Ceilidh. He lived for this place.

The moment he opened his front door, I was caught up in the smell of him. Fae always had a scent but working in a bar brought plenty of pheromones from both sides, I had never differentiated their smells. His was sweet, as if I had stepped foot into a bakery.

For some reason, I had expected Finian to smell like leather and spice, but maybe that was due to him wearing a long leather jacket.

While he had an air of importance about him, he did his best to blend into the crowd he served. He wore his jacket, a simple shirt underneath, and worn pants. Everything about his look screamed the opposite of sweet, but it wafted over me, making my insides relax.

"Welcome to my home."

Through my time working with Finian, I never imagined myself up here. "It's lovely. Thank you."

His open floor plan showed off his gourmet kitchen and cozy reading nook. He had a television and a large collection of movies on display. Finian watched movies. *Interesting.* The Fae had never seemed fascinated by our history or pop culture, but Finian's film collection appeared to be a cherished feature in his home.

I couldn't remember the last time I sat down to watch a movie. Idle time and electricity became a luxury most couldn't afford in the fallout. As much as Finian took care of his court to keep the wilds out, the electricity outside of Ceilidh's walls was spotty. He was trying to fix it, but he had never come up with a solution. The war destroyed plenty of the infrastructure, and as other courts rose around Ceilidh, they drained further resources from the area. Finian's court consisted of his club and the hollowed-out lands, which were still recovering in the aftermath.

Instead, he focused most of his energy on the club, hoping the extra coin would eventually be enough to fix the rest of the court.

"This way." He led me to the left door off the living room, opened it, and gestured to the guest room. "I am right across the living room. Let me know if you need anything, okay?"

"I might want to eat, if it's not too much to ask."

The corner of his lips rose as his eyes swirled to life. "I can put something together for you."

"Thanks. I mean it." I wandered into the room and opened the wardrobe and dresser. Finian hadn't been lying. There was so much *stuff* in here. Men's and women's clothes, a variety of undergarments, deodorants, and cleaning products. It was like a luxury hotel. And the bed… it was a giant king-sized canopy bed with a huge fluffy comforter. Normally, such a thing wouldn't be necessary in the middle of summer, but Finian's club was always at a pleasant temperature. People said it was from his magic.

Apparently, I was staying the night. I was about to change and enter the kitchen to see if I could help him with food, but I heard hushed voices from the living room. Narrowing my gaze, I wondered if he had someone else staying here with him. It wouldn't matter either way, but I didn't want to intrude.

Instead of barging into the conversation, I decided to shower first. I smelled like stale beer and fried food, and it would be worth the extra time to get myself cleaned up, especially since I didn't need to take the fifteen-minute walk home.

Finian Raskos

The thought of her in my apartment, eating my food, wearing my clothes, awoke something feral inside me I thought I had shed long ago. It took effort to not use my power on the humans around me, as influencing them sometimes happened accidentally. I never wanted my employees to feel forced into an uncomfortable situation, so I avoided proposals. The invitation to stay here bordered my rules. Tonight, I had watched my words, making sure I never pushed her with my magic.

Holding back my power felt like wrapping my body in chains, but it was worth it to ensure my employees' safety.

When Jules agreed to stay in my guest room, a part of me nearly died of shock. Jules had been unobtainable. I had asked her to enjoy a morning coffee with me after a particularly late night performing inventory, and I had asked her to dinner before one of her shifts. At those moments she had been on Faerie wine. She could answer me honestly, and every time, she turned me down.

But Nightmare walked into our lives, and she said yes.

Opening the fridge, I pulled out cheeses, meats, and several fruits. I shoved the door closed with my hip and jumped back as my eyes met with Night's fierce gray ones. He looked disgustingly healthy from his feeding off Scarlet the Fae Slayer. I worried Devoss may have my head over the whole stunt, and as Night gazed at me, I realized my mistake putting those two in touch.

He had gleaned way too much power from her.

"Get the fuck out of my apartment." I dropped the array of food onto the counter and pulled out a cutting board. "In fact, get out of my club and stay out of my life." My magic pulsed around me, but it rolled off his skin with an annoying dissolution, exactly how it felt when I tried to use it on Scarlet.

Stupid Dream Walkers.

"Now, is that any way to treat a friend?" His arms crossed over his chest as he leaned against my counter, far enough away to avoid being an immediate threat, but close enough to prove he could become one in a second.

"How did you get here?"

"I shadow walked, obviously. And I touched her. Where she goes, I go. You have a nice place here, *Finian*."

"Don't you dare."

"Isn't that what she calls you?" He stood up straighter, and I took a few hesitant steps back. "What do you prefer? Finian or Raskos?"

"Raskos to you," I spat.

He placed his hand on his chest and sucked in a breath. "I am wounded. I thought we were closer than that."

"Closer? Night, before you were creeping around my club, you terrorized my court in Faerie. How am I supposed to... *live* knowing you are within spitting distance?"

"You have delicious subjects. What can I say?" His eyes darted toward the closed door. The water turned on, and I hoped Jules's showering would buy me time to get this asshole out of my apartment. Knowing he had touched her made my skin crawl.

I snatched a knife from the block and brandished it in front of me. Night stared at the gleaming steel. "You touch her again, and you die."

"Big words from someone with little power in his bloodline."

"Get out of my fucking apartment," I hissed again. "Unless you want to lose an eye."

He held up his hands, lip twitching with amusement. His eyes twinkled, and I hated the smugness on his face. "You know it's too late, right? The moment I put my hands on her, I had control, and now I always will."

"Night." I stepped forward, holding out my weapon. "If I blink and you have not vacated the space in my apartment, I will kill you." An empty threat, and he knew it.

His hand reached toward me, and I slashed the knife across his palm. He caught the blade. The metal scraped against his bone as he ripped the weapon out of my hand and tossed it across the room. "Use your magic, *Finian*. Prove to me you can protect her. If you can make me leave right now, I won't have a delicious snack tonight." He licked his lips.

My magic flared around us. It muted the sound of the shower and shifted the atmosphere. I clenched my fists at my sides, wishing I had any hope of summoning an element.

"The thing is, I've been alive longer than you can remember. Which means I've seen your line. You are sympathizers. Your ancestors fell in love with humans, more than once."

My jaw clenched.

"There's nothing wrong with it, Finian. Quite the opposite.

Your family felt a certain connection with the creatures, but it did harm your line. You may have some Fae powers, but you are nowhere near as strong as you would have been with a full-blooded line."

"And you?" I snarled. "You're better because you're the *last of your kind?*" Forgetting myself, I stepped toward him. "You are on the verge of extinction, and you dare to challenge me in my own home?!"

Night moved again, getting within an inch of my face, but I slammed my forearm into his wrist. My leather jacket prevented our skin from touching. "So protective of yourself, but I wonder what will that cost her tonight? I need to eat." His eyes flashed blue as his hunger set in.

"Find somewhere else. Go to Lady Burke's." It would take out two problems at the same time if he listened to me.

"Her court is boring. They are already living their worse versions of themselves. Your court is... well, people have hope, but they have also lost it among their own regrets. It's quaint. They could fix their problems if they stopped over-thinking. It's a fantastic place for me."

"And her? Why are you making this personal?"

"You said it yourself. I am on the verge of extinction. What the fuck do I have left to lose?" He shrugged, and when I blinked, he had left the apartment.

Or at least my kitchen.

I rushed to the guest room and hesitated in the living room. Barging in would be a huge invasion of her privacy, but I had to know she was okay. "Jules?" I extended my magic, making my voice carry on the airwaves so it was like I was standing outside the shower.

"Finian?" she gasped. "Where are you? It's like—"

"Sorry, I wanted to make sure you were okay."

"Am I taking too long? I forgot to ask about the water or—"

"You're fine. Is there, uh, any cheese you don't like?"

"If there's mold on it, I don't want it."

I lowered my brows, but nodded. "Okay. I'll have dinner ready in a few minutes."

"Sounds good. And... thanks."

I listened to the water cascading off her skin and pattering against the acrylic shower floor. Forcing out a breath, I cleaned up the blue blood, the knife, and the evidence of Night's appearance. Then, I set about making the plate, slicing up everything and placing it on a tray.

Once she was out of the shower, she joined me in the kitchen. Her long, dark brown hair hung in loose wet waves around her shoulders, and her warm brown eyes considered the tray and me. "It looks nice, Finian. Thanks."

She was in one of my shirts and pants. Granted, they weren't *mine*, but she had chosen a loose fitted t-shirt and some flannel pants that I owned. Seeing her in typical male clothes made me swallow on a dry throat.

The way she said my name also made me want to shut down the club for three weeks and give her my complete and undivided attention for as long as she would allow me to. No human ever had this effect on me.

Over the years, I had never used my magic against humans. I preferred genuine interactions over platitudes. Something about Jules was a challenge, and perhaps it was because for as long as I had known her, she had never jumped into bed with other Fae or humans who had caught her eye. Sure, she spent hours flirting, and maybe she did things off hours, but while she was in my club, she kept things professional.

14

Never crossing the line with me, either. Which frustrated me to no end, because my baser instincts screamed at me to make her mine.

I breathed out as she took a cracker and a slice of cheese and popped them into her mouth. Night was right. My lineage was full of human sympathizers, which was exactly why my magic wasn't as strong as it should have been. The last thing I needed was to dilute it more.

And yet…

"I didn't think your apartment would be so…"

"Sparse? Empty?"

"Homey. It has just enough to feel comfortable, but not overwhelming. I thought you might have been more ostentatious. But why do you have so many extra things?"

"In the guest room?"

She nodded.

I shrugged. "In case I ever needed to shelter an employee from anyone else."

"Are you sheltering another person tonight?"

I shook my head. "Why would you ask?"

"I thought I heard you talking to someone before I got in the shower." She shrugged, delicate shoulders rising underneath the shirt. What I wouldn't give to strip her of those sleeves. "I didn't want to interrupt, so I took a shower instead."

"That was nothing. Not someone who was welcome to stay."

"I don't want to be in your way."

"You're not." I watched as she ate, her fingers picking with extra care at the plate. Being able to nourish her aroused pride within me. I wanted to do this every day. "Where do you stay?"

"My home?"

"Yes, is it safe?"

"It's within the court boundaries, so it's safe enough."

I hated that answer. The court outside of Ceilidh was not like other places. We didn't have the walls or the reconstructed town, but we had a large force of Fae willing to protect the club. We had my wards, which my magic fueled regularly. While the roving bands of hoswisps kept a wide berth around my court because of my shields, there was always the chance one of them would cross the border I had created.

My magic allowed for a few things, and one of them was a repellent. At the least, I had that going for me. It unfortunately did not seem to work on Dream Walkers, else I would have never seen Night's face again. I tried casting him out, but for some reason, my magic seemed to draw him in, like he was attracted to the sense of danger my power created.

Ceilidh worked because people feared me. That fear was a mask. It was an impression of my magic. In reality, I would be helpless in a direct attack from any Fae or human. I could create a shield, but shields meant nothing in the long run. Night could have easily overpowered me, yet he didn't.

"Tell me about Faerie. We've never really sat down and talked about your history."

"There's not much to say."

Jules gave me a look that suggested I had plenty to say.

I appreciated her thinking as much, so I tried my best to conjure a story from yesteryear. "Before the king cast the curse, my court was in this valley called Hydref. It was stunning in the springtime, with wild blooms cascading down the countryside and a lush landscape. I think you would have liked it. We had a few patrols to keep the hoswisps in check, but they did not have the population of today. We also had water Fae to put out any fire from the pauldrins. Other creatures roamed too, all of which lived in symbiosis. One reason why the hoswisps started multiplying was because the royal assassins overhunted the caltula population to extinction." I let out a breath, remembering how everything had cascaded into decay soon after that. The ecosystem unbalanced further after the king's curse. Devoss had never taken part in the hunts, but his line was guilty of destroying the world.

Especially his late father.

"Tell me something good about Hydref," Jules said, taking a grape off one cluster. She rolled it between her fingers.

"We had this monastery that represented the Mother."

Jules practically choked on the grape as she let out a laugh. "I'm sorry, a monastery? As in monks and worship and stuff?"

"Not quite so human a comparison, but it was a place of reflection for those who needed it."

"And you went from that to running a nightclub?"

I shrugged. "The landscape in Hydref lent itself to be a more spiritual place. When the wilds were in sync, it had this energy about it. You couldn't deny the draw to a sense of oneness."

"Did you worship too?"

"Most Fae did to the Mother, back when the magic was stronger, before the curse."

She nodded, chewed, and swallowed. Her warm eyes roamed over me. I wanted to put my thumb against her neck and feel her throat move underneath my grip. "Things I never would have guessed about you, Finian."

I ran my hands through my hair, realizing how messy it had become. Normally, I pulled it back, up and away, but toward the end of the night, I allowed it to hang wildly around my shoulders. "Would you believe it if I told you before I took over my court, I was in training to give my life to the Mother?"

That laugh sounded from her again. "Not that you are corrupt or anything like that. It's just… you always seem so…"

My lips quirked. "What do I seem, Jules?"

Her lips paused over another grape, leaving them parted enough to show me her pink tongue. My thoughts were getting the better of me. "Like a man who knows what he wants."

"You know most people don't call us men?"

"Why is that? I never understood it."

"Because we're Fae."

"You're still a man."

"Male. Not a man. I am not *human*." My eyes flashed in a reminder. My magic swelled into the space between us.

She shrugged. "It doesn't make a difference. We all have sex the same way."

My jaw hit the floor.

"What? I'm not some innocent girl. I know how sex works."

"And you have had sex with a Fae?"

She looked down at the tray and shifted in her seat. "Once."

I fought the urge to grip her chin and force her to look at me, because something in the way she spoke the word made me want to kill whoever made her feel ashamed of her history. But there was another part of me that enjoyed how she had only been with one other Fae. Only one.

Maybe two.

Someday.

"What happened?" I asked.

"I don't know. He made it seem like… I did something wrong. But I slept with a few other men too, and it all felt the same."

"Sex with the Fae felt the same as humans for you?" I tilted my head to the side. "That's unusual."

"See? It's like there's something wrong with me, and it's not appealing to go into sex thinking I am broken."

"That's not what I meant." I held up my hands at her cross expression. "I'm sorry. Just most... most people, outside of the Fae Slayer, don't want to stay away from Fae after they've slept with one. A lot of humans describe it as euphoric, which is why I thought you might have never slept with any of us."

"Well, I have, and I don't see how you are different from anyone else."

"I would certainly be different." The words tore from my mouth without thought.

Jules's eyes went round and wide as she considered the meaning. "Finian..."

I blinked, forcing my heart to slow. "No pressure. I want it to be clear, however, my offer is there if you ever want it." I took a slice of meat from the tray and swallowed it. "We don't have to talk about it further, and you don't have to answer me. I had to say it." More like it slipped out on my traitorous tongue.

"Okay."

"Okay." I nodded.

"I mean, okay. As in, maybe I'll consider it. I don't know, maybe I missed something the first time. The guy was hot, you know? I mean, all Fae are. But maybe I missed something because I didn't have any connection to him."

A slight bump sounded from her room. My eyes darted to her door, but Jules had heard nothing. My jaw clenched. *Night*. He was not going to leave her alone. While I claimed my apartment was safe, he was anything but.

"Sorry if that's weird. Gosh, I am making you sound like an experiment instead of a person with actual feelings. Ugh, forget I said anything."

Refocusing, I grabbed her hand so she wouldn't misunderstand my silence. "I am shocked, but not disappointed in the slightest. If you feel you could be comfortable enough with me to experiment, I will not say no." Her hands were still in mine, and she squeezed my fingers back. "And did you insinuate that we have a connection?" The corners of my mouth quirked.

Jules rolled her eyes and yanked her hands back. "We were having a moment."

I smiled in full. "Were we?"

"Yes, we were. But it's over." She stuck her tongue out, but a delicate blush rose to her cheeks.

"Well, if you want any other moments, you know where to find me." I gestured to my room. She glanced at the door for a second before pressing her eyes shut. It felt like she was envisioning the possibilities behind her lids, and it made me ache to show her the passion that welled within me.

When she opened her eyes, her gaze steadied on me. "I will think about it. For tonight, I am thankful for this."

Her thankfulness was going to disappear if she learned any of the thoughts roiling in my brain. They ranged from shoving her against the refrigerator while ripping off her clothes to bending her over the very stool she sat on and having my way with her until her voice was so hoarse, she couldn't scream my name any longer.

I swallowed. "Anytime, Jules."

Three

NIGHTMARE

Raskos was becoming a problem. While contemplating my next move, I watched from the fire escape across the street. I had planned to follow Jules home. I had planned to figure out what it was about her. There was something inside this woman, something which had brought me to this forsaken court, leading me straight back into Raskos's life.

Not that I minded the last part.

In true form, the male had been livid when I showed up at his club. We had history, him and I, and not a very good one. His court almost turned against him in Faerie after he was unable to get rid of me by using his power. I had fed on his subjects. A lot. Terrorized them, really. And here we were on a new planet, threatening to be on the precipice of the same problem. It was no wonder why he had slashed my palm open.

The metal knife had scraped against my bone. It was an annoyance more than anything.

21

He meant business when it came to keeping her safe, even if he didn't have enough power to back up his arrogance. I looked at the wound on my hand, which was already stitching itself together. I could feel my energy draining, even with the Fae Slayer's nightmares fueling my body.

I needed more. I always needed more.

My gaze shifted back to the window, where Jules leaned over the kitchen bar and plucked another grape from the cluster. She popped it into her mouth and laughed at something Raskos said. A smile quirked on his lips, but there was an unsettled furrow in his brow.

He should be worried, because that woman would be mine no matter how much he tried to protect her. I had already gotten inside her head, inched into the edge of her consciousness. Now, I wanted her to go to sleep so I could see what dreams she invented before they became my nightmares. Dream walking was easier if I was touching her, but I only needed the first touch to establish a connection. Still, I found myself wanting to be nearby, to keep an eye on what was mine.

Raskos had created a challenge, a game, and I was not here to lose. This was also how his magic made me feel. He tried to create a barrier to keep me out, but it only ignited the passion to stay within the confines of his court. The more he pushed against me, the stronger the fear welled inside me, and the more I wanted to linger. His magic created artificial fear, and I reveled in it.

After a few more moments of watching, I grew tired of Raskos having all the fun. He had lured her into his apartment, but I refused to walk away without my piece. Of course, I would have her as soon as she fell asleep, but that wasn't enough.

Slipping into the shadows, I crossed the street and reappeared in the guest bedroom inside his apartment. The whole place smelled like him, and I prowled around the room. He had stocked everything, making it clear to any guest who came here that they were more than welcome. I scowled, because at this rate, Jules may not go home. If she had everything she needed inside this room and this apartment, why would she bother going back to her place?

His apartment held the air of royalty, even if the furniture was a little sparse for my tastes. I rifled through the drawers and closet, admiring the array of items he had to choose from. It was a comfort, really, because he hadn't done this for her. He had done this for any guest who stepped foot into his apartment.

I breathed easier.

My eyes caught on the folded clothes on the bed. I shifted my gaze to the door. No movement, and small murmurs still sounded on the other side. Jules laughed again at something he said, and my insides turned cold. I crossed the room and picked up her shirt.

It smelled like her—apples roasting over a fire. I inhaled her scent, and in doing so, a smaller piece of fabric fell out. Curling my fists, I smiled. While Raskos might have her inside his home, I was going to take home a very different prize. I snatched up her panties, stuffed them into my pocket, and walked through the shadows to the other side of town.

If I had thought that Raskos's apartment was sparse, he had nothing on the complete absence of items inside Jules's home. She lived in a hole in the wall apartment on the opposite end of the town. The place smelled like her instead of the soap that Raskos provided, but it was run down. If he knew she was living like this, he never would let her out of his sight.

The apartment walls were crumbling. It was a glorified closet— one large room with a tiny kitchen added on as an afterthought. The bathroom was even smaller. I walked around, obsessing over her choice of colors—grays for everything. It was like she knew I was coming for her, and it pleased me.

Though, I still couldn't put my finger on *why* I cared so much. Normally, I got into someone's head, then rummaged around their worst nightmares. Their nightmares satiated me, and once fed, I got out. As I ran my finger along the laminate counter and pulled back a layer of grime, I realized that this wouldn't do.

If I was going to chase this woman down in her dreams and haunt her nightmares, then she needed better living conditions. As I waited for her to fall asleep at Raskos's apartment across the court, I cleaned hers from top to bottom. She would walk inside, and her heart would pound at the thought of someone else being inside her space. She would feel like it was an invasion.

Good. I wanted her to be scared. I craved it more than the blood running through my veins. By the time she drifted to sleep, I had organized her place. Every stain was gone from the walls and all the grime was scraped off the cabinets.

And she was missing several more panties from her hamper. If she hadn't wanted a Dream Walker in her house, she should have never touched my hand. Raskos certainly avoided me.

I shadow walked back to the guest bedroom and waited for her steady breathing to even out. Once she was in a dream, I smirked. While I didn't need to touch her once she was asleep, I wanted to. Stepping out of the shadows, I stood over her and pushed her hair away from her face. I drifted into the darkness with her. Her dream surrounded me as I transitioned into the other world.

I frowned and growled instantly. We were in a storeroom filled with bottles of beer, wine, and other liquors. It smelled like the club, and I realized this was her version of whatever storage was back at Ceilidh.

But what was making my fists clench was Raskos's hands wandering through Jules' hair. He released her locks from the ponytail on top of her head, letting her dark hair trail over his fingers. He brushed his lips along her neck. She gasped and arched into him. Her eyes closed as she lost herself in the feeling of his body.

"Fuck this," I growled. It took me no time to cross the distance between myself and Raskos. Twisting his head to the side, I watched as he dropped dead at my feet. A strange feeling welled inside me from seeing him die like that, but this was a dream.

My dream now.

Jules gasped, but it wasn't one of horror. Her eyes widened in disbelief and shock, but none of the terror that usually struck dreamers traced its way through her irises. "Night?"

"Obviously," I snarled.

Her eyes flitted to Raskos's prone form on the tile floor, brown eyes assessing. "He's not really dead."

"Oh, he is."

"No, he's not. This isn't real." She pressed her hand on my chest. "But... it *feels* real."

I grabbed her hand in mine, crushing her fingers together. "It is real. He's dead, and I'm going to leave you here with the cleanup. Everyone will blame you for his death."

I waited for it to hit me, any sense of being full, of my veins becoming satisfied from the most recent meal. I wanted it to expand my chest and make me feel like I could breathe again. Most people were easy—show them their worst nightmare, and their fear electrified me.

But from her—nothing. She stared at me with her hand pressed against my chest. Her palm was so warm, fingers so light against me. The way she looked at me, it was... wholesome.

"Why aren't you scared?" I growled.

"Because this is a dream." She took a step back and waved her hands. To my absolute horror, Raskos's head settled back on the right way, and he sat up, looking dazed, but still very much so alive. "And if it is a dream, then I can do whatever I want." Jules closed the distance between us, a smile curling up her lips. "Tell me, Night. What do you want?"

I was hungry, and my jaw clenched. I could only think of one thing. "Food."

"Can I be of service?" She bit her lower lip, sinking her teeth into her skin. She probably thought I was a dream too, that she was caving into some fantasy she had about Raskos and me getting with her.

My jaw worked, not sure how to feel about this new development. "And how will you help me if there is nothing here that will terrify you?"

"Because you feed on fear?"

I nodded, pulling her the rest of the way into me. Raskos remained on the floor, forgotten by Jules's subconscious mind. I pushed us back until she was jammed between the shelves and my body.

"Yes, and there's a reason you should be afraid right now."

"And why is that?"

"Because I am *very* real." I pressed my hand against her throat, feeling her pulse racing against my thumb. Normally, I didn't get involved like this. Their nightmares would take shape around me, and I would fill myself. But now, this felt personal. This felt like I needed to.

She was preventing me from eating.

And I was *starving*.

I squeezed.

Her breath raced out of her, and our surroundings shifted, like she was trying to run away from me. Eyes widening, she moved the shelves away from her. Jules stumbled backward a few feet out from my grasp.

Fear rose around her.

"How is this possible?"

"I'm a Dream Walker." I prowled toward her. "Surely Raskos mentioned that?"

Nodding, she staggered back a step or two. Her confusion rose around us—Raskos had told her, but she didn't understand what it meant, not really. Not until now. Her dream kept changing shapes around us, and she conjured several obstacles in between us. I removed them, because she had no control here. I wouldn't allow her to be. Dreams were my domain. Dreams belonged to my race.

"Why me?" As she backed up farther, I projected myself behind her. Her back bumped against my chest. Her body went rigid. I wrapped my arms around her as she let out a scream. My hand clamped on her mouth as she tried to kick me.

"Because you smell *really* good." I ran my tongue against her cheek as her body trembled underneath my touch. My lips brushed her skin. "Jules, I must ask you something important. If I told you to run right now, would you?"

She nodded.

I smiled. "Perfect."

As I released my hold on her, I watched her scurry away from me, knocking things into my path as she went. I breathed in, sucking life into my bones. I licked my lips, because now it was time for the chase.

And I loved a good chase.

JULES

The moment he let go of me, I dashed away, forcing objects to collapse behind me. My logical brain knew I had to wake up, but there was this other part of me that felt oddly... alive. The fear was real. I didn't know what would happen if he caught me.

But there was something *exciting* behind it.

Night had stared at me with hunger, and no one else had ever consumed me with a simple look. The depth of his gaze was intense, rolling over my skin like I might ignite. It was unlike the looks Finian gave me, which were coated in respect and awe. Night looked like he wanted to *eat* me.

Which, at the moment, he probably did.

Like I had told my boss, I worried there was something wrong with me. The sex I had with the one Fae had been just... okay. Nothing life altering, nothing new.

I wanted the mind-numbing, body-exploding, heart-stopping

sex other people said happened with the Fae. I wanted to feel myself come apart from an orgasm so extreme that I forgot how to breathe.

And in this dream, when I had placed my hand on Night's chest, something dangerous prickled underneath the surface. There was an emptiness inside him—hunger and desire so strong, it acted like a current. His *need* contributed to my fear because I now understood how deep it went.

He would stop at nothing to get me where he wanted me, and his desire was insatiable.

Every impression I had gathered from the single touch. It might have been dream logic, but I knew it to be true.

Regardless, he was a stranger to me. I couldn't do this with a stranger, could I?

Maybe I wanted to.

The club dissolved around us, and I dashed through the streets to avoid my chaser. Glancing over my shoulder, he wasn't there. I wasn't stupid enough to think he stopped or I had outmaneuvered him. Night made it very clear—I wasn't to get away.

As I tore down another alley, I focused on the world around me. This was a dream—*my* dream—and I could control it to an extent. I created this world, and I could shift it. I made walls around myself, blocking my path with a maze within the world. The farther I ran, the less my heart pounded against my ribcage. After another few moments, I slowed to a walk, erecting more walls just in case. I took a few stabilizing breaths and turned the next corner.

I yelped.

Night smirked. He crossed his arms over his chest, leaning against the brick wall as if he hadn't run for a single second. He reached up and ruffled his silver hair, watching me with his blue, blazing eyes. Had I been imagining the gray in his eyes earlier? It also looked like his pallor changed.

"Did your eyes change color?"

His irises flashed. "They do when I am hungry."

"And now?"

"Starving."

I swallowed, wondering if it would hurt. My pulse thrummed. "Are you feeding from me right now?"

"Absolutely." His eyes narrowed as he closed the distance between us. I backed up against the wall, feeling the cool bricks digging into my skin. "Wouldn't you, if presented with something delicious?"

"I wouldn't know."

"What do you call them… vampires?" He smiled, showing his gleaming white teeth with absolutely no sharpness. "I'm like that, except it's your fear I find irresistible."

"What happens if I stop being afraid?"

"I can always make you afraid." He spun a lock of my hair around his fingers. "If running is boring you, we could change to something else."

"Do you always get… this close?"

He frowned. "No, not always. It depends on the nightmare. Most of the time, I'm an observer."

"But you got involved with me."

"Yes."

"Because of Finian?" I couldn't help asking, because it felt like this had nothing to do with me and everything to do with the Fae Lord.

His jaw worked. He ran a hand through his silver hair. Everything about him screamed danger, from the sharp angles of his cheekbones to the lean muscle of his shoulders. While he looked human, his muted skin and ethereal eyes gave him an otherworldly appearance.

And it stirred something in me.

"Are you jealous of him?"

The frown marring his lips told me that whatever game he had been playing ended the moment I made the suggestion. He leaned impossibly close, his breath icing over my skin. "Jules."

"Yeah?"

"If you don't scream and mean it right now, I might just kill you." Out of nowhere, a knife appeared in his hand, poised straight over my heart.

As the metal dug into my flesh, a scream ripped through my chest.

"Get the fuck out of here, Night!" Finian's voice. The nightmare faded, leaving me with heavy lids. "Jules? Wake up." His warm hand dusted over my forehead, smoothing my hair away from my face as I opened my eyes. "Jules," he said, my name soothing on his tongue. He said it with absolute conviction, like he could protect me for the rest of my life.

I had screamed, but it hadn't been fear I felt. My heart pounded, but this was something different. It was like tipping over the top of a roller coaster.

Finian's hand was on my cheek when I placed mine on top of his. Turmoil coiled inside me, two feelings warring against each other. The gentleness of his gaze against the dark pits of Night's danger.

"Finian," I breathed, still uncertain *what* I felt. "He was in here?"

He nodded, a grim set line on his lips.

Of course, we wouldn't get rid of Night that easily, not that I was sure I wanted to.

Until the knife had shown up, what I felt hadn't been genuine fear. Besides, the gleaming metal had caught me off guard. From touching him, I felt like he had wanted the chase more than he wanted to catch me. Seeing the steel poised over my heart unleashed darkness in the dream. His eyes had flared to life with wicked gray beauty as he latched onto my emotions and pulled them into his soul.

It had been haunting and alluring.

I had screamed, but... underneath the covers, my legs pressed together. Traitorous, that's what my body was. I sat up, Finian's hand fell away, and I drew my knees to my chest, wrapping my hands around myself. He leaned back, giving me space, but a frown marred his perfect face.

His jaw worked. "What can I do to help?"

I wasn't sure there was anything to do. Confusion muddled my thoughts. "Tea?"

"Chamomile?"

I gave him a wry smile. "Sure."

He left the room, but I felt inexplicably alone. Night had been here. I felt it, but I wasn't sure where he was now.

While I lived by myself in my apartment, the space was small, never making me feel tiny. But Finian's guest bedroom was practically bigger than my little space in the world, and without him in the room, it felt empty.

It was a wonder I had fallen asleep in the first place.

The first breaths of dawn had swirled into the morning sky. I took a deep breath, threw off the covers, and padded after Finian. The kettle was on the stove, and his lips pressed into a thin line as he watched the water.

"Watched pots never boil," I said.

"Huh?"

"It's an old saying." I plopped down on a bar stool, eying him over the kitchen island. "If you watch the water, it never boils."

"Fae rarely have that problem." He crossed his arms over his chest. "Most use their magic to make it go faster."

I sat in silence, letting his words sink in. He wasn't using his magic, and it seemed to bother him. I wasn't sure why he didn't. He kept the club feeling nice, the drinks cold, and plenty of other things from his magic. It swirled around the court, but I had never seen him use anything other than what was required to keep Ceilidh going.

"Sometimes it's nice to have the silence," I offered.

"The silence?"

"Of waiting," I shrugged. "You can find out a lot about a person by the way they wait for things."

"And what do you learn?" His eyebrow arched as he slid me a look I could only describe as grateful.

"The amount of patience someone has. How quick someone is to anger if you get something wrong or make a mistake. Sometimes, I can figure out if someone is faking their politeness by their body language." Another shrug, and I had to look away as Finian's eyes settled on me. His gaze was too assessing, too intense.

"I meant, what have you learned about *me*?"

I flicked my gaze toward him again. His moss-colored irises blared to life with bright green. Staring at him was like falling headfirst into a jungle. There was a wild edge to Finian, and he wanted to be uncovered and explored. "I don't know."

"Try me."

"You're my boss. I've tried to... not think about it."

"But you're willing to consider sleeping with me?"

"Well, yeah, okay. There's... mutual trust, and then there's thinking about you like, uh..."

"Like what?"

Like someone I want to unfold like a treasure map and excavate their secrets.

"Like a potential partner?" It came out as a squeak, because his eyes scanned my body.

"You haven't wanted to think of me sexually."

I straightened. "Exactly, because you're my boss."

He sighed and leaned against his stone countertop. "What do you want out of life, Jules?"

"What do you mean?"

"You work in my club, you live in a small apartment in my court, you don't have a partner, and you don't seem interested in dating. What do you want?" His eyes flared, and I felt his magic trace along my skin, but he pulled it in, snapping it back into place like he surprised even himself. "Sorry. Ignore that."

"No, it's okay. I know how hard it is for you to control it when asking questions." I gave him a soft smile. "If I had superpowers, I would imagine I would have a difficult time, too."

"Superpowers."

"What?"

His lips curled up, eyes sparkling. "It's adorable how you think they are superpowers. Most humans don't."

"Well, what am I supposed to call them?"

"Magic."

I rolled my eyes. "If it were magic, then every Fae could study and learn more of it. While it *is* magic, your powers are more like superheroes from a comic book or something. They are finite, and they come with a cost."

He shook his head, but that quirky little smile stayed on his face. "And what would my superhero name be?"

"I would need to think about it, but probably something to do with a shield."

Finian turned back to the kettle, which whistled softly. He turned off the burner, picked up two bags of tea, and tossed one into each mug. As he poured the water, I obsessed over his long fingers and how delicately he moved. I wished he would serve drinks with me, because watching him behind the bar would be a sight.

"You never answered me."

"Hm?"

"What do you want out of life?"

I frowned as he slid one mug over to me.

"It's not supposed to be a horrible question, Jules. I am curious what you'd want if you could have anything in the world."

No one had asked me that before. The Fae door opened when I was turning sixteen, and I was approaching thirty now. Just over one more year, and I'd be there. My parents had me in their twenties, but I wasn't close to finding a romantic partner, let alone having a family.

But I missed my family. I missed the way my parents would look at each other with this *knowing* before they responded to a question I asked. I missed the way our family functioned on trips. I ached for the dynamic of being surrounded by people who loved me.

After the Fae door opened, everyone had to start over. I was no exception. Several people I knew died in the war, but my parents had both died to insanpheria. I could have been furious over it, but after seeing the tragedies that befell others, I decided to accept what had happened. I grieved, and I moved on.

Besides, I still had my cousins. We were distant, but I still had family alive. And it had been over a decade since I had lost my parents.

"I'd like to have a family of my own someday."

"What's stopping you?"

I shrugged. "When you work as a bartender, everyone looks at you like you are their next ticket to oblivion or they are saving one for the spank bank."

"Spank… bank?" He tilted his head to the side and blew on his tea. His magic coiled around him as the liquid touched his tongue.

"Are you protecting yourself from burning?"

"Yes. Do you want the same?"

I smiled and shook my head. "Like I said, patience. And a spank bank is like… memories you save in your head to masturbate to late—" I yelped as the handle of his mug shattered in his grasp. The mug would have dropped to the floor, but his magic flared and suspended the cup in the air.

Finian's teeth gritted. "They do *what* to you?"

Lifting the handle-less mug, I moved it back down on the table. "I don't know if anyone is *specifically* doing it. I meant in general." My fingertips were hot when I shook them. I tapped my mug a few times. Finian's jaw worked as he got a hold of himself. "Trust me, if some guy was acting like a creep, I would get the bouncers to remove him in a second. No questions asked."

"You deserve to be worshipped."

"I don't know about that…" I spun a lock of hair on my finger, looking anywhere except at Finian and the shattered pieces of ceramic that he was now scraping into his palm.

"If there is one thing I am certain of in this world, it is that you are deserving of so much more than… that job."

"You gave me that job."

"I know." His gaze was solemn and full of regret. "But that was before I knew about this thing called a spank bank."

"Oh, come on. You've never stored up memories for a little fun later?"

FINIAN RASKOS

The way she said it made me want to get onto my knees and confess. I was one of those males. More than once, I had watched as she tapped another keg. More than once, I had watched how her body moved when she shook another drink to serve. I admired her toned muscles, the way her skin remained soft, her scent.

More times than I cared to admit, I watched her suck a taster into her mouth to make sure she had correctly mixed the drink before serving it. Her tongue flicked out, running over the toothpick and sucking it dry.

I understood exactly what she meant, which was why I hated when other males or men looked at her like that.

I tossed the shattered ceramic handle into the trash and dusted my hands on my pants, using the motion to adjust myself.

"I suppose I have."

"See? We're all guilty of it. What matters is if you act like a total creep because of it." Jules blew on the top of the tea and took a delicate sip of chamomile. The way her lips parted had me licking my own.

I poured the liquid from the old mug into a new one and tossed the old one into the trash. I'd have to watch my anger around Jules. In the past, I had been careful. She needed the coin, so I made myself scarce from the bar frequently. My presence as an overprotective male would generate a lot less income for her.

But now, with Night lurking, heat simmered inside me.

"Couldn't you find someone to put it back together?"

"I wish those kinds of Fae were easier to come by." I gave her a sad smile. "Maybe I could find some super glue. We could puzzle it together if you want."

She grimaced. "I would be terrible at that."

"Why? I thought you had patience."

"I do."

"A puzzle is the ultimate form of patience."

"Ah, but it is also spatial awareness. Which…" She gave a half-hearted shrug.

Jules was good at her job because of her tenacity. The few times she tried to get fancy with her drink pouring, she had broken more than her fair share of glasses. Thankfully, she broke none of the liquor containers, which was where most of my expenses came from.

With Lady Burke increasing the prices, I may have been angry with her if that had been the case.

But replacing glasses was annoying, and my patrons broke more than their fair share. If I caught them, I required coin for payment. I didn't allow drinks on the dance floor, but Fae did what they wanted.

"Then it's decided. The mug stays in the trash."

"May it rest in pieces." Her voice hitched up in a giggle, and I wanted to strip her bare right then and there. Jules rarely laughed, but when she did, it made me want to show her what exactly I meant by worshipping.

"Do you think you'll be able to get back to sleep?"

Her fingers roamed around the outside of the mug, as if absorbing the heat from the ceramic surface. It was hot and muggy outside, indicative of a last summer heat wave for this area, but my club and apartment were within the range of my magic. On top of creating shields and being able to repel creatures with wards, I could control the temperature. It was the same concept—shielding from whatever we needed to avoid. In this case, it was the heat, so my apartment was cool and comfortable.

"I'm not sure. It wasn't that I was scared."

"You were screaming." My brows lifted.

She sucked her lower lip in between her teeth. "I know I was, but that was from it being unexpected."

"Do you want to tell me what happened?"

Shifting in her seat, her brown eyes stayed glued to her mug, watching the steam rise off it. "Not really."

I wanted her to look at me, to tell me everything. But I would let her lead this conversation, even though I wanted to push her.

"I am here if you need me." I took another sip of tea, trying not to read into her unwillingness. Had it been that awful? Because if so, I would kill Night the next time I saw him. Or try to. I frowned, wishing I could do more to block Jules from his next attack.

Outside of a rare occurrence like Cumina and her ability to mess with memories, the Fae held no jurisdiction over dreams. Her magic only worked when she was nearby, and it drained her energy to use her power. Dream Walkers gathered strength as they fed. That was the only reason I trusted Cumina over the Dream

Walkers—it cost her to use her magic. Once Night had a person's mind, he could do whatever he wanted for as long as he wanted.

Once the curse of the Fae door settled in, the Dream Walkers had been hunted to the point of oblivion. The Fae were virtually invincible because of the Fae King's curse, but the Dream Walkers hadn't been so lucky. We finally had power, and we had used it.

Night was the last of his kind. If he wasn't a prick, I would feel bad for him.

"I appreciate that. More than you know, but I have to process what happened."

I nodded like I understood. I didn't.

With a sigh, she pulled her knees up to her chest, sitting perched on the stool like a bird. "I think I am more disturbed by the way it made me feel."

I wanted to ask, but she already said she didn't want to talk about it—anything she wanted to tell me now, I would give her the space to do so.

"I uh…" Her cheeks reddened. "I didn't think I would be into anything… kinky." The last word squeezed out of her lips as if it hurt her to confess.

"That's what you're worried about?"

She shook her head but paused and glanced at me. Her nod was slow, as if still considering her feelings. "I always thought of myself as kind of… I don't know, boring? I mean, that's what my partners have said to me. But tonight, when Night chased me…"

I gritted my teeth together to stop myself from saying anything.

Jules ran her fingertips over her knees, as if the fabric of her pants could illuminate what was going through her head. She stayed so quiet.

I set my mug down, not sure if I could hold it without breaking the handle again. Night *chasing* her. The image made my blood rage.

"I'm sure you're not boring." I had to choke back the hatred for her ex-partners in my voice. No one should degrade a woman that way, even if the sex hadn't lived up to their expectation. There was honesty, and there was brutality. Those were very different. "And those men you slept with sound horrible."

She laughed, but it came out clipped. "They weren't great, that's for sure. But it doesn't change how I'm handling this. I don't know what to do with this new information. Like… did I like it because it was a dream? Or did I like it because I would want something like that to happen in real life?"

"You need a partner who understands and respects you, someone who empowers you to explore yourself and your desires, not someone who shames you for being… unsure."

"Shouldn't I know what I want at this point in my life?" Her eyes rose to meet mine, and the flecks of honey hues in them melted my heart. There was earnestness there, but also openness I hadn't seen from her before.

"I think we find out new things about ourselves daily. It doesn't matter how old you are." Like how patient I could be. Like how I could stare at her for hours, and that would be enough to satisfy me. How I knew I had more control than I gave myself credit for, because my magic wanted to whirl inside her.

"Thanks, Finian." She gave me the sweetest smile, a subtle upturn to her pink lips. "I think I'll take the tea and try to sleep, or at least rest." Her eyes darted over to the giant windows on the side of my apartment. "It's so bright in here."

The sun had crested over the horizon, streaming in through the windows. For people who worked at the club like Jules, they likely slept for most of the day. "There are black-out blinds. There's a remote on the nightstand."

"Of course there is." Her warm eyes crinkled at the edges. "I'll see you this afternoon?"

"Definitely."

She cast me a final gaze before closing the door between us. And it took less than a second for Night to materialize in front of me. I swung at him, but he caught my hand, and I stumbled backward as his warm skin pressed against mine.

"You forgot the biggest rule about being around a Dream Walker, *Finian*." He prowled toward me, pressing against my fist, until my back was flush against the refrigerator. He was a breath away from my face. "You shouldn't touch us."

"What are you going to—" I didn't get to finish, because we both tumbled into a nightmare of his creation.

I stood in the middle of nothing with darkness and destruction around me. My club was leveled, with pieces of it lying in smoldering piles and ashen remains. Twisted limbs and charred bones wrapped through the rubble, unidentifiable in the ruins. The rest of my court was untouched. Just my club had become a bombed-out shell of what it used to be.

"This is it?"

"Fuck off, Night." The amount of anxiety creeping up my chest and gripping my throat was unreasonable. I had spent a decade of my life perfecting this place, creating somewhere my employees could be safe, and in the last few years, where Jules could be safe. I had fought Lady Burke for the rights to distribute her liquor stores and production she had created in Port City. My court and Ceilidh had been built from nothing.

And now it was decimated.

"This is what you are so scared of? Losing a club?"

I swung at him again, but he caught my fist easily. He pulled me into him, and I stumbled forward, trying to wrench myself away from this male. His eyes glinted a deep, vicious blue. I could feel his magic twisting around us as he fed from me. As my emotions flooded into him, his irises turned into glittering silver pools.

"I never thought I would meet someone so shallow. Most Fae and people panic over losing loved ones, but you fear losing a nightclub?" He spat the words.

"If you don't understand how this is more than a club, then I question your ability to read true fear."

Night snarled, dropped my hand, and took a step back. "I know what I see in front of me, Raskos. Your nightmare is predictable, made up of selfish notions, just like you."

"You don't know me." My voice dipped low, becoming a growl. He arched one of his silver eyebrows, as if to say he knew me fine. "What about you, Night? What has piqued your interest with Jules?" I advanced, stepping right up to him until we were nose to nose. I had already done the damage of touching him for the first time, so what the hell did I care about getting this close anymore?

"I find her interesting. Don't you? Though I wonder how much you care, seeing as how the club is the only thing destroyed here."

"She's *part* of the club, idiot." I gestured around us. "There are bones in the ruins. She's part of this." I clenched my fists at my sides. "You say I am selfish, but I am betting you wouldn't know love if it hit you in the face. You're incapable of such a thing."

His lips curled and brows lowered. "What's the point of love when it all becomes the same thing? Disappointment. Our species are too different, so are the humans. I am the last of my kind, and as you so helpfully put it earlier, I will die someday." He stood his ground, but his eyes roamed over me. I felt exposed as he assessed me and my surroundings again. "I suppose I expected more... horror from you."

"You're judging my fears now?!"

"It's... fairly mundane. I've seen everything, Raskos.

Everything. Do you know what clowns are?"

"Of course I do."

"Yeah, well, it seems like people are terrified of them."

I snorted.

"I am so absolutely *bored* with the mundane fears of humans. But you... I was hoping for something more feral, more entertaining. This is just... sad."

I turned my back on him but could feel the heat of his presence pressing against me. "Because it's real. This could happen, Night. And with it, I am certain I would lose the part of me that makes me... me." I glanced at him over my shoulder.

His silver eyes flickered, and as quickly as we had fallen, we were back in my kitchen.

"Get off him!" Jules screamed.

The mug soared through the air, tea still in it. The steaming mess was going to slam into Night's back, but my magic flared up. It encapsulated the mug and placed the liquid back into the ceramic.

Night eyed me curiously, and I had no idea why I had stopped the mug from hitting him. I shoved him off me and snatched the drink out of the air.

"I said it before, and I'll say it again. Get out of my apartment."

"But it just became entirely more interesting."

"I won't run."

Night glanced at Jules. "What?" His nostrils flared.

"In the dream, you wanted me to run. You wanted to feed off the fear, but I won't do it. I won't run if you keep messing with Finian." She crossed her arms over her chest and pushed out her chin.

She was sticking up for me, defending me. No one had ever done that before.

A lazy smirk spread across Night's lips. "Scratch that. Now it's the most interesting thing I have borne witness to. I'll see you later, *Finian*." Night stepped into the shadows, whisked away into nothing like he had never been there to begin with.

Jules crossed the room, eying me as if she expected to see an open, gushing wound. "Are you okay?" Under her scrutiny, I could see the two dark birthmarks near her right eye. They crinkled with her skin as she narrowed her gaze. "Do I need to hurt him?" Her hands wrapped around my chin as she glanced at my jaw and neck.

"Hurting a Dream Walker. What an interesting concept." I let out a breath as her fingers trailed down my arms. "Jules."

"Seriously, are you okay?"

"I won't be if you keep touching me like that."

She ripped her hands away as if she had felt hot coal. "I'm sorry. I know we're... Uh, we haven't..."

I cupped her jaw in my hands. "If this is too much, you tell me so. You tell me no, and I will listen." I brushed my thumbs gently along her lips. "Tell me what you want."

Her lips parted. "I'm not sure."

My fingers went to the nape of her neck and pulled her forehead against mine. "Is this okay?"

She nodded.

"Jules."

"Finian."

"I've tried to be a patient male, but I saw the world without..." I blinked, because I couldn't very well admit my nightmare had been losing *her*. Night was right—it would have been self-centered if it had just been about my club, but it wasn't. She had been in the club. She had been the person I feared losing the most. Something had pulled me into her orbit a long time ago, and I was done fighting this feeling. "I don't feel very patient right now."

"I think that's okay."

I closed the gap between us and whispered against her lips, "You think, or you know?"

"Yes," she breathed.

I didn't care which she was saying yes to. I had waited too long, and she was melting underneath my touch. If she asked me to stop, I would, no matter how much it hurt me to do so. My fingertips gripped her neck as I sealed my mouth to hers. The kiss was electric, soaring through my body and piercing into my soul.

Nightmare

I watched as increasing unease settled throughout my body. While Finian believed I shadow walked out of his apartment, I had stayed, watching the scene unfold before me. There was something about Jules I couldn't put my finger on, something that frustrated me. Perhaps it was how she challenged my dreams, the way her subconscious didn't bend to my will. It was a half-meal, one that was topped off by my brief state of being inside Raskos's mind.

Neither of them satiated me.

But when Raskos pressed his mouth against hers, wildness stirred inside me, a possessive notion I had never felt with another being. As I narrowed my eyes at them, watching their lips move against one another, I debated interference. I debated ripping them apart from each other.

And from some unknown depth, I debated *joining* them.

Jules let out a soft hum and pressed herself against Raskos's chest. She seemed to soften underneath his touch, but just as quickly, she placed her palms against him and opened the space between them. "It's too much. I'm sorry. I—"

Raskos let out a low growl, and her eyes widened. I was ready to step out in front of him, but he swallowed and shook his head. "Sorry, Jules." The words sounded pained, like they had ripped their way from his throat.

She blinked. "I want to, I think. Eventually. It's just… I am too shaken up tonight to get my head on straight. Plus, I don't have too much time before my next shift starts."

"I happen to know the boss."

"Oh, yeah?" She smirked. "And do you think he would be upset if I came in late?"

"He wouldn't mind. Not at all."

Jules ran her fingers down his shoulders, along his arms, and over his hands, savoring the touch as they stayed connected.

I frowned, because if I had my way with this woman, I would not stop at a kiss. In fact, I would make this moment so memorable she'd never be able to look at another male without thinking about me.

Of course, I would get my moment with her. I had to be patient and wait until she left the room. Raskos wouldn't let me near her during their time together—at least, not without interruption. However, as soon as he was in another room, she would be vulnerable.

Despite his shields, he wouldn't be able to keep me away from her. His powers were too weak. Between the night club temperature, sound regulation, and hoswisp wards, his magic was stretched too thin. He had nothing on me.

"Thanks again for letting me stay," she whispered, her eyes going soft around the edges.

"Anytime. I mean that." His green eyes glowed with the color of the Faerie moss right after the spring rain broke. When the Faerie moss bloomed, the air was still moist, and the ground became carpeted with dew each morning. The air held such promise, I could taste it.

His irises reminded me of home.

I wanted to hurt something.

A blush rose on Jules's cheeks. With a nod, she took her tea back to her bedroom.

I followed her, walking through the shadows and eying every movement she made like it would be the last time I saw another living being. I was drowning in the idea of her, wanting to clamber inside her dreams and watch her as she screamed again.

I liked her emotions. I wanted her anger, and I craved her fear.

It wasn't enough. I worried it would never be enough.

With a sigh, she placed the tea on the nightstand and sank onto the bed. She ran her hands over her face and stared at the ceiling, as if in deep contemplation. Her exasperation made me want to chuck Raskos across the room. Granted, he hadn't done anything I wouldn't have tried, but the unfocused look in her eyes made my knuckles clench.

With another few sips from her mug, she climbed under the covers and brought them up to her chin. Her brown eyes gazed at the door as her lips parted. She bit down on her lower lip, dragging it slowly between her teeth as her hand drifted under the sheets.

Lower and lower.

Her eyelids fluttered shut as her hand moved against her flesh. Her hips rotated while seeking the pleasure Raskos had left her wanting.

Had she wanted him but denied herself?

No, I decided this woman would not be thinking about Raskos

while in a state like this. I slipped out of the shadows and leaned over her bed.

Her eyes snapped open. While her lips parted to let out a sound, I had already gripped her mouth and nose shut. Her brown irises shrunk as her pupils widened, not with horror or terror, but a strange sense of absolution.

"What's going on in that mind of yours?" I asked, as we stumbled into her dreams.

Oddly enough, we stood in the same ruins of Raskos's nightmare. The court was in shambles, and she stood in the middle of it. Loneliness emanated from her, wafting around her like a dark cloud.

"What's so scary about things that don't exist?"

"The mind makes it feel real," I answered.

She shook her head. "It doesn't feel real. It feels like a dream, an annoying one. Do you want me to say it? Yes, I am scared Raskos's court will face ruin, because this job has been the closest thing I've had to a normal life since the Fae door opened." Twirling toward me, she put her hands on her hips. Her lips curled with annoyance. "I am terrified of losing this. It's not family, not yet and not really, but…"

"But you want it to be." The desolation in her soul stretched across the landscape. As much as I was trying to influence her dreams, it felt like she was influencing *me*.

"Do you remember your family?" Her eyes flicked around the ruins. "My parents, before the insanpheria, they were doting. They were attentive. I remember how they loved each other, but maybe that's rose-colored lenses and all that." She waved her hands.

"Do you want to see them?"

Jules narrowed her eyes at me.

"I feed off nightmares, but I can sift through your memories and let you relive them."

Her brows lowered.

I wouldn't trust myself either.

"A memory of yours for a memory of mine. I don't remember my parents. It was too long ago, but I remember my sister. I remember her face when we were hunted by the Fae, turned invincible by the curse of the Fae door. Her eyes were as bright blue as a summer sky, as she hadn't ventured out to feed in days. With paper thin skin, she was easy for them to blow apart. She became the same as this court, torn into shreds like her life had no meaning."

Jules's eyes roamed over me. "How do I know you're telling the truth? How do I know you aren't killing me, and this isn't some weird DMT trip before I die?"

I shrugged, but held out my hand. "If you're already dying, then what do you have to lose by jumping farther into oblivion?"

Her tongue flicked out, running along her lower lip. I steadied myself as she eased her fingers onto my palm. The brush of her skin was so light. I couldn't remember the last time someone touched me with care.

Latching my fingers around hers, I pressed my eyes closed and searched her memories, clinging onto one and bringing it to life around us.

Jules was fifteen, coming down the stairs to a living room lit up by flickering multi-colored lights and a tree in the middle of it.

"Christmas." She breathed out and dropped my hand. Marching across the room, she pulled back the curtains and frowned. "There's nothing outside."

"It's your memory. If you never looked outside, then there's nothing to pull back to the present."

Jules let the drapes flutter shut and glanced at the younger version of herself. Her saucer eyes glittered as she took in the presents under the tree.

"I remember it was snowing this day, though. Which made it so special. It hardly ever snowed on Christmas day." A frown marred her lips, and I wanted to make it snow so much it suffocated us. "But at least there's this." She skipped to the fireplace. It glowed with red and orange hues. The flickering flames cast long tendrils across her skin.

A few moments later, two adults walked into the room. Both shared a likeness to Jules. The woman had long, flowing brown hair, and the man had honey-hued eyes that glowed with the reflection of the fire. The man held two mugs of hot chocolate, one topped high with whipped cream and a gleaming red cherry on top. He bent over near the tree, kissing younger Jules on the forehead and pressing the mug into her hands.

"We couldn't afford much this year, honey, because we're saving for your eighteenth birthday."

Jules's smile widened. "Am I getting the car?"

Her parents exchanged a glance. "We're going to try, but we're hoping you like what we got this year."

Without waiting another beat, Jules ripped open a few presents. None of them seemed expensive or from the heart, but she beamed anyway.

"I got you guys something, too." Jules reached over to an envelope. "I know you said I should use my summer money on something important to me, and well…" She passed the envelope to her parents.

Her mom gave her a curious smile before opening the envelope. She let out a little gasp and handed it to her husband. "Jules…"

"If you are saving, then I want this to go into the savings, to help when it comes time to get the car."

"We're going to the bank tomorrow. We'll open an account for you. You can keep your own savings and spend it when the time comes, okay?"

Jules gave them a wide smile. "I'm getting a car. You'll see."

"I believe you, honey." Her mom smiled sadly.

The memory faded into the background, and we're transported back into the ruins of Raskos's court. Jules sighed and sat down on a piece of broken foundation. "They opened the account with my name and my dad's, but when I went back to take money out, they told me it had been closed. They needed the money to pay for our oil bill that year and never had the heart to tell me the truth."

"They hurt you because of that."

Jules shook her head. "No, I enjoyed the warmth. But they could have been honest. I wasn't as innocent as I looked."

"I can try again, give you something better."

"No, I think the rose-colored lenses are probably better than knowing the truth." She curled her legs up to her chest and wrapped her arms around herself. "Were you ever in love with someone so much it hurt?"

"I've never been in love."

Jules glanced at me, and there was an endless amount of knowing in her quick assessment. "That's a shame. I think you might be good at it."

"Oh?"

"You're the first man to listen to me since… well, other than Finian."

"That's a pretty low bar to set, especially seeing as how I was inside your room and watching you pleasure yourself."

Her brows lowered as her jaw dropped open, her mouth making a perfect o shape. "You were in there for that long?"

"What were you thinking about?" I took a step toward her,

towering over her small frame. "Was it Raskos, or was it me?" I bent down. "Or if your bar is that low, was it someone else?"

She breathed out while staring at me. The slow exhale made her chest collapse. There were so many things I wanted to do to her. "Finian. I was thinking about Finian."

I straightened. "That won't do."

I erased the landscape, plunging us into absolute darkness.

She blinked and waved her hand in front of her eyes. "Fun trick. Do you perform at parties?"

"This is the part where you are supposed to run."

"I told you I wouldn't." She leaned back, and while she couldn't see anything, she arched her back. Jules looked up into the nothingness and flicked her tongue out, licking her lower lip. "I said I wouldn't give you what you wanted."

"And what do I want?"

Her eyes stared in my direction, but she was looking through me, unable to see. "Someone who is scared." Her fingers traced down her sternum and over her stomach. "Someone who wants to run." She paused at the hem of her pants. "But the strange thing is… the idea of running—" Her hand dipped under the waistband. "—makes me really wet." She eased past her panties and moaned as she reached her core.

Fuck.

I changed the dream and shined spotlights straight at her. She blinked into the brightness, her pupils becoming pinpoints.

"You want to watch?" Jules inched her pants down her hips, moving the fabric lower as she wiggled the elastic band against her skin. "Do you *like* watching, Night? Would you watch if it were me and someone else?"

Something swelled inside the dream, and Raskos appeared behind her. His hands cupped her breasts above her shirt. His thumbs traced circles around her pebbling nipples. She sucked in a breath as she writhed her ass against him. Raskos hardened. A smug smile crawled across his lips as he stared straight at me with his bright green eyes. Jules's dark brown hair cascaded over his neck, joining the wild waves of his. As her hands traveled lower, she fully exposed herself to me.

Raskos's hands followed right behind hers, wandering over her skin until he grasped her hips. His fingertips dug into her skin as she slipped a single finger into herself.

I forced both of us out of the dream and stumbled back a few feet into her room. Blinking, I forced the image from my mind. Jules sucked in a breath and brought the comforter up to her chin.

"Now that we're in real life, you lost your confidence?" I sneered.

"It's not a dream," she said, her voice holding none of the bravado of the woman a few moments before. "And you? You didn't want to watch anymore?"

"If I were to watch you and *Finian*, make no mistake, I would be the one directing the show. Not you."

Her throat bobbed as she swallowed.

I prowled toward her. "And if I were to bet, you are wetter now than when you started this whole thing, because as much as you want to claim innocence, you crave debauchery. Show me how wet you are."

Jules blinked, but her right hand let go of the covers, and she reached between her legs. She shuddered as she dipped into herself, and she brought her fingers back up. As she showed them to me, her body froze while her hand trembled.

Her two fingers were soaked. As she was about to wipe her arousal away, I snatched her hand and sucked her fingers into my mouth, pressing my tongue against her skin. She tasted just as she smelled, with a hint of late autumn sunsets. I lapped up every drop of her, feeling each groove of her fingers against my tongue.

"Raskos has no idea what he's missing. And now that I do, you'll never get rid of me." I grinned and stepped into the shadows, leaving her with a shocked expression and eyes that told me they wanted so much more.

JULES

A low tone escaped Night's throat. "Raskos has no idea what he's missing. And now that I do, you'll never be able to get rid of me." His manic grin made my muscles clench as he slipped into the shadows.

I shut my mouth as I stared at the space Night once stood in. He was a stunning man. He and Raskos had similar statures, both being taller than me. They were on the thinner side, but seemed to be nothing but toned muscle underneath their clothes.

That was where their similarities ended.

Night had molten silver eyes that turned blazing blue over time, and they signified his hunger. Half of his silver hair was messily cropped to his head, while the other side swept against his ear. A single lock drifted across his forehead. The smugness of his expressions led me to believe that whatever game he was playing with me, he was going to win every time. He had a light amount of stubble that played across his jaw. Kissing him would be as rough as his voice was deep.

If he even kissed. No, judging from my interactions with Night, he devoured.

Raskos, however, had a more serious expression, like he was contemplating the existence of the universe in between each of his breaths. His brows furrowed over his moss green eyes too often. He had a rounder face, but his cheekbones were still visible. He held such poise over his movements, it would have made a dancer jealous.

It felt like both men wanted to protect me, even though for Night it was likely because he was territorial over his food. I didn't understand what Night could be interested in, especially since I didn't seem like an easy meal for him. Ever since I was a kid, I had lucid dreams. I always knew when I dreamed, and whenever Night tried to twist my imaginary worlds, it seemed obvious.

Surely, another person without lucid dreaming would be easier for him to feed off.

But even as I thought this, I couldn't deny the awful truth of my predicament. I *liked* how Night wanted to chase me. His attentive gaze felt like I was getting peeled apart for the world to see.

And there was the new complication of Finian. He had been my boss for years. Throughout our time together, he made sure I had Faerie wine, accommodations, and safety. He checked in on me. He had become a friend, someone I trusted.

And now, we had kissed.

My lips still tingled thinking about it.

I groaned and pulled the covers over my face. I was almost thirty, and apparently had been single for entirely too long, because I wasn't possibly thinking about two men at the same time. It was becoming impossible to ignore the thrill both sent through me.

It was a lot of tossing and turning before I fell back asleep.

❧ ✄ ❦

I woke up just before the sun sank below the horizon. The smell of coffee wafted from the living room, and I threw on a change of clothes before heading out. To my surprise, the space was empty when I got there with a note propped on the counter. I snatched it, eyes darting over the lazy script of Finian's hand.

Jules,

I figured you might need some coffee after the rude awakening last night. It's from my private stores, but if you don't like it, there's plenty of tea in the upper right cabinet.

There were some financial items I had to handle in the club this evening, so I am sorry I could not join you for breakfast. There are eggs in the fridge, bread in the oven, and cheese, depending on what you are in the mood for. Help yourself. You can stay as long as you want.

Finian

A stupid smile crept over my lips. He had opened his home to me with no requests for anything in return. Well, okay, maybe he had alternative reasons for wanting me here, but I enjoyed his attention.

I helped myself to the food and nearly went to heaven when I tasted the coffee. It held caramel and chocolate notes, and I groaned as I poured a second cup. I boiled an egg, slathered a few slices of bread with the spreadable cheese he had, and lost myself in ecstasy for a few moments.

"You eat like you're going to die at the end of the meal."

"No," I said, chewing on a giant bite of bread. I sucked in a healthy mouthful of coffee and washed it down. "This food is too good to be ruined by you."

"Who said anything about ruining?" One of Night's eyebrows rose. "On the contrary, I was hoping to enhance it. I wonder, will you make that much noise when my face is buried in between your thighs?"

I pointed to the mug of coffee. "It is too early for this."

"It's never too early for sex."

"We're not having sex."

"We will." Night pulled a stool next to mine and faced me. He sat down and watched me with such intensity my body shivered.

I tore off another large mouthful of bread and stared at him as I chewed. "You seem very full of yourself."

"Not as full as your mouth should be."

"Is everything going to be an innuendo with you?"

"I can try, if that's what you want."

"What I want is cheese, bread, and coffee. And for that egg to magically peel itself. Can you do that?" The egg was cooling on the countertop, still inside the pesky shell.

"I could give you a dream where you are surrounded by peeled eggs, but I must admit, the only eggs I'm interested in—"

I held up my hand. "Nope! No. You are *not* talking about my ovaries during breakfast."

"Shouldn't this be dinner, anyway?" Night plucked the egg off the table and, with small taps, chipped away at the shell. "It's late."

"Someone made me sleep in late."

"Did Finian get to taste you after I left?"

My pussy betrayed me by clenching. The way Night said it so casually indicated absolutely no jealousy, which was surprising, considering he seemed to contain such a possessive personality.

"No, I went to sleep."

"And how long did it take you to fall asleep, I wonder?"

I glared at him as his fingers roamed over the shell, flaking off piece after piece. "Don't you know?"

"I know. The moment you fell into your dreams, I sensed it. Just like I could sense how Finian never went to sleep. He was too terrified that I would infect his dreams."

"Would you have?"

"What would be the point? The only thing he seems to be worried about is losing his club."

I flinched.

"Oh, did you expect something different from a Fae like him? His club is everything. More meaningful to him than he is to himself." Night held up the perfectly peeled egg.

I snatched it out of his hand and placed it on my plate, frowning. "You aren't very nice, are you?"

"I never claimed to be."

"Then why spend so much time here, if you are just planning to feed on us?"

"Why do ranchers take care of their herd?" A smirk spread across his lips. "I have a reason to be invested."

"There are easier meals."

"Yes, well, maybe easy doesn't interest me."

I picked up a knife and slid it through the middle of the egg. Keeping one half, I offered him the other. "Do you eat real food?"

Night stared at my outstretched hand, as if no one had offered him a meal in his life. It made me shrink away from him, but his fingers wrapped around my wrist before I took back the offer. His eyes met mine, and with his other hand, he took the egg from my palm. His fingertips brushed my skin, and I had to breathe out to remind myself that I was still alive.

"No one offers a Dream Walker food, out of fear of becoming such themselves. I can eat, yes, but it is more for enjoyment than sustenance." His eyes assessed the egg as he took a bite of it. Watching him chew was mesmerizing, and it got worse when he swallowed.

I tore my eyes from him and placed a small amount of salt on my half, tossing it into my mouth in one bite. When I glanced his way, his jaw was tight. The muscles along his neck clenched.

"What?" I muttered around my overstuffed mouth.

He shook his head as the front door to the apartment opened. Finian was about to step inside but froze as he took in the two of us sitting at the kitchen island. He had folders in his hands but dropped them. His magic kicked up, and instead of them spilling onto the floor, they flowed gently into a pile away from the rage reddening his face.

"I told you to stay the hell out of my apartment."

"I don't recall agreeing to those terms of a deal."

"There was no deal." Finian marched across the room and yanked on Night's shoulders, pulling him out of the stool. Night winked at me and disappeared. Finian growled and whirled around the room, staring into every corner.

"Come out and fight me."

I blinked as Night's arms wrapped around me from behind, and I squeaked as he pulled me off the stool toward him.

Finian's face dropped into anguish. "Night."

"Raskos."

"Let her go."

"And if I don't?" With me pressed against his chest and one hand against my neck, his other arm wrapped around me and pulled us flush together. "What are you going to do? Shield me to death?"

Finian flexed his fingers. His eyes swirled with brilliant shades of green. "Let her go."

Night's fingers found the hem of my shirt, and he played with the edge. "I have an idea. If she tells me to, I will." His words caressed my ear as he pressed down on my throat, threatening to cut off my air. "Say the word, Jules, and I will let you go."

I whimpered as his tongue brushed against my ear.

Finian's jaw worked. "She can't say anything if you are choking her."

Night released his hold on my neck, dropping his hand straight to my breast. His other fingers brushed my waist, and I swore it felt like I was being torn apart. I watched as Finian's face went from anger to... something else. Disappointment, maybe?

I swallowed. "Not like this," I whispered, finally.

Night released me instantly.

I missed his warmth already, but it was the right move, because Finian's glare settled on Night once again. Maybe Night didn't care about sharing, but my boss certainly had feelings about it.

"Get out," Finian said again.

Night stepped into the shadows, and the gleam of his silver hair was the last thing to fade from my vision.

Finian rushed to me, grabbing onto my upper arms. "Are you okay? I will kill him. Him using you like that—"

"Finian," I tried.

"—it's not right. No person should ever find themselves in that position."

"Finian," I tried again, a little louder.

"And this is all because he's trying to mess with me. I haven't figured out why, but maybe—"

"Finian!"

"Jules," he said finally on an exhale and pulled me into him. I could hear his heart racing as my ear pressed against his chest. "Are you okay?"

"I'm fine. I—" How could I explain it to him? I liked his gaze on me while Night touched me. I liked his jealousy and shock. Heck, a guilty part of me liked his disappointment. I blinked, not sure what to do with any of these feelings. "I am fine, and he didn't do anything that I didn't want."

"What?" Finian pulled back. His hands found my shoulders once more as he searched my gaze.

"I mean… I don't know. I like you, but there's also something about him."

"A Dream Walker?!" Finian spat out the words, clearly disgusted. "We are nothing alike."

"That's kind of… why."

He blinked, but I might as well have slapped him. "Nothing good can come from dating someone who feeds on fear."

"Some humans say the same thing about Fae."

Finian scowled and dropped his hands from my shoulders. Without either of them touching me, I felt cold. "You always were too nice to see the dangers right in front of your face. No matter what Night says to you, I will make sure you see the truth about him. Dream Walkers are almost extinct for a reason, Jules. They are dangerous."

"I know."

"You know."

"He's made me see nightmares, but he's also been in my dreams."

Eight

FINIAN RASKOS

My nerves ignited at once. "He's been in your dreams," I repeated the words, because they didn't make sense. I wanted them to pierce through the thoughts in my mind and settle on something logical.

Jules was differentiating dreams and nightmares with Night in *both* kinds. She had claimed she hadn't hated it, or... something like that. Her hesitation to tell Night to stop had been apparent, and now she defended him.

Defended a monster.

"If I had been someone else, maybe it would have been frightening, but I don't know. I knew it was a dream. I've had lucid dreams since I was a kid. It wasn't... scary." Jules shrugged. Her shoulders were toned from working in the bar, and her shirt showed off her curves. It made my blood boil to think of Night touching her, tasting her.

Jules was supposed to be mine. I had waited for years. And he

66

came in like he owned her—like he owned *me*.

I clenched my fingers against my palms. My fingernails cut into my skin. "Jules, I have to ask…"

She gave me such a long and innocent look.

"Did you want him to touch you?"

Her lips parted, and I waited on bated breath, hoping she'd say the one word I needed to hear. Night could not become a regular fixture at my court again, and his obsession with Jules was ruining my chance to explore whatever this was we had.

On the other hand, I would not stand in the way of her potential happiness. As much as it would pain me to step back, I would.

"I don't know," she said after a moment. "I know that's not what you want to hear, but—"

I waved my hand, opening the space between us. Her shoulders slumped. "I have to get ready for the rest of the night at the club. We should make a lot of coin tonight, since we have another court visiting this evening. I hope you are well rested and ready." I winced at the emptiness of my words. She wasn't, of course. I was running on no sleep, letting my magic keep me afloat. It was taking so much of my power to keep up the shields around the court and stay awake.

"I'll be ready," she said finally, sucking in a breath with watery eyes.

I turned toward my files, picking them up in one smooth motion. I paused at the door. "If you want to talk about it later, after the club closes, I'll be here." I tossed a glance over my shoulder.

Her brown eyes held such hope as she nodded. I ached to hold that hope in my heart as well.

Pressing my lips together, I swept out of the apartment. I didn't want to leave. I had brought my work home because I wanted to be close to her, ask her for her opinion on the receipts in my hand. Letting out a breath, I realized I would have to do this on my own.

That was until I took a few steps down the stairs and my eyes caught on silver hair. "What do I have to do to get rid of you?"

Night's gaze flicked to me. "Well, if your nightmare is any indication, if your club goes, I go."

"My true nightmare would be you standing next to me in the fallout after that." I marched down the rest of the stairs and stood toe to toe with him. "Why are you here? And no bullshit, Night. What are you doing back in my court?"

His eyes darted toward the closed apartment door. He started to step into the shadows, but I wrapped my fingers around his wrist. He stilled.

"You're touching me, Raskos."

"Damn right I am. What are you doing here?"

"You know I can shadow walk with you holding onto me? I would dissipate under your fingers."

I yanked him closer still, voice dipping into a growl, "Tell me what you are doing here."

"Jules is an interesting person, don't you think?"

"Of course you would look at someone with so many facets to their being and boil them down to *interesting*." My lips curled, disgusted by the simplicity in which he viewed the world.

"How am I supposed to put it? I just met her. It's not like I can claim anything more than that. Yet."

"You'll never be able to claim anything, because you are not the type of being who can feel."

He placed his other hand on his chest. "Ouch, *Finian*."

"What is it about her?"

Night's eyes darted back to the door, but I grabbed onto his chin and forced him to stare at me.

"You don't get to look at her or touch her. You don't get to do any of that without my permission."

His brow arched, and a slow smile spread across his lips. "Oh, this is going to be so much fun."

"What?"

"Why don't we make this into a game?"

I snarled.

"The first male to sleep with Jules wins."

"She is a *person*."

"Which makes the game all that more interesting." The easy smile spread wider on his face. "Unless you are too scared to play. Worried that a stranger is going to steal what you've been working on for the past few years?"

My nails dug into his chin. "You are horrible."

He smirked and disappeared right out from underneath my fingers, and I stumbled forward a few inches before catching myself.

"I am only as horrible as your nightmares make me to be." Night sat on the steps, farther up near my apartment.

"You create the nightmares!"

He leaned forward, resting his head on his hand as he considered me. "You're right on many accounts, Finian. But I'll do you a solid, okay? I'll give you the night to seal the deal, but the moment your girl falls asleep, she's mine. And believe me when I say I am going to be looking forward to it, because she tastes delicious." He winked and shadow stepped out of the stairwell.

The folders in my hands felt too heavy. I wanted to forget about the club and apologize to Jules for being curt. But I also wanted to rip Night's head off his shoulders and make his corpse watch as I had my fill of Jules.

My relationship with her wasn't a game.

It wasn't until I had reached my desk that the last part of what he said hit me. *She tastes delicious.* Like he had already had her in some way. Had she not realized it was a dream? Had she allowed him to taste her?

No. I had to banish these thoughts from my mind, because if I didn't come up with some way to deal with the overextended trade routes with Lady Burke, I was going to find myself without my club and without Jules faster than a fire pauldrin launched flames.

I sighed as I considered the mountain of paperwork. It was going to be a long night.

∝ ✂ ∝

An hour after the club closed, a quiet knock sounded on my office door. I blinked away the bleariness that crept up on me. Hours. I had spent hours in this room, combing through documents to see if I was making enough coin to pay off my debts to Lady Burke's court.

Every single assessment came back with the same inevitability. Lady Burke would come to collect, and with her, she would bring a message of what happened when you sidestepped your debts. I wasn't prepared for that day, and I likely never would be. Night was right—my shields hadn't kept him out, and even though I tried to repel anyone who deemed to do harm against my court or Ceilidh. I had to wonder if my power was waning more since we left Faerie.

I let out a sigh. "You can come in," I said as I swept the papers into a large pile on the corner of my desk.

Jules cautiously poked her head inside. We hadn't spoken since earlier this evening. In truth, I hadn't wanted to hear about how she might *enjoy* Night. We had known each other for years, and

Night's possessive hands had already been on her more than mine had. Something about it drove me to anger, and I hadn't been the most sensible male at breakfast because of it.

"You didn't come out for the court's visit tonight, so I wanted to make sure you were okay." She inched into the room and let the door snick shut behind her. Her eyes searched every inch of the office as she refused to look at me. "Katie asked me to check on you, since she was upset she had to manage the special event by herself."

"I'm sure she did fine." I fought back an eye roll. Katie had likely made a lot of coin because of her lucrative side business that she thought I wasn't aware of.

"Are you avoiding me?" Her eyes flicked towards me, but she looked away just as fast.

"Not necessarily. I am, however, trying to avoid how short I was with you earlier today, and for that, I am sorry."

Her arms crossed over her middle, and I hated how she was hugging herself, as if she had to save herself from me.

"Jules, I am sorry."

Her lips parted like she was going to say something else, but she nodded instead. "It went well. She's a good manager when she doesn't leave early."

I nodded, understanding her frustration, because Katie often sneaked out before closing duties were finished. When she did perform, she did so flawlessly. "It's why I keep her around."

Jules ran her fingers over her arms, as if searching for a distraction. "What you said earlier, I was thinking about it. And you're right. I don't know Night, not like you do, and I guess I should listen to the people around me when they say someone is trouble."

"Did something happen?" I rose from my chair, ready to ignite the world, even if I had to use matches to do it. Screw magic. There were plenty of human items that could light things on fire.

She shook her head. "Nothing in particular. Just a guy who I thought was harmless, but he cornered me in the bathroom. Jersey shoved him out fast because Katie had been watching the guy all night. Nothing happened." Jules held up her hands as my magic flared around me.

My magic wasn't strong enough to do anything. For someone to make it past my wards, come into my club, and try to hurt my staff meant my magic was getting weaker. I was getting weaker.

If Burke tried to collect her debts now, it wouldn't end well for me.

Forcing a breath, I sat back in the chair. "Tell Jersey to get me his description. We're throwing him to the wilds, and I'll notify the other nearby courts that he is not welcome. We'll see what happens to him when there is no one providing him safe harbor."

Jules nodded. "I don't know why I always see the good in people, and I guess I'm a bad judge of character." Her exhale broke off a piece of my heart.

I couldn't take it any longer. "You know he wants to fight over you?"

She blanched, her gaze unwavering from my face. "He... what?"

"Night. He wants it to be a contest. He doesn't care about how you truly feel. According to him, whoever sleeps with you first gets to claim you."

Her cheeks turned flaming red, and I thought perhaps I had overstepped. I didn't need to be so inappropriate with my honesty, but she had a right to know the type of male he was. There was no redemption for someone like Night.

"No one gets to claim me except me." Her hand reached into

her pocket as she fished out the key I left for her earlier today, as if her anger needed to well up inside something. She slammed the small piece of metal down on my desk.

"Jules—"

"No, I have my own apartment, and I need to figure out my life before I have two men coming in here and messing it up."

"I'm not trying to mess it up."

"That's part of the problem!" Her voice arched upward, sounding desperate. The sheen in her eyes as she gazed down at the key was full of regret. "You are so nice to me, and I don't really understand why. I've never been particularly nice to you, and I've never expressed interest, and yet, you are still here. Why haven't you left?"

"Is that what you want me to do?"

Her eyes remained fixed on my desk. "It's what every single man has done to me in the past. It's what everyone will do in the future. I'm just shutting it down before it gets to that point." Jules turned toward the door, but I was faster.

It hadn't occurred to me how quick I could be, because I hardly ever relied on my speed. But she hadn't taken more than a step before I was in front of her, the key in my hand.

She blinked. "Please move."

I took a step toward her and grabbed her wrist, forcing her hand up between us. Pushing the metal into her palm, I closed her knuckles over it, not letting her move an inch under my grasp. "You don't have to stay with me if you don't want to. But I am not trying to ruin your life, and I am not going anywhere. I like you, Jules."

Her throat moved as she swallowed. Her defiant and resolute eyes melted into something softer as she looked me over.

I pulled her into me, wrapping my arms around her. "I'm not

going anywhere. But I won't push this. I won't push you. Whatever you want or don't want. You name it."

Her fingers traced fine lines up my back. She gripped my shoulders and let out a ragged breath. "I'm going to grab some things from my apartment. If you are comfortable having me as a roommate, I'd like to stay here."

"Anything you want."

Jules pulled back. Her lips pressed into a tight line. "I feel safe with you, and I don't want to lose that."

"You won't."

Her expression warred against her disbelief as the frown widened on her face. I would do anything to show her how eager I was to have her in my life. "Okay. I'll put some trust in this…" She gestured between us, as if not sure what to call us. In truth, I wasn't sure, either. "I'll see you in a bit."

I gave her shoulder another squeeze before she slunk out of my office. I wanted to give Jules the future she deserved—one inside a safe court surrounded by comforts. She shouldn't have to work to live in luxury. I should be able to provide all of that to her as a Lord of a court.

Except, as I turned back to my paperwork, dread washed over me. I had to keep the club open, because if I lost the club, how could I keep her sense of safety? If I lost the club, would she dare to trust me again?

If I lost the club, would I lose her?

$\mathcal{N}$ine

NIGHTMARE

I followed her back to the tiny closet of an apartment. She unlocked her front door and glanced over her shoulder, straight toward where I stood. My eyes never left her. A funny little smile played across her lips as she second guessed her instincts. They must have been screaming at her—*danger, predator, run*—and still she calmly twisted the key in the building's lock and opened the door.

Through the shadows, I drifted into her apartment before she opened the interior door and waited. It felt like days passing instead of mere minutes as I waited for her to turn the deadbolt in her apartment.

I sat on her bed, still in the shadows, and kept my eyes on the worn wood. When she finally pushed the door open, her jaw dropped. It had been well worth the wait.

Her fingers curled into fists at her sides, her right one still clutching the metal keyring, one of which was Raskos's apartment key. I swallowed a growl as her eyes darted over her belongings. Slowly, she prowled around the room, opening cabinets to see if everything she owned was still present.

There were only a few items I had stolen.

After a few moments, her brows came down over her eyes. She marched over to her dresser and opened the top drawer. Slamming it shut, she turned in a circle and yelled, "Night!"

"You called?" I slipped out of the shadows, still seated on the edge of her bed.

"Where are they?"

"Where are what?" I smiled.

"My fucking *underwear.*" She took a step toward me, anger furrowing her brow. "And since you are in here right now *watching* me, you can cut the innocent act. I know you came in here and messed with my shit, and I am not in the mood for whatever excuse you are about to give."

"Such a mouth. I can think of plenty of other things you could do with it instead."

Her cheeks blazed red. "Where are they?" She spat each word through gritted teeth.

"I don't know what you are talking about."

"Give them back." With two strides, she was across the room. Her hand rose, and she slapped me across the face.

I didn't so much as flinch, but my smile spread wider. The sting was marvelous. "Maybe you should put some claws into it next time, tiger."

"You are impossible." Her hands went to her hips as she towered over me.

This wouldn't do at all. Kicking out my legs, I wrapped them around the back of her knees, making her stumble into me. I caught her easily, bringing us both down onto her bed. It squeaked in protest.

She grunted and placed her hands on either side of my head, trying to scramble off me.

My fingers wrapped around her wrists and held her firm against me. "I don't think so."

Jules growled, her eyes narrowing to slits. "Did you challenge Raskos to see who could sleep with me first?"

I shrugged. "It wouldn't be the worst thing I have done."

"I am not a toy."

"I disagree."

She reared back, but I shifted, slapping my hand over her mouth at the very moment she spat. I clamped my fingers down over her nose. My palm was covered in her spit, and she couldn't breathe in the current position. It smeared around her face, just how I wanted.

My other arm pulled her body close against me. Her eyes widened as she realized how hard I was. I didn't mind a fight. In fact, I craved it.

"Are you going to apologize?"

Her face turned a deeper shade of red as she shot daggers at me.

"No? You tried to make me dirty, Jules. And I think you'll find that the only one who is going to become filthy in this scenario is you." Digging my fingers into her cheeks, I dragged her face toward me. "And I can promise to make you *extremely* messy."

The skin on her face turned purple, and her hands clawed at mine, trying to pull me off her. One of her nails caught on my skin, and she tore through. Blue blood blossomed from the wound, but I refused to let go of her, not when she was so close to me.

She muttered something underneath my hand, and it sounded an awful lot like "fuck you."

"Let's make this lack of oxygen last a little longer, shall we?"

I stumbled us both into her mind. Dreams lasted longer than reality, and she could stay on this cusp of deprivation for as long as I needed. Despite what she may believe, I fully intended to make her mine by any means necessary. And I had a distinct feeling this woman liked it when I treated her this way.

We stood in the middle of the court's fallout again, and she slapped me across the face, gasping for breath even as her eyes watered from the lack of air in the real world. I was going to enjoy this.

"What the fuck, Night?! Are you trying to kill me out there?" She swallowed as if searching for her inability to breathe. "Are you still controlling my breath?"

I nodded, a smirk spreading across my lips. "I figured you might want some time to think about what you tried to do before you passed out."

Her fingers curled into fists as her body shook. "Originally, I was pissed at Finian for telling me in such a calloused way. I thought he was trying to be the knight in shining armor by making you look like a total douche, but now..."

"Now?" I took a step toward her. "What do you feel now?"

She looked down at the ground. I lifted her chin, forcing her to look at me. That blush was back, spreading across her face. "I, uh, am..."

"Tell me." I pressed into the recesses of her mind, projecting her innermost thoughts around us. Sucking in a breath, I took a step away from her and opened the space between us. Her darkest dreams were all on display for me. I blinked. "Raskos won't like that. He won't like that at all."

"And you would?" She shook her head and pressed her palms against her eyes. "I don't know what's wrong with me."

"There's nothing wrong with you, other than the complete lack of oxygen your brain is getting right now."

She let out a soulless chuckle, dropped her hands, and glared at me.

I grabbed hold of her and spun her around, dipping my fingers into her pants. "But I don't think you mind that at all, do you? If your next breath depends entirely on whether I *allow* it?"

Her head fell back onto my shoulder.

"Say it." I played with the hem of her panties. "Tell me what I'm going to find." My fingers edged underneath the last layer of her clothes.

"Ah, I'm… I'm horny, okay?"

With my middle finger, I traced a line past her trimmed hair, straight to her clit. She bucked against me as I moved over her nerves and traveled lower still. I parted her, dipping my finger into her center. She was fucking dripping. I bit her ear, and she moaned. "So wet, and all because of me?" Her cunt throbbed against my finger. I pushed one inside her, making a long stroke in and a slower retreat. "What's he going to think of you getting finger fucked by someone who stole your panties?"

"I knew it." Jules slammed her fist back into my face and leaped away from me.

I growled and rolled my thumb over the wetness still on my finger. "You may act pissed, but we both know the truth. And there is no reason to be ashamed."

"Just because it turns me on doesn't mean I want it to happen with *you*."

"And you think Raskos will give you that?"

She rolled her eyes. "I am not trying to get anything from Finian! You two are impossible. But you want to play your little game? I'll play. I'll sleep with him first so you lose."

I snatched hold of her neck and pulled her face to mine. She huffed out a breath, nostrils flaring. I growled. "You can do whatever you want, Jules, because at the end of the day, you will be mine."

Bringing us back to reality, she wrenched out of my hold and stumbled back, sucking in a breath. Color came back into her face as she screamed, "Out!"

"No," I said. "Besides, if I shadow walk, I'm going to be right behind you, anyway. There's no getting rid of me, Jules." I stood up and closed the gap between us, placing my hands on her cheeks. Crashing my lips against hers felt like the calm after a thunderstorm. All the energy swept out of me, streaming into a single moment that held her captive against me. Her lips parted, and I swept my tongue along her mouth, tasting her. Her face was covered in her own spit from earlier, and I didn't care.

She was gorgeous, even as she raked her nails along my arms and tried to shove me off. Her breath cut short into a whimper as she melted against me. She could fight me all she wanted, but I knew her dark truth.

And I liked what I saw.

I pressed my forehead against hers. "If you can prove you aren't wet, if you slide your fingers against yourself and come up dry, I will leave you alone for the rest of time."

Jules shook her head, but made no effort to create distance between us. "You and I both know that won't happen."

I breathed her in. "Then I'll see you around, Jules." Stepping into the shadows, I left her apartment and drifted back to Ceilidh, because if nothing else, I played fair. If I knew her secrets, then Raskos needed to know too.

Winner would take all.

I stepped into his office as he flung a paper airplane across the room. It thudded pathetically against the ground two feet in front of him. I hadn't walked through the portal by the time airplanes were taken out of commission by the Fae. I never got to see one in real life. In dreams, however, I witnessed glorious crashes. The things never seemed safe.

"What are you doing here, Night?" Finian let out a breath. His top knot was loose, and strands of his hair cascaded along his neck.

Crossing my arms, I leaned against his bookshelves. The shelves held nothing but binders full of inventories and notations. Raskos cared too much about this place. Between the desk covered in haphazard leaning piles of paper and the blinds drawn over the windows, there was no personality in this room.

And for some reason, Jules still summoned this man into her dream with me.

"I thought I would deliver some information to you."

His gaze flicked up to mine, brows lowering over his eyes in a glower.

I took a step forward, but slammed straight into a wall. Pressing my fingers to my brow, I glared at him. The asshole had put up a shield to keep me away from him. "I can shadow step this in a second."

"You told me my powers were worthless." He had the audacity to look smug.

My nose did feel tender. "Do you want my help or not?"

"What could I possibly want your help with?"

"Jules," I growled.

He stood up from the desk, and a few papers drifted to the floor from the pile. They were covered in red ink and numbers. I wasn't one for holding down a business, but that amount of red usually wasn't a good thing. I wondered how she would feel if she knew her livelihood was in jeopardy.

"What about her? Is she okay?" He spoke the words so fast, they slurred together into a single syllable.

"She's fine, but fair's fair. I told you the first person to sleep with her wins."

"I am not playing this game with you, Night."

"Oh, but the game got entirely more interesting when I dipped into her brain and coaxed out her dreams."

Raskos's jaw dropped. "You can do that?"

"I'm a Dream Walker, *Finian*."

"But you've never done anything except nightmares in my court. I've heard the stories. I—"

"Just because I feed on fear doesn't mean I can't see someone's wildest fantasies." I smirked as he eyed me.

"Why should I trust you?"

I shrugged. "You can ask Jules herself when she comes back. I'm sure she'd be excited to tell you. Or not, as it were. She seems very adamant to uphold this idea of purity she has about herself."

"Spit it out or get out." His eyes spun as he created a ward around his office, one that inspired existential dread.

I felt these needling thoughts prickling at the edge of my mind. *What happens if I'm wrong? What happens if I cannot find another Dream Walker? Why does the future of my race lie on my shoulders?* My nostrils flared as I sucked the negative energy straight into my soul. I gritted my teeth as my vision brightened.

"How the fuck do you do that?" Raskos shook his head, scowling. "My wards keep creatures away, they scream danger. But you…"

His magic tasted good; I would give him that much.

Licking my lips, I said, "She wants to be chased."

"I'm sorry?"

"Jules wants to be chased. She wants to feel so much passion under the hands of her lover that it borders on pain. And if the world burns around her while she's coming, she won't care. Her ideal lover borders on toxic."

Raskos's brows ducked low over his eyes. He tucked his hair behind his ear as his magic dropped, allowing me to step forward freely. But I thought it'd make a better point not to physically crowd him. "I'm not that type of guy. You are."

"Oh, here's the best part." My smile widened. "She also wants the guy who is so sweet it borders on disgusting. She wants to be doted on and asked how her day was. Romance and domesticated life and all that." I waved my hand.

"Those are…"

"Polar opposites? Exactly what we both are *together*?" I pointed between both of us as the smile spread up my lips. I couldn't help it, because our future was clear. At least to me.

"I am not sharing someone with *you*."

"Ah, but you are open to the idea of sharing."

"Is she?"

The grin split my face in two.

"Night, what did you see?"

"Only the things you could imagine in your wildest nightmares."

Raskos flung a shield out, and it shoved against the door, opening it with such force, the wood slammed into the wall. The impact shook the building. "Get out, Night."

"Why? You see the predicament we're in. Neither of us could satisfy her on our own."

"I am not sharing anyone with you. Not if we were the last two beings on the planet and not upon threat of my life. I would rather die."

I shrugged. "Your loss. It could have been easier to win her over, because on our own, she's still hesitant about either of us. Though, I have to say, she certainly tastes good." Slipping into the shadows, I didn't wait for his response, but his scream of anguish and rage hit me as I drifted back to escort Jules to the safety of Raskos's apartment.

She glanced over in my direction. Her dark brown hair now lay in wavy layers past her shoulders. A small breeze kicked up and made the strands dance around her face. Her brown eyes searched the darkness, as if she could sense me. A smile spread across her face as she carried two bags back to Ceilidh.

JULES

B y the time I arrived back at his apartment, Finian was sitting at the kitchen island. The door was unlocked, so I let myself in, but immediately regretting not knocking. It felt too invasive, as if I had punched a hole straight through our friendship and turned it into something intimate. I hesitated over the threshold.

His eyes wandered to take me in before wandering back to the dark amber liquid in his hands. "I never understood the appeal of alcohol for the Fae, at least not the human kind. I think I'm understanding it now, though."

"Are you… okay?" I shifted on my feet, not sure what to do with my belongings now. The air weighed heavy.

Finian's fingers ran along the rim of the glass. "It kind of numbs everything. Is that why it's so expensive?" He glanced over at me. His tight-lipped expression contained pure devastation. His hair was in disarray and the look in his eyes was haunted.

I had never seen him like this.

"What happened while I was out?" Though, I had a feeling I knew. Night had seen into my dreams, and the man seemed to gloat whenever he could.

Finian downed the liquid, slamming the empty glass on the table. He snatched the decanter and poured more into the glass. "I'm trying not to let it bother me."

"Let what bother you?" I dropped both my bags near the entrance, because I wasn't sure if he still wanted me here. The air around him was tense, so unlike how he usually was. I approached with caution.

"Everything." Tipping the cup to his lips, he drank deeply until the liquid disappeared again.

I placed my hand on his shoulder, and his body froze. Since he hadn't shaken me off, I pressed my luck. "Tell me, Finian."

He turned toward me. Red rimmed the whites of his eyes around his irises as he placed his fingers so gently on top of mine. The look on his face was pained, and I had to suck in a breath to keep myself from speaking.

"I want to give you everything you need, but I am realizing now that because of my…" His eyelids fluttered closed. "I won't be able to give you everything."

I let out a sigh. Of course Night came over here and focused on the *kinks* inside my dreams. I grasped his fingers in mine and tugged him up. He followed me as I walked us over to the couch. I sank onto the cushions, and he joined me, but dropped my hand as soon as we were settled. "Do you want to know what I really want?"

"Are you saying it to placate me?"

I shook my head. "I want someone who makes me feel comfortable enough to discuss those secrets with. The rest of it will happen over time."

"And if I know I cannot provide everything you want? If I know that today, right now, the type of male I am could never cross certain thresholds?"

"Like what?"

Warmth emanated from his body as he turned toward me. His fingers roamed over my knuckles. His skin was so hot, it was practically on fire. "Like chasing you, dominating you…"

"And is that all Night said I wanted?"

"No, but—"

"I won't get bored."

He tilted his head to the side. Some of his dusty brown hair grazed his shoulder.

I tucked it behind his ear and let my fingers linger along his jaw. I traced the lines of his face, keeping my touch featherlight. Finian's moss eyes shut as he leaned into my hand. A smile curled across his lips.

"That's what terrifies me the most."

His eyes opened. "What?"

"Of *you* getting bored." I ran my thumb along the stubble of his jaw. The intensity and closeness of my touch made me drop my hand, feeling self-conscious. "All my partners did before, so why would you be any different?"

Finian closed the distance between us. His lips brushed against mine as his fingers ran through my hair. The tender way he held me while the smell of whiskey surrounded us made me melt into his grip. His hands massaged my scalp as his kiss grew deeper, pressing into me until I opened my lips for him.

It wasn't invasive like Night's kiss. It wasn't demanding or all-consuming, but it was sweet and delicate. His kiss was the type that curled my toes and made my thoughts drift into oblivion. I gasped as his fingers trailed down my neck and onto my shoulders. He brushed the bare skin underneath my shirt. His touch was so light, it shot straight into my core.

Fuck, I was going to sleep with Finian Raskos tonight.

"Finian." His name escaped my lips on a gasp.

His tongue flicked against my lower lip as he laid me back down against the couch. With delicate movements, he pushed against me, using his lips to move me backward. I tried to wrap my arms around him, but his fingers roamed up my wrists. He threaded his fingers through mine and held our hands down. The possession wasn't about control, because when I looked at him, he had nothing but admiration.

"I don't want this to be about me. I want this to be about you." He nipped at my lower lip and pulled away, glancing at me. "Are you okay with that?"

After a mind-numbing kiss, I was fairly certain I would be okay with anything. Finian could have asked me to go clean out the grease trap in the kitchen, and I would have said yes in all my frustrated glory.

"Lift," he said, hooking his thumbs underneath the hem of my pants. His skin grazed against mine as I brought my hips away from the couch. Kneeling in front of me, he lowered the elastic on my joggers, grabbing my panties in the same motion. He was methodical, painstakingly slow in his attentiveness of removing my clothes. By the time my pants were off my body, his gaze had already singed holes into my skin. His irises swirled as he let out a low moan from his lips.

"You're stunning."

"I'm okay."

"Stunning." He pressed his hands on either side of my thighs and pushed me apart. His hungry gaze was level with my core and his tongue ran along his lips. "If you want to stop—"

"I won't."

"—just say so." Finian stared at me until I nodded, because he wanted confirmation. His hands moved inward, grazing along my skin and causing goosebumps to rise as my body tingled with anticipation. His thumbs crossed to my center first, and he moved with meticulousness, finding every place that made my body shiver beneath his touch. He nudged me apart with his thumbs. I let out a breath as his tongue flicked out and ran along my center and up to my clit. He sucked me into his mouth, shooting pleasure straight through me. My hips bucked off the couch, but he growled as his hands held me steady.

His irises swirled with the deep green of a moss-covered forest as he hummed against me, licking every part of me like a man starved. One of his thumbs traced the exterior of my pussy, teasing my entrance. I moaned as his teeth grazed against my skin.

"Finian, please…" I didn't know what I was begging for. I needed more. I wanted more. Grabbing onto his hair, I rode his face as he held me against the couch, not allowing me any more of him than his wicked tongue. As my hands clenched his hair, he shifted positions and pushed two fingers inside me. He searched with the same tenderness that he explored my exterior, and it didn't take him long to find a spot that made me suck in a breath.

He smiled against my clit, but didn't pause in his tongue's steady rhythm. Roaming circles around my nerves, he growled as my body shook against him. My grip tightened, my body clenching as I rode his face, screaming out his name. Every scrap of tension I had flooded out of me as I came. I fell back against the cushions, feeling a wave of exhaustion.

Finian sat back and gazed at me, a satisfied smile on his lips as he stared at my arousal coating his fingers. He stuck his tongue out, licking himself clean.

It shouldn't have turned me on as much as it did, but... my body wanted to go again, craved to have him inside me. I needed to be filled by Finian more than I needed anything in the world. I had never felt that amount of lust for anyone before in my life.

"Thank you, Jules."

"You're thanking me?"

He shifted back, settling on the coffee table as he lifted my pants for me to get back into. I couldn't hide the disappointment running through me, because even though that was a great orgasm, I wanted more. "I am thanking you for giving me such a gift."

I snorted. "You're too much."

His teeth flashed with his smile. "And you seem to like it just fine."

"I... do." I lifted my hips and allowed him to pull up my pants. "What about you?"

"What about me?"

I shifted my gaze down to his pants.

He grimaced.

"What is it? What did I do wrong?"

Finian shook his head as he cinched the drawstring on my waist. Grabbing one of my hands, he placed it against his hard cock above his pants. "You have done nothing wrong, but you also haven't had Faerie wine. If you do anything more than this right now, I cannot guarantee that my magic will stay tucked away. I cannot risk losing control with you. If I ever made you do something—"

Taking my hands back, I cupped his chin and forced him to look at me. The look he gave me was so full of longing I believed every word he said. I believed he would *stay*. "I trust you."

Closing his eyes, he leaned into my hands, placing his on top of

90

mine. His fingers curled along my palms. "And I will try to never betray that trust." When he opened his eyes, it was with a sigh that made any trace of magic leave his system. "If you are willing to do this again—"

"I am."

"So eager." He smiled and ran his hands up my arms. "Then next time, I will make sure you take a dose beforehand, so we don't have to worry."

"Next time… not now?"

His gaze turned solemn. "I need you to understand something very important. While Night might have made that stupid bet, I don't want it to overshadow anything we do together. I don't want you to think this is about me winning a stupid competition with that Dream Walker, okay?"

"I don't think that."

Finian cupped my face in his hands and kissed me. His lips searched mine, and I sighed into him, opening for his tongue. The taste of me lingered on him. His forehead pressed against mine as he pushed a stray lock of my hair behind my ear. "I try not to live with any regrets, and I don't want you to, either. If you still trust me in another day, we can do whatever you want."

"Promise?" I bit my lower lip, probing his earnest gaze.

"Promise. Go get some sleep, Jules."

"Can I sleep in your bed?"

Finian's brows furrowed as he pulled back from me. His pensive eyes took me in. "You want that?"

I nodded.

"Okay, well, get yourself ready, and I'll see you there."

Grinning, I scrambled off the couch and grabbed my bags from the front door. I placed them in the guest room, as that felt less invasive. Once I was prepared for bed, I went back into the living room and knocked on Finian's door. It opened with a flip of his fingers from his magic.

"Hi," I said, suddenly feeling shyer than when he had me shamelessly displayed in front of him. He wore a baggy shirt and loose-fitting pants that hung low on his toned hips, and I saw everything. My body begged to jump him, but I also understood where his fear came from. I had seen a lot of relationships with humans and Fae over the years. Their compulsion could kick up whenever they wanted something, which was why Faerie wine was so necessary for employees at the club.

Most Fae tried to be respectful. The one I had been with hadn't compelled me, but he had kept a tight hold on his magic.

"Hi." Finian pulled back the covers and gestured for me to get inside. "If you are still certain."

I glanced around his bedroom. It was simple and cozy, with a dark wood four-post bed, light gray covers, and a light hardwood floor. A circular area rug covered most of the floor space, encompassing the entire bed. Two nightstands with decorative square lamps stood on either side of the bed, and a bathroom with dark tile was on the opposite side of the room.

"I am." Crossing the room with more confidence than I felt inside, I slipped under the covers.

Finian slid in behind me and pulled me tight against his chest. His nose nestled against the skin of my neck, and he breathed in. "What changed your mind?"

"What do you mean?"

"I've asked you out before. What made you change your mind?"

I felt a blush creep across my cheeks as his lips pressed against my skin, leaving light kisses in his wake. "Would you hate me if I said Night?"

Finian stilled.

"Not like that. Like… when he invaded my dreams… oh, this is uncomfortable to explain."

His grip tightened around me. "I think you should tell me so my brain doesn't go to horrific places." His voice strained.

"I knew they were dreams, so I kind of… summoned you to piss him off."

"Summoned me?"

"The memory of you."

"Did you make me touch you in front of Night?"

I swallowed. "Maybe?"

"And did you tell him you're mine?"

I felt his hardening length against me, and I wasn't sure how to approach the next part. Because while I wanted Finian, I also loved Night's eyes on me when I made the dream version of Finian touch me. But judging by the hold the man had on me, I wasn't sure he would like to hear the truth.

"Finian, I will be whatever you want me to be if it means I get to come on your face again."

He chuckled and lightened his grip, running his hands over my arms. His touch made goosebumps rise across my skin. "I think you are leaving out some naughty details, but I'll let you keep your secrets. Maybe I'll make you admit them to me the next time you are clenching my fingers between your thighs."

My traitorous body hummed at his threat. I became a useless puddle as I melted under his touch. As much as I had tried to avoid engaging with Finian over the last few years, I had to admit the truth. I was falling for my boss.

I was in big fucking trouble.

NIGHTMARE

Well, weren't they fucking cute? Jules curled against Raskos, and his arms clenched around her as if she was the air he breathed. I had been so tempted to get involved the moment he guided her back onto the couch and held her down. Our girl didn't want just one of us, she wanted both.

The question was... how could I make Raskos see this? I had already decided how this relationship was going to go. Now, I needed them to fall in line.

As far as I was concerned, I was claiming both of them. Jules was mine, and she wanted Raskos as much as she wanted me. That meant Raskos was mine, too. Besides, I had a few theories I needed to test, and I had no way of doing that without slipping into Jules's dreams again. And while I could jump into her dreams and go unnoticed without touching her, where was the fun in that?

No risk, no reward.

I waited in the shadows, watching as their breathing leveled out.

Jules sighed underneath his touch. I stepped into the physical world. My hunger was getting the better of me, and I knew it. Touching her would strengthen the connection and my ability to control her dreams, make her afraid, and feed on her.

None of Raskos's club goers were cutting it. The nightmares of humans were becoming mundane. Recently, there were so many clowns, falling, and oddly enough, log truck catastrophes. I was getting bored. Monsters and Fae had invaded the human world, and they still feared the make believe—supernatural fucking clowns.

I *hated* clowns.

My fingers pressed against the steady thrum of Jules's pulse. Her skin was warm, and it made me want to do a lot more than just touch her. There would be time for that. My patience waned with every rustle of the covers caused by Raskos's uneven breaths, but still, I wasn't about to go anywhere.

I slipped into her dreams.

At first, her mind stretched out as a dark, empty void. I embraced it. The endless nothingness, the cavernous space devoid of existence and lost to time. If a Dream Walker wasn't careful, one could lose their mind to this—the in between where neither the conscious nor subconscious existed. It didn't take long for the world to crop up around me, because as soundly as she slept, Jules had an active and vivid mind. And this time was no different.

Her dreams burst forth with color, bringing swatches of brightness out of the emptiness. She fell into an old memory, one of the world when she had been younger, and the sky sang with birds. Her dream self was the same age as she was now, but the memory belonged to her youth.

Not for long.

She sat on the end of a dock overlooking a large lake. Her legs swung over the reflective surface of the smooth water. The sun shone brightly across her, causing her tanned skin to glow. Her almond-shaped eyes stared into the distance, contemplative. Her gaze lifted, and she waved at someone, a bright smile widening her lips.

A smile I longed to provide her, but also one I wanted to strip straight off her bones. She waited a moment, but a frown marred her lips as she turned toward me. The warmth she held a moment ago seeped out of her skin, making her shoulders hunch with more weight than I cared to watch her bear.

"Night," she said.

The dream stilled. The birds ceased their songs, the water stopped the gentle laps against the dock, and the wind died, no longer brushing her hair over her shoulders. I hated how cold it grew with a simple glance at me.

She had no idea what I was capable of. Yet.

"Jules." As I said her name, a split occurred between her. There was the woman sitting on the dock, waiting and watching to see what I would do next, and a ghost of her taunting me with heavyset eyes and a sneer on her lips.

She wrinkled her nose. "Are you here to ruin a good time again?"

"Depends. Who is the good time?"

Her gaze slipped to the teenage boy who stood frozen mid-stride, a half-smile cresting his lips and his hand up mid-wave. Her emotions had stopped the dream.

"No one who matters anymore." Letting out a breath, she stared back at the pond. The second being—the ghost—crossed her arms over her chest with an eye roll. "I don't know why I'm thinking about him. It's not like... Well, I'm sure you saw what happened."

"Did I?"

"Didn't you?" Jules placed her hands behind her and leaned back, allowing her head to dip full into the sun as she pressed her eyes closed. The ghost watched me with a smirk and wide eyes. "I could feel you watching us."

"And how did that make you feel?"

Her tongue flicked out, and both versions of her licked her lips. "I'm not sure."

I walked down the dock and sat down next to her. While her feet skimmed the surface, mine plunged into the frigid water. Not a single ripple spun outward from my feet. "How do you want to feel about it?"

"Society before told me I should be angry or annoyed or scared. You're essentially stalking me."

"Except?"

"Except I feel none of those things." Her eyes sliced open, and she peered at me. The ghost's smile grew wider with mocking. "I know what I should feel, but none of that sense of wrongness or danger is coming through. So, either I have a terrible survival instinct, or you aren't anyone to fear."

"Do you want me to terrify you?" Pressing my power into her dream, the sky darkened above us, making the lake become liquid black. "Do you want to feel your heart pounding so hard inside your chest that you know without a shadow of a doubt you are alive? Do you want the adrenaline to take over your veins so thoroughly you forget everything else?"

Lightning shot across the sky, creating deep blue shadows against her skin. Thunder cracked through the silence, threatening to splinter the dock underneath us. The storm made her come back into full focus as one person, one entity. The Jules who I had met on earth and the one I faced in her dreams melded into one person, but was a part of two worlds.

"I could make your body become fear. I could envelop your soul."

Jules cocked her head to the side and split again. One opened her mouth, carrying the innocence I wished to tear apart. The other's nose curled with indignation; I wanted to punish her for it.

"And how would you do that? Through some flashing lights and loud noises?" Both versions of her gestured to the storm. "I've lived through worse." Her nose wrinkled, as if the thought of her history disgusted her. "You know, I remember the world before it all happened. I had just secured a small scholarship. I had my life ahead of me. People kept telling me, 'It will get better once you're older.' I was waiting for the day those words became reality, and then the portal opened." One version let out a sigh. The other stuck out her tongue. "I am tired of waiting for the day it gets better. Why not today? Why not now?"

"And what do you think will make it better?"

She stretched her feet all the way out, and her toes dipped beneath the surface. Her arms burst with goosebumps. "Feeling something more than... this."

"Than what?"

"Wishing it was different." She looked at me again. One gaze bore straight into my soul; the ghost threatened to tear my skin off. "Don't you ever want it to be different?"

Without my concentration, the storm I had erected overhead dissipated as quickly as it had come. "No, not really. I don't wish for things that never were. I don't wish for a past that can never be. But I suppose if I were told to wish for something, it would be one thing."

"And what's that?" Her voice had split. One curious and innocent, the other dripping in venom. The first needed corruption, the second needed subjugation, and I was in a giving mood.

A smile stretched across my face as the storm rolled back in, the wind whipping at the lower strands of her hair. She fought against the pull, one side of her widened her eyes, and the ghost smiled maniacally. A war broke out in her mind. She was here with me, both parts she had yet to fully understand, the conscious mind and the unconscious mind meeting in the middle.

Excitement coursed through me as I saw the lines blur between them.

I placed my hand on top of hers, curving my fingertips into claws. The sharp edges dug into her skin. Her pulse kicked up as blood seeped from her wounds. Both versions of Jules snapped into one solid figure as her adrenaline shot through the roof. Her emotions tore apart the seams of the world.

"The one thing I want is for you to *run*."

Casting out my power, I solidified a strip of land heading across the lake. Jules ripped her hand out from under mine, creating long gashes in her skin. She leaped up and bolted down the rocky terrain. Her fear whipped around me, burying straight into me and ebbing my hunger.

But on top of the fear, she was *excited*.

I pressed my eyes closed and breathed in. Her scent left a trail for me to follow.

When I opened my eyes, Jules had sprinted nearly halfway across the lake, showing no signs of stopping and no signs of looking back, like the good girl I knew she was.

"If I catch you, I am going to win that bet. You hear me?" My voice echoed around us, filling the cavernous space of her frozen dream.

Jules made no acknowledgment, but she kept running.

I stood, stretched my arms over my head, and walked along the land I created. She could run all she wanted, because I wasn't letting her out of this dream until I taught her a thing or two. And we had plenty of lessons to cover.

JULES

Earth surged up from the lake, and my feet were under me before I had time to process what I was doing. I dashed across the landscape, feeling the rocks cutting into my feet. My hand ached from where his fingernails pierced my flesh. So much blood.

I hadn't been scared at first, not when Night first got here, but seeing red break through my skin made something inside me turn feral. All I knew was panic. It spread up my spine, coiled into the base of my brain, and took over my body. I was a puppet, nothing except the pure emotion rushing through me.

I didn't dare look back, but I could feel him. Night had his eyes trained on me as the ground rumbled up from the bottom of the lake. Every time I took another step forward, more land would appear under my feet.

This was from his magic.

Wait.

This was *my* dream. Which meant it could be *my* ideas instead.

My fists curled, but I didn't stop. I did, however, make my brain focus on an alternative path. Night was herding me away from him, toward the other side of the lake that was surrounded by a large field with nowhere to hide. If he wanted me over there, he was going to have to try harder.

I thrust my mental energy into creating another path, this one curving off to the right and toward the forest. As soon as I was done thinking about it, the path split in two. I tore down the new stretch of earth to the right.

Not knowing where Night was made my heart skip a beat as my breathing became faster. My feet flew down the path. I forced the ground to become flatter and more compact. No rocks. Then I dreamed up shoes for my feet. I smirked, feeling satisfied by my discovery. Lucid dreaming was powerful, especially against someone like Night. My adrenaline urged me onward, but I had a modicum of control.

A sigh sounded behind me in the empty world. "Very clever, tiger, but it's not enough to escape."

Maybe not, but that reminded me of something I needed. As I crashed into the forest, I restarted the world. It was strange hearing my ex-boyfriend say my name, only to sound confused because I had disappeared. The birds started at the same time as the wind and water. Everything came back and settled over my senses, blocking out the sounds I made as I stumbled through the woods. In my wake, I stitched the forest closed, making the ferns stretch and underbrush grow, expanding until there was nothing left of my tracks.

Night grunted, but his voice sounded like it was everywhere. "Isn't it exhausting? Putting forth this much effort when you know you're going to fail?"

My heart thundered, and part of me wondered why I was still running. Night was attractive, and a part of me wanted to explore whatever he desired to toss at me. That part of me wanted to toy with him as much as he played with me.

The other part of me remembered what my skin looked like bleeding under his fingernails.

And a smaller part of me wondered how Finian would feel if he found out. The shame I felt was not as strong as I wished it had been. Finian was a good man, and he deserved someone who was all in, someone who would care about him without a second guess.

Not that I was second guessing. I liked Finian, too. But liking two different men felt… wrong.

I screamed as I slammed into Night's chest. Reeling back, I tried to dart away, but he grabbed hold of my wrist and pulled me into him.

"How the hell did you do that?!"

"Your thoughts are more like screams inside this world." One of his arms snaked around my back, pressing me against him, and the other one intertwined with my hair. He pulled my locks so hard my scalp ached and my eyes watered. "I believe I won our little game."

My heart kicked against my ribs. "And what are you going to do?"

He leaned forward, brushing his lips against my cheek. "Whatever I want." Night's tongue ran along my ear. "But that's what you hoped for, isn't it?" His teeth sank into my lobe, and I pushed against his chest. It was impossible. He was an immovable object.

Plus, it wasn't like I wanted to go anywhere.

"And if I say no?"

He forced my head back, so I was looking at him. His lips

pressed against mine with bruising force, and I gasped, parting for him. His tongue flicked out, and he might as well have been consuming me.

"As I said, your thoughts are loud." Night pressed his eyes closed, and the air around us shifted. One minute we were standing in the forest, the next we were in the plains he originally had been guiding me to. "I'll give you one last chance. If you want to get away, now is the time."

"And if I don't?"

Night's blue eyes flared silver. He dropped to his knees, grabbed onto my ankles, and yanked me toward him. I fell backward and landed in the grass. The wind knocked out of my lungs, but Night didn't give me a moment to orient myself. His fingers traced the hem of my shorts and tore straight through them. Top to bottom. He tossed the ruined material away into the field.

His eyes flickered to mine as he pushed my bathing suit aside and sank a single finger inside me. "So wet. It's amazing, considering how satisfied you seemed after Raskos had his way with you."

"I was—" I gasped as he curled his finger inside me, not getting to finish my thought.

A smirk quirked his lips as he kept moving, testing, and probing for reactions. "You might not understand this yet, Jules, but you are *mine*." He took his finger all the way out and toyed with my entrance. His other hand ripped my suit straight off my skin. My breasts popped out, and my shoulders ached from where it had torn, but now I lay exposed to him.

I tried to cover myself, but Night's smile grew as vines trailed over my wrists. "No, you don't." The vines grew thicker as they tightened and pulled, spreading my arms out wide above my head. I gasped, feeling wetness seep out of me. How the hell was he doing this?

"You're gorgeous like this."

"I'm sure you say that to all the girls in the dreams you invade."

"Is that what you think?" His face was so close to my clit that every word he said cascaded over my nerves. "That I go around chasing everyone?" He didn't give me a chance to respond as he pushed two fingers into me. Pumping a few times, he flicked his tongue out and licked me. I jolted, wrists stretching against the vines.

Somewhere inside me, I knew I could break free. This was *my* dream; I had control. But I didn't want control as his fingers slid out of me again.

"You didn't answer me." His silvery blue eyes assessed me as head tilted to the side. His silver hair contrasted against the stark yellow field around us.

"Yes." My voice came out as a whimper. "If you feed on fear, then—"

"I don't create fear, Jules. It's already inside them. They give it to themselves, and I take the energy it creates." He tested my entrance with three of his fingers, tongue running against my nerves again and making my body buck underneath him. "I rarely get involved."

"Lucky me," I gasped as he pushed all three fingers just an inch inside me.

"Yes, lucky you." His eyes flared brightly as he shoved them the rest of the way in.

I screamed. He fucked me with his fingers, pressing his mouth down on me and sucking me in between his teeth. The sensations of his thrusts and his tongue were too much. I thrashed, trying to close my legs. He growled, and vines wrapped around my ankles too. I moaned as I was pulled open wider for him. His steady, hard rhythm never stopped, as he pushed me toward the edge. As soon as I was gasping and unable to catch my breath, he pulled away—stopping right as I was about to come.

"Tell me, Jules, what do you want right now?"

I swallowed as my body clenched. It didn't escape Night's observant eyes as his fingers ran along my thighs. I needed and wanted more. His sudden absence was like a hole drilling straight into my core.

"Tell me," he demanded.

"You."

"In what way?"

I swallowed as his hands roamed around my hips, up my stomach, and settled on my sides, waiting for an answer. It looked like he could wait for ages with that smirk cresting his lips. My body shuddered again.

"Needy, aren't you? Tell me. In what way do I get to have you?"

"Fuck me."

"If I fuck you here, I'm fucking you in real life."

"Like, while I'm asleep?"

"Oh, no, tiger. You'll be absolutely awake when I take you in real life. I am telling you the conditions of my game."

"Does everything have to be a game with you?"

"Yes. And I'll give you a hint as to how I play." He nipped at my thigh, and another shuddering breath escaped my lips. "I always win."

"Fine. You can fuck me here, and in real life, but when I'm *ready* for it. And I want a safe word."

"Demanding for someone tied up."

"You know I could escape."

He smiled, pressing his thumbs along the inner portion of my thighs. "You could. But you won't. What do you want your word to be?"

"*Tiger*," I challenged.

"You got it."

"What's yours?"

"If you think I need one, you haven't learned anything yet." He rose to his feet and stepped out of his clothes. Literally stepped out of them like he had become nothing more than a shadow. They fluttered to the ground, and he stood above me in his naked glory. His angular face tilted as he considered my gaze. My eyes swept over his body, and all my muscles clenched. Arousal dripped down me. He was gorgeous, with angles and muscles pointing straight to his cock.

I couldn't understand how someone like him existed. I was soft in comparison. My arms were strong, but that was from lugging around kegs, wine, and beer. I never worked out outside of my job, so my stomach had lost tone, but his man...

"I feel like I should thank you."

"For what?"

"It's been a while since anyone has looked at me with anything other than disgust. You might regret it." Night positioned himself between my thighs and with a flick of his wrists, my legs lifted into the air, the vines pulling them straight up, making me level with him on his knees. My back arched uncomfortably, but my pussy clenched with anticipation. "Fuck, you're really wet, Jules. I can go harder next time. I felt like your first time shouldn't be the worst that I can give." He ran his tip over my entrance, smearing my wetness around. His hands wrapped around my hips as he lined himself up.

He thrust inside me, and I forgot how to breathe. The three fingers hadn't prepared me for this. The stretch, the fullness, and the—

He chuckled. "You like it?"

"What the hell is..." I wiggled as he pulled out of me and pushed back in. Two piercings. I had been so distracted by his muscles that I hadn't noticed the metal sticking out of his dick.

"You'll learn to love it. Might have to get Raskos his own."

I gasped as he shoved his cock back in. I wasn't ready for a conversation where Night was perfectly okay with me exploring things with Finian. It felt disconcerting when I had Night's dick buried inside me.

Night picked up his rhythm, holding onto my hips with a bruising force to thrust harder. His piercings rubbed against me, adding to the intensity. He hadn't let me come yet, pressing me closer and closer toward the edge until my brain felt like it was nothing but scrambled emptiness. I clenched around him, and he relinquished his hold on one of my hips so he could run his thumb over my nerves.

"Night," I screamed his name on the end of a breath as my world exploded. My thighs clenched. My body came apart as he kept pushing more and more. He didn't stop, didn't let me catch a breath as he pounded into me. His hand traveled up my body, in between my breasts, and wrapped around my neck.

"Scream my name again." He was relentless, continuing the ruthless pursuit of his own pleasure as my bones turned into nothing but rubber.

Somehow, he coaxed his name from my lips another time as his fingers curled into my pulse. His grip was so possessive that my body wanted to do nothing else other than obey. With a final clench around the metal that was rubbing me raw, I came undone.

With one more thrust that pushed so deep I had to suck in a breath, he released inside me. The vines slipped from my wrists and ankles. Night pulled out of me slowly and settled me down onto what was a mattress. He had shifted the world once more, putting us inside a bedroom. Something about it felt so much more intimate than the field.

He growled as I tried to close my thighs. His fingers swiped up the mess we had made, and he pushed it back inside me, pumping a few times as I groaned. My gaze settled on him, eyes widening as I considered what he just did.

"Relax, tiger. You can't get pregnant in a dream."

What the hell did it say about me that I liked him pretending to try? Even though the thought of having children scared me, I still wanted a family someday. But with a stranger?

Was he really a stranger anymore? Because I felt like somewhere deep inside my soul, I understood him.

Night pressed his lips to my forehead. A move so gentle compared to the rough way he took me. "I'm afraid someone is awake and pissed off."

"What do you mean?"

"You're about to see. Back to the real world."

FINIAN RASKOS

I ripped Night off Jules, slamming him back into the wall with such force my apartment shook. "What does *stay away* mean to you?" The words snagged in my groggy throat.

I had woken a few moments earlier. I had expected to roll over and kiss Jules good morning. Perhaps I could have coaxed another orgasm from her. Instead, I found Night bent over her, tearing into her dreams with color coming back into his skin as he did whatever horrible thing he could within her subconscious mind.

"Finian." Jules's voice was thick with sleep as she tugged on my arm. "It's okay."

"It's not okay. I told him…" Another growl ran through me as Night smirked—the asshole had the audacity to smirk.

"I have something important to tell you, *Finian.*" He had no trouble speaking the words, even with my palm crushed against his windpipe. Fucking Dream Walkers.

"Don't you dare drag me into a dream right now." I gripped his throat so hard I punctured his skin. Blue blood oozed from underneath the wounds. "I will destroy you."

Night swallowed and instead of thrashing or trying to get out from underneath my choke hold, he pulled me closer. My body slammed against his, and he let out a grunt against the wall. He was hard between us, and he twitched in his pants. The triumph on his face grew.

Snarling, I pushed off him, giving us both space.

"Finian, can we talk—" Jules's voice cut off as I turned my gaze on her. Her mouth hung open, eyes widening with surprise.

My heart sank when she looked at me like that—like I scared her. Clearing my expression, I shook my head. "I'm sorry. I am furious with him, not you."

"But I think we need to—"

"Jules?" Night asked. He reached out his hand, but as he was about to brush against her skin, his silver eyes glanced over at me. Whatever he had done in her dreams, he was full. And she was here, not screaming at him.

Night swallowed whatever emotion he had and dropped his hand instead of closing the gap between him and her. "Would you mind terribly giving Finian and I the room? I believe we have some matters to discuss." He said my name without a snarl, and it made my skin prickle.

Jules crossed her arms over her chest, making her tits pool out of the top of her tank top. And if I hadn't been focusing on Night, I would have missed the way he noticed her movements the same as me. "If this is concerning me, then I should be involved, shouldn't I?"

"Ultimately, I do agree with you, but I have some things that Raskos needs to know before he makes a woefully painful mistake during this conversation. I'd rather you not be here for the aftermath."

"Are you protecting her from *me*?!" I snarled the words, gesturing at the absurdity of that statement. "I'm not like you. I would never put Jules in danger."

His eyes flashed into a brilliant silver. I had to be missing something. Night was fully fed, and Jules didn't seem horrified by whatever happened in the dream with him. His face was unreadable, and hers was… she looked sad? Contemplative?

"I trust both of you," Jules said.

And hearing those words might as well have been a stab in the heart. Someone *trusting* Night as much as they trusted me. He waltzed in here a few days ago, and she already trusted him the same way, despite knowing me for years.

"I think you should give us time," I conceded, mostly due to how much rage boiled inside me. I didn't want to risk turning this on her, because I couldn't help my compulsion when I was this emotional. I had promised to be careful with her, and right now, I couldn't be trusted with that care. "We will talk to you after Night and I share some words." I shifted my gaze back to the silver-haired man, but not before catching the glimpse of hurt running across her face.

"I'll go shower. Try to figure out whatever this is before I'm done. I'm hungry, and I would like to have breakfast in thirty minutes." She stood, crossed the room, and slammed the door shut behind her.

I threw a magical shield up and shoved it at Night's face. It hit him in the nose, which burst with blue blood.

"You fucker," he growled, readying a stance for a fight. Night charged me, and I threw up another block. He barreled straight into the force field and stumbled back a few feet. "Fight me like a fucking male."

"This is how I fight, asshole."

"With shields?!"

"Shields can be quite powerful. Ask your face."

A smirk spread across his lips, allowing the blue to pool in between his teeth. He wiped some of the blood off, but kept his gaze steady on me. "It's a neat trick, *Finian*."

"You said you had something to tell me." I crossed my arms, keeping a firm hold on the barrier between us. No way was I going to risk him getting into my mind when Jules was in the other room. Who knew what he had been doing to her in the dreamscape, but I would not let this man mess with me too.

"I do. It's an interesting story, not one I think you'll want to hear, because it will change the dynamic between us forever."

I lowered my brows and considered him. The overconfidence, the way his lips curled up, the healthy flush over his skin. Grabbing my hair in one hand, I yanked it up into a quick top knot, not wanting to admit where my mind had gone, what the most logical conclusion was.

"Oh, yes, that happened too, but I'm afraid that's not the point."

"It doesn't count if it wasn't in real life." Even though I had never agreed to the terms of his deal, I wasn't ready to let her go without a fight. Not since she spent the night in my bed, not since feeling her come apart on my face.

Night's eyes narrowed. "That wasn't the deal."

"Physically sleeping together is different than…" I pressed my eyes shut, but that was a mistake, because all I could see was her coming undone—not under my hands, but under his. It made me want to murder him. Shaking my head, I turned my glare back at him, refusing to back away from this.

"Besides, the deal matters little. I am proposing something else due to the new information I've received."

"New information." My jaw twitched.

"Let me tell you the story." Night sank onto the bed, the very spot Jules had been sleeping. It took everything I had in me not to tackle him and pummel his face into oblivion. "I came to your club this time not to terrorize your patrons—"

"Which you've done before."

He ignored me. "—but to follow an instinct, a baser level draw I felt to your club. I wasn't sure why, but there was this lure, and it made me want to come back to this very spot. I had been here a few times before, but left instead of pissing you off more."

"How many of my people have you fed from?" My nails dug into my palms as my fists shook.

Night pretended I hadn't spoken. "But every time I left, something told me to come back. Finally, I listened to it, partly because the Fae Slayer has created havoc in the courts and I didn't want to deal with the politics, and partly because there was something here."

"And what is here?" My teeth threatened to crack as I wanted him to get to the point.

"Jules."

"Obviously," I snarled. "What does that have to do with you?"

"She's Dream Walker." Night's smile grew wider. My jaw dropped open in shock and disbelief. I wasn't sure I heard him correctly. "She's like me. Diluted, yes, but she's the last of my kind—of *our* kind." His eyes drifted toward the door. "So, you understand, the previous terms of our agreement no longer work for me, seeing as how she's the only way my race will continue to exist."

I stared at him.

"You can say something now."

My brain had broken. *Dream Walker.* I had met Dream Walkers, and I had killed them. We had been taught that they needed to feed on nightmares and fears to survive. We had been taught to never let them touch you, and I had—

She had tasted sweet. Unbelievably so, nothing like what the stories had said. She had not sucked me into a world full of fear but had made me hard with wanting.

"Raskos?"

"Shut up and let me think." I sank onto the far end of my bed and pressed my fingers into my brow. "Does she know?"

"No, I only confirmed it just now in the dream."

"How?" I looked at him, unsure if I should trust him. I gauged the tilt of his head, the open expression on his face. His brow remained smooth.

"There were two sides to her in the dream. The conscious and the subconscious. Dream Walkers do that before they learn to control their powers. They are two entities inside their own worlds. There's the Jules who you are falling for, the innocent woman who is searching for love in a world full of endless vapidness, and there's the Jules I have been watching, the one who wants to toy with darkness and open herself to it." Night let out a sigh. "Which brings me to the next point, which I believe you will like even less than the first part of this conversation."

What could be worse than finding out the woman I liked was a Dream Walker?

"I said it before, but I am more certain now than ever. Neither of us will satisfy her alone."

My brows lowered over my eyes.

He held out his hands. "I know. I would much prefer toying with you and dangling her like a carrot in front of you as I devour her pussy like you did last night—"

"I *will* kill you."

Infuriatingly, he still ignored me. In my own apartment. "—but her conscious and subconscious minds have different ideas of love. And I don't think the two of them will merge, because she has such a small amount of Dream Walker in her. Until that rectifies, if she chooses either of us over the other, I think she'll be... unhappy."

"And you didn't want her involved in this conversation because?" My voice dipped low. "It involves her and her decisions."

"That's my point. I think we need to decide if we're okay with this."

"Okay with what?"

"Don't be daft." His eyes set on mine.

"Tell me what you want, Night."

"It's what she will inevitably realize, not what I want." His tongue flicked out between his lips, and the hair on my neck rose. Night gazed at me with hunger. Out of our confrontations over the years, he had never looked at me with such intensity.

"You *want* this."

He continued to stare at me, refusing to speak.

"But what I don't understand is why. You hate me."

"Do I, Raskos?" His signature smirk quirked at the side of his lips. "I'll leave you to think about it. And if you decide to tell her about her new identity, I'll be there when you do." He slipped into the shadows.

"You don't get to do that," I growled, whirling around the room and trying to see him, despite the impossibility. "You don't get to have the final word and disappear. She deserves to know."

Resounding silence answered me.

I sighed and exited my bedroom, padding my way over toward hers. I knocked on the door. No answer, and the water was still running. I nudged the door open and called out, "Jules?"

"Yeah?"

"Are you…" I swallowed back my jealousy, my rage, my fears. She deserved more respect than that. We had never established what we were and certainly had never discussed what I expected of her inside her dreams. She had no idea she was part Dream Walker, and I wasn't sure how I felt about it.

My feelings matched those of when I was a youngling, being dared to jump off a waterfall back in Faerie. The water looked welcoming and warm, glistening under the sun, but if I jumped, so many creatures could be lurking in the depths, ready to drag me down. It was a game played by the bravest of the young Fae, and I had never been particularly brave.

But right now, did I care if I drowned?

"Can we talk when you're out?"

"Of course."

"Coffee?"

"Yes, please." Her voice visibly went up, and it made my stomach settle to hear it. Jules was still herself, despite what Night told me. She would continue to be her, regardless of her genetics. She was kind. Her smile brightened a room. She brought out the best in me.

Night had to be wrong. He was playing another game. There was no way someone who created such joy could come from a race of nightmare creators.

"I'll have it ready for you."

As I was about to close the door, she called, "Finian?"

"Yeah?"

"You're really, really nice. You know that? And I do really like you." The words sounded like a plea, as if she wanted me to understand all the confusion welling inside her.

117

I pressed my lips into a thin line. If what Night said was true, then she probably had no idea why she was feeling this pull toward both of us.

My murderous thoughts toward Night waged war against my feelings for Jules. It was her decision what happened at the end of the day—not mine, and not Night's. I loathed the suggestion of us together, but I wouldn't force her to choose or force her to decide on me.

From the sound of it, Night seemed to hold the same thoughts, despite his claim on her being the last of his kind.

The words held more weight than he let on, because if we agreed, Night still needed her for the future of his kind, which meant younglings *with* Night.

I pressed my eyes shut and said, "Thanks, Jules. Coffee will be ready soon." I closed the door, feeling a piece of my heart break off with it.

JULES

As I towel dried my hair, I wondered what I was going to say to Finian. Despite Night telling me it was only a dream, I swore I felt sore between my legs. I was wetter than usual, but having an incredible sleepover with not one but two men would do that. As I pulled my hair into a ponytail, I sighed and chose comfier clothes for the day. I had a shift in a few more hours, but I could change into something cuter later.

Right now, I needed to have a hard conversation with my boss.

In one night, I had messed up my working relationship with Finian by crossing a line with him to make things physical, and then I had slept with his enemy.

Well, not physically, but... I gritted my teeth. The dream felt real to me, and Night had been there. It might not have occurred in the real world, but it was a real experience.

And I needed to discuss what all this meant immediately. I would not shy away from the tough conversation.

After shoving on a t-shirt and jogging pants, I walked into the kitchen to the smell of coffee. Okay, maybe I needed two sips of coffee before we spoke. I slid onto the barstool, and Finian passed me a steaming mug along with some sugar and creamer.

"I believe we have some things to talk about." His voice came out as a cool whisper, and I lifted my eyes, feeling horrible about everything that happened. "The first being about why you look so guilty."

I swallowed my first sip.

"I am flattered, Jules, that you would feel any guilt over what happened in a dream." His jaw clenched, and I could practically see the pain this caused him etching across his brows.

I opened my mouth to apologize, but he put his hand up. Why was he making this so easy?

"Things have changed a bit, and I think you need to be… in on the changes."

"If you need me to move out—"

"What? No." He looked horrified by the suggestion.

"You suck at this," another voice said. Night leaned on the opposite end of the island, glancing between both of us. His eyes crinkled at the edges as he looked at me. "So let me spare you both because it is getting painful to watch. Tiger, Raskos is aware we fucked last night, so don't go wearing that look of shame for a moment longer."

I glanced back at Finian and caught his murderous gaze on Night, but he picked up the mug with practiced patience and took another sip. With his magic, he pulled out another mug from the cabinets and slid it over to his rival, filling it to the brim with the black brew. Night took it and nodded at Finian.

What the hell was going on? I glanced between the two of them.

"And while I know I originally said whoever slept with you first won, things have shifted a bit. It seems you have two romantic desires—two different ideas for what your ideal love life should look like. Isn't that right?" Night asked.

My cheeks turned bright red as Finian tapped his fingers on his mug. He watched me, assessing my reaction.

"Um… I like how sweet and thoughtful Finian is. He's always made me feel safe and comforted." I swallowed, not really knowing how to describe the warmth he made me feel.

"But you also like how I'm going to treat you like nothing more than a place to put my cum."

I glanced at Night. He held absolutely no shame in presenting it so vilely. In fact, he looked smug as he watched Finian's fingers curl tighter around his mug. Besides, I knew the truth. While, yes, Night saw me as someone to conquer and own, there was a softer side of him too—whether or not he wanted anyone to see it.

"The problem Raskos has is that he knows the truth about you. You cannot *just* be his, and I am willing to share under a few conditions."

"Another one of your games?" I narrowed my eyes.

"Jules," Finian pressed. He let out a breath and shook his head. "It's not a game. Under any other circumstances, I would have to fold to Night completely."

"My future isn't for you to decide." I straightened. While I was happy they had come to terms with no longer fighting with each other, I didn't like how it seemed like there was a secret between them.

Finian's eyes held endless sorrow as he lifted his gaze to meet mine. "You're part Dream Walker."

"Which means, by rights of Faerie, you're *mine*, Jules."

I glared from one to the other. "I'm human. I've been here

since before the portal opened, so have my parents, and—"

"And that means nothing. Plenty of Fae and Dream Walkers came over before the curse. While I thought it was impossible for us to breed with humans, one of your ancestors must have found a way, because you're partially Dream Walker." Night shrugged.

I blinked.

"You're the last chance to save our race."

I pinched my brow and shook my head. "I have not had enough coffee for this shit." My hand shook as I tried to lift the mug to my lips. "How can you be so certain?" I forced myself to take a long swig.

"The control you have over your dreams. Humans cannot do what you do."

"Lucid dreaming is a thing."

"Yes, it is. But creating entire universes out of nothing more than your subconscious mind is something else. You could live out lifetimes in your own mind if you wanted, and if you practiced, I think you could learn to jump into the dreams of others too."

Finian pulsed his jaw. "It makes sense."

"Why?" I turned my gaze to him.

"You said you never felt that spark with Fae like other humans do. After you slept with a Fae, you should have been eager to do it again. You should have fallen for the Fae... and I've never tried compelling you. I've given you Faerie wine, as I did to all my employees, thinking you needed it, but perhaps you never did."

I blinked, trying to sort through this new information. "Dream Walkers can't be compelled?"

Both shook their heads.

"Then do it. Compel me to do something. That will prove that this is... wrong." My heart thudded inside my chest, because I sure as hell wasn't going to restart an entire race of beings with Night.

Finian glanced at Night, and I wondered what the heck they had talked about while I was in the shower. Go figure that the two of them would finally stop fighting when they came to an agreement about *me*.

"Give the lady what she wants." Night gestured for him to move forward with it.

Finian turned toward me, placing his mug on the counter. His eyes swirled with the green of unfurling ferns after a rainstorm. "Kiss me." The command rolled over my skin, making the hair on my arms rise. I wanted to kiss him simply because he commanded me to, but not because I had to.

"Tell me to do something else, because I want to do that."

"Jules."

"What?"

"You would be throwing yourself over the island to follow my instructions if you were fully human."

I shook my head. "I mean, I still want to kiss you. Try something else to see how much it affects me."

"Strip."

Again, the sensation crawled across my skin. From his command alone, I could feel myself getting wet, and I wanted to listen to him. A blush crossed my face. "Stop making it sexual."

Night snorted, crossing his arms as Finian glared at him.

Finian pressed his eyes shut, thinking. "Pretend to be a hoswisp."

This time, the command had no effect on me. The magic caressed my skin, but nothing more.

"She wants to strip for us." Night bit his lower lip as his eyes trailed along my body. "I don't think we'd have to beg too much."

Finian turned around and gripped the counter.

"Don't be too upset, Raskos. She's still yours."

"You don't get to speak for me, Night," I spat the words out. "But Finian… if you'll forgive me, then I would like to see where this will go."

"Forgive you?" When he turned back around, his eyes were blazing. "There's nothing to forgive. You are partial Dream Walker, which means you were always going to be drawn to Night. Like calls to like. I'm not sure if I can sit on the sidelines and watch this happen. You're welcome to stay, Jules. I don't like you being on the outskirts of town right now, regardless of what happens with Night, but I need some time to… think." He breezed out of the room without so much as a backward glance, and when the door clicked shut behind him, I swallowed.

"I didn't mean to hurt him," I squeaked.

Night watched the closed door with a haunted look, and his brows pressed tight. "Strange. Me neither." I didn't have time to process that before he slipped into the shadows.

I supposed if they needed time to think, I should take the time too. I stared at the milky coffee and blinked several times to fight the welling tears.

How could my parents not have known? Who in my ancestry had slept with a Dream Walker before the Fae door curse? Prior to the curse, there had been ways to cross over, but the Fae had kept mostly to themselves. No one I knew who was alive today remembered a time before the Fae door. Which meant it must have been my great grandparents or further down my lineage. And despite the truth staring me in the face, I struggled to believe it. Especially since Night didn't seem to have any answers for me.

Sighing, I brought my coffee over to the television and pulled out a movie from Finian's collection. As soon as I settled onto the couch, Night appeared next to me.

"If I were anyone else, I would have chucked this coffee in your

124

face." My nerves felt like steel right now.

Night frowned. "I am not used to having longer conversations. It's a habit to… leave."

"Is Finian okay?"

"How would I know?"

"I thought that's where you went."

"I was here."

"Watching me from the shadows?" I arched a brow.

"Like I said." He shrugged, as if that explained enough. And perhaps for a man who fed on people's nightmares, it did.

"Sure. Have you seen this one?"

Night narrowed his gaze on the screen. "If this has a fucking clown in it, I am throwing Finian's movie collection out the window."

"No, it's… You know what? Let's just watch."

He closed the gap between us and snatched my ankles again in one hand. I yelped as he grabbed my coffee. He pulled until my feet were in his lap. My neck landed against the armrest, and I was about to yell at him when he offered the mug back to me.

I took it as I watched his eyes fix on the movie screen. His hands moved over my foot, pressed against my skin, and massaged the tension out of one, then the other. I melted into the couch cushion, wondering how the heck I found myself on the couch with someone who was supposed to be scaring me half to death in order to survive. The man who had chased me, dragged me into a field, pulled me apart with vines, and ravaged my body. The man who also assuredly touched my feet as if he had every intention of doing this for the rest of his life?

Night fed on fear, but I loved it when he did—and I loved seeing this side of him too, the one that claimed me in any way he wanted. Even the softer side of him contained an edge, because he trapped my feet with the same strength he had in the field. He was doing this so I would fall for him, as his future depended on it.

But despite knowing that, it was still working.

FINIAN RASKOS

I stayed on the other side of the door, back pressed against it as I took several breaths to steady myself. While I had been attempting honesty, I hadn't quite gotten there. In truth, I was jealous. Jealous they shared something I couldn't begin to understand. Jealous of how Night had more of a right to her than I did. But more than that, I felt this odd sense of confusion that Night seemed open to whatever Jules wanted.

And how could she want me after they had shared… that?

Regardless, I didn't want to stick around to witness whatever was blossoming between them—if Night was capable of building a relationship. That male had ruined my court in Faerie. He had hung around unwanted for ages and was unwilling to move on anywhere else. He preyed upon my patrons, giving my court a horrible reputation. I had been unable to defend anyone, so why would it be different on earth?

This court had been a chance to start over. I had removed the reputation from Faerie with a rebrand of the club, making it into what it was today. It was a place where humans and Fae could interact. Fae caught using compulsion were not welcome back, as my shields kept unwanted visitors away. Which was supposed to include Night.

Except…

I pushed off the door with a sigh and went downstairs to the club. After pouring myself a tall cold glass of beer, I wandered over to my office, sliding the key in the lock.

My door, however, wasn't locked.

Placing my drink on the floor, I turned the knob and pushed the heavy door inward. It groaned on its hinges, revealing a Fae with quaking purple eyes staring at me.

"Close the door, Finian."

I barely had time to slip inside the room before the door slammed shut, cutting me off from the rest of the universe. Magic flared up around us.

"Evander." His name cascaded from my tongue. I wished it were anyone else sitting in my office chair. If he was here, it was on the orders of Lady Burke, and if that were the case, it meant nothing good would happen next. "To what do I owe the pleasure?"

His eyes whirled as he pushed the chair on the other end of the desk toward me. "Take a seat, will you?"

"And if I do, will I be able to stand again afterward?"

"When I am done with you, yes."

I was fucked, but there was no way out of this. My shields could only save me from so much, and part of my deal with Burke was that while I was in her debt, I couldn't turn her court away from my club, no matter who the Fae was.

I sighed as I sank into the seat.

"I'm honestly surprised you didn't break your end of the bargain." Evander leaned forward and put his chin on his hand. "I would have, if I were in your position."

"What am I without my word?"

"Hasn't meant much before, has it? Didn't you try to turn the previous king against our current king?"

I rolled my eyes. "That was covering my ass. The late king asked me a very specific question about the Fae Slayer's whereabouts, and if I were to deny answering, it would have resulted in my swift demise. More so than now."

Evander laughed and shook his head, a wide smile offsetting his tan complexion. "We go way back, Finian, do we not?"

"We do." I nodded.

"Then you must know, I would never take a job where the result was ending you." His eyes narrowed. "I do, however, answer to my Lady, much like you had to answer our late king. So, I am sure you understand what will happen next."

I swallowed.

"Twenty thousand coin behind on payments, Finian. What message should I send back to Lady Burke?"

"I am only behind because of the increased prices. If we could go back to the previous—"

Evander held up his hand. "I cannot do that, nor will she. The increased price was to accommodate the workers' demands for higher compensation. You know as well as I do that the new king put a large strain on the Lords and Ladies."

I shook my head, knowing it was more convoluted than that. Most courts would have been fine if the Lords and Ladies had dipped into their own pockets instead of placing the burden back onto the consumers. After Voss took over and sent out the missives, I put my rebuilding projects on hold to cut back on costs.

I had been paying my staff all along, so not much changed there, except for the cost of supplies. I had raised the prices of my drinks and admission by a modest amount, but it hadn't matched what Burke had increased everything to. Her prices soared, and the demand stayed the same.

"How are her construction projects going then, Evander?"

He narrowed his gaze. I had hit the mark. Burke had cut nothing from her lavish lifestyle. She always was one to come out on top, and with as many Fae and humans as she had in her pocket, it was no wonder why. I despised her as much as I admired her.

"I see the time for pleasantries is over. I'll take what is due." Evander rose, and I leaned back in the chair, refusing to show weakness during our locked gaze. He circled around the desk and knelt next to me. "When are you going to make the next payment, Finian?"

"As soon as I have it."

He nodded, pressing his lips into a thin, straight line. "Of course, for Burke that isn't good enough. But I appreciate knowing I might not have to do this again." With a resigned sigh, he straightened. His magic flared, circling around his fist. He drove a punch straight into my face, and my head snapped back. My body would have fallen backward from the blow, but Evander settled the chair with his other hand.

My cheek and jaw throbbed, and I could feel the swelling of my bleeding tongue.

"Two more," he said. His magic kicked up again, and with one hand still holding the chair to the ground, he drove another punch into my guts.

I heaved, coughing as bile rose up my throat.

Evander didn't give me warning for the last one, and a part of me was grateful I had no time to prepare for the third hit. He slammed his fist into my eye. One of his rings cut into my skin, and blood flooded my vision. I blinked blearily, feeling ten times smaller than I felt before. Burke had me wrapped around her finger, and I hated that bitch.

Straightening, Evander shook out his hand. "I do appreciate you, Finian. You never give me what the others do."

"Which is what? Begging for mercy?"

Evander smirked. "Because you're smarter than that. You know there's no mercy where she is concerned. I hope you make the debt back soon. She's expecting ten thousand coin in the next week."

"That's impossible."

He arched an eyebrow. "I've seen how many people you have come here. Are you telling me that increasing your revenue would truly be that taxing on your business?"

I clenched my teeth. Blood ran down my chin as I spoke. "I am not in this for profits."

His eyes narrowed as he tilted his head to the side. "Then what the hell are you in it for? You're a Lord. You could simply tax the people living within your bounds and come up with the coin overnight."

"If you think that is a reasonable solution, then we don't know each other as well as you thought, Evander. Get out of my club." I used my magic to open the door. He bowed and left the room. Slamming the door shut behind him, I coughed. Blood splattered out of my mouth, tossing droplets across the desk and the papers I had been poring over for days.

No matter how I cut it, I either needed to increase my prices over four hundred percent or needed to tax my people, something I had never done due to the conditions everyone was living in. My court was meager, living on the revenue from the club and not much more. Burke was price gouging because she could. She had the supply, the followers, and the means. I had nothing.

"Fuck!" I slammed my fists down on the table and coughed again. Wiping the blood from my mouth, I stood up. My body ached, my face was on fire, and rage rushed through my system. I wanted Burke's head on a platter, but more than that, I wanted reasonable prices for the people who counted on this place being a haven from the woes of the wilds.

Our world was horrible enough—why did we have to increase the price of blowing off some steam?

With shaking fingers, I pressed against the two spots on my face he had hit. My magic swelled as I tried to coax my skin into knitting itself back together, but I had never been particularly gifted with healing. My vision righted itself, and I counted that as good enough. I wasn't sure what I was going to do next.

One thing was certain: this day couldn't possibly get any worse.

"What the fuck happened in here?"

Except it could because Night's voice sounded from across the room. I hurled the first thing I wrapped my fingers around at him.

NIGHTMARE

He threw a fucking tape dispenser at my head. Who even needed a tape dispenser? Finian fucking Raskos, who tried to play the role of human club owner when he was a Fae Lord. I caught the black thing easily before it hurtled straight into my skull. He had an arm on him. I had to give him that because my palm stung from the impact.

"Raskos," I hissed. I crossed the room and grabbed his shoulders, whirling him toward me. "What the fuck happened?"

He let out a low growl, likely looking for another office supply to pelt at my head. His eye was black and blue, a cut had already scabbed over above his brow, and his jaw was swollen about double the size of its normal angular cut. The way he hunched over told me there was another injury I couldn't see.

Rage overtook my body. "Who did this to you?"

"What does it matter?"

"It matters because you're *mine*."

Finian's brow unfurled. "What did you just say?"

Gently, I grabbed both sides of his jaw, running my thumb along the blue bloom on his skin. My blood raced as anger spun throughout my body. "You're mine. I chose your club because I chose you. And the fuck if I'm going to let anyone else mess with my territory."

"You chose Jules."

"How long have I been annoying the fuck out of you, Finian?" I shifted my thumb over his lips. One half was swollen. It made me violent.

I dove into his subconscious.

He leaped away from me inside the dream. "Letting myself get touched by a Dream Walker again." He spat the words, but it missed the usual liquid venom.

"You're no longer in pain."

The crease reformed on his brow as his fingers went up to his jaw. He moved his mouth, flexing and relaxing, but I didn't give him time to mull this over. I closed the distance between us, grabbed the nape of his neck, and pulled him in for a brutal kiss. My mouth closed over his, claiming his lips as my own. I breathed in his scent, his fear and anger, his essence. Everything that made Finian exist ran straight into my veins. He growled, but I applied more pressure on his neck, and he softened underneath my touch, opening his mouth and letting me inside. I licked the edges of his teeth.

I wanted to do more, but I had more pressing matters now. There would be plenty of time for us to catch up on our elongated game later.

"As I said, how long have I been annoying you?"

"Over a century."

"And have you known any Dream Walker to stake a claim on a

territory for that long?" My forehead rested against his. His green eyes swirled as he licked his lips. I could sense the doubt settling over him, so I dug my nails into his neck. "Have you?"

"No, they moved around. They weren't territorial like that."

"We aren't, unless we feel like we need to *protect* something or someone. I claimed your territory a long time ago, Finian, and in doing so, I claimed you."

"What the actual fuck, Night." There were more questions he wanted to ask. Disbelief crept into the corners of his eyes and became apparent on the downturn of his mouth.

I chuckled. "So, I'll ask you again. Who did this to you?"

"Lady Burke sent one of her men."

"What's the name?"

"Evander, but he's not the problem. Burke is."

"Tell me everything."

Finian tried to take a step back, but I dug my nails farther into his skin. He winced.

"Everything, Finian."

He started from the beginning, and I decided he was right. Evander wasn't the problem; Lady Burke was. I wouldn't mind taking revenge. When the Fae waged war on the Dream Walkers, Lady Burke had taken part in more than her fair share of murders.

Dream Walkers had never been accepted by the Fae. The rift between our races had existed since before I was born. The Fae hated when we fed on them, and the Lords and Ladies hated their lack of control over us. That changed when the curse of the Fae door made them more powerful. They had hunted my race to extinction—until now.

Burke was heartless, sitting behind the massive walls of her court and dictating how the rest of the Fae should conduct their businesses by increasing meaningless numbers. She was going to ruin society—ruin what was mine.

"Night," Raskos said when he was finished. "What are you planning to do?"

I smirked. "The same thing I do to everyone, see what makes her tick."

"She has a lot of allies. If you do anything impulsive—"

I pressed my thumb against his lips. "Unless you are going to open your pretty mouth again to take my dick down your throat, I suggest you shut the hell up."

His nose twitched. A pissed off Raskos was the hottest version.

"That's a good boy. Let me handle Burke. Do you trust me?"

"No."

My smile grew. "As you shouldn't."

I tossed us back into the real world, and Finian stepped away from my touch. Once he was healed, I would show him what I thought of his retorts. I would teach this man a lesson about what it meant to belong to me.

"You should talk to Jules."

Finian pressed his eyes shut and let out a breath. His shoulders slumped.

"She's going to either see you now or after her shift, and if you wait, she'll be angry you hid it from her."

"I'm not hiding anything." He leaned against his desk and crossed his arms over his chest, closing himself off. "I'll wait a few more hours, so the swelling goes down. I'll catch her on her lunch break."

"Sure, when she can't do anything because she immediately has to go back to serving customers."

"What do you know about customer service?"

I smirked. "Oh, Raskos, don't you know? It's the thing humans fear third—falling, clowns, then customer service." I stepped into the shadows, going back up into the living room with Jules.

She had curled her feet onto her side of the couch and had thrown a blanket over her body. Her brown hair cascaded over her shoulders, and I wished to wrap it in my hands.

I stepped behind her and draped my arms over her shoulders.

"You are wearing entirely too many layers."

"Oh?" She tilted her head back and stared at me with those wide, innocent eyes.

I got the urge to spit in her mouth and force her to swallow. Someday soon. It was a promise I would keep.

"Where did you go?" she asked.

"To check on Raskos, but unfortunately, there is something that has come up, and I am going to need to leave the court for a while."

She reached for the remote and paused the movie, turning to face me in full. "What's going on?"

"I have to teach a certain Fae some manners."

Her brow furrowed. "Do you need help? I mean, I could help, right?"

"Have you learned how to shadow walk yet?"

Her lips pressed together.

"Or how to tap into someone's subconscious and unlock their biggest fears in order to manipulate them?"

"Obviously not," she huffed.

"Then my answer is the same as yours."

She frowned, and the pout across her lips made my dick twitch. How I wanted those lips wrapped around me instead of leaving them behind.

"You'll learn." I took a single step into the shadows.

"Night?" Her voice came out strained, so quiet despite the confines of the apartment. I paused, half enveloped in the shadows and half with her. "What if I want a family, but the idea of having kids scares me?"

With a sigh, I stepped fully back into the apartment. A bitter taste crept into my mouth. "Then that's something we should discuss."

"I'm almost thirty, and I've never really... thought about it. I've wanted a family, but I've thought more about the partner I would have, you know? Plus, bringing an entire species back into the world seems like a lot of work."

Chuckling, I climbed over the couch, crowding her with my hands placed on either side of her head. "It will be, but Dream Walkers don't age."

She shook her head. "I'm aging. I'm mostly human, and I—"

"Correction. You won't age once you learn to feed. We'll work on the rest later." I leaned against her. "And I think Finian is going to like the idea of sharing you." Cupping her chin in my hand, I ran my thumb over her lower lip, sliding her lips apart. She sucked me in, running her tongue over my skin. I pulled out as I gazed into her warm brown eyes. "You better get used to the idea, Jules. I'll see you in a few days." Before she could interject anything else, I slipped into the shadows.

I needed her to be comfortable with carrying my young, but she would get there eventually. She would be mine in every way of the word, and I intended to continue my race with her. It didn't have to be immediately, but it would be.

Finian was a bonus.

What an unexpected happenstance to corner him after so long. It turned out I needed the woman that he wanted. After playing them against each other and using them in a game, they were finally seeing my side of things. The three of us were better together.

We would be happy.

Just as soon as I terrified a certain Lady who was overstepping my boundaries.

It took me a few hours to step out of the shadows in Lord Alpin's court. He hated it when I visited, but he had one request, which I felt was only fair to grant. I stepped straight into his office.

The white-haired Fae glanced at me and turned toward the two people he was meeting with. Alpin cleared his throat, gathering the attention of the two in the room. "Excuse me, gentlemen. We'll have to continue this conversation another time. Seems I have a guest." I wasn't sure if the other two realized who I was, but they scurried out of the office like scared rats.

"Night."

"Alpin." I leaned against one of his bookcases with my arms crossed. "I see not much has changed."

"I suppose it wouldn't, since I run the borderlands fairly."

"You and Raskos seem to have that in common."

Alpin's eyes rolled. The freckles on his darker skin danced along his nose. "I have nothing in common with that weasel."

I crossed the room in a moment and wrapped my hand around his throat. "Say it again."

Alpin's wide eyes swirled with bright orange. "Kindly unhand me before I do something we both regret."

"Not until I get what I came for."

"Not so violently." He offered his wrist. "You know the rules. I don't care how much you like that scheming male."

I breathed out, pressing my eyes shut. "He's not—" Shaking my head, I dropped Alpin's thick throat and shifted to his wrist. Perhaps someday I could make other Fae see what I saw in Raskos. He had a large heart but didn't have the power to do much about it. It was why he had created so many underhanded deals. He had to because his magic was diluted. None of the other Lords understood his history, not like I did.

"Why do you allow me this?" I asked, looking at the older Fae. He had a square jaw, one that held an air of superiority, but he hardly wielded the magic I knew he had.

"Because it's better for my court if you only feed on me. I can handle it." His eyes glowed in a challenge, like I couldn't give him anything he hadn't already seen.

Alpin was a strong Fae. He ran an honest court with mostly honorable people inside it, kept strong by the court's borderland status. He became a hub for trade, but mostly in textiles and small trinkets one might need. I wished Finian could do business with him instead of Burke, but she had made herself the head of a lot of industries, especially those involving alcohol.

When I traveled through here before, Alpin had the gall to confront me in the middle of one of my feedings. Instead of demanding that I leave as most Lords and Ladies did, he offered me his wrist. He said if I needed sustenance in order to move on, he would allow me to tear his mind apart.

I respected him after that.

I did not respect, however, his opinion of Finian.

With no more fanfare, I dove into his subconscious. Normally, I wouldn't extend my session with Alpin, but today, I felt a little generous over his comments. Once I had enough strength to take the rest of the journey, I reveled in his nightmares for a few minutes longer. Then, and only then, did I move on.

Seventeen

JULES

Lifting the keg with a grunt, I secured it where the previous empty tank had been and tapped it within moments. The time it took me to change the beer out had lasted less than five minutes, but that was five minutes too long judging by the patrons' demanding gazes. Both Fae and human became irritable whenever the alcohol stopped flowing.

"Come on, lady."

"What is Raskos paying you for?"

Another number of jeers taunted from around the bar. The unruly crowd would be satiated once I got their drinks in hand. While it took a lot more than a few beers to make the Fae drunk, they were typically more demanding. While the Fae respected Finian enough to keep their magic to a minimum inside the club, that's where the respect stopped and their haughtiness started.

But the worst part about the Fae wasn't their attitudes—they were shitty tippers. Maybe tipping the bartender wasn't normal in

Faerie, and on a typical night, I swallowed back my annoyance.

Tonight, however, I was about to lose my cool. I had plenty on my mind. Like… if Finian was serious about my staying with him, could I get out of my lease and move in permanently? Would he open up again? Or had I missed my chance?

I ached to talk to Finian after my conversation with Night. Hope spread in my chest—maybe the Dream Walker was right. Maybe Finian would be okay seeking a future where we could be together, *and* I could explore whatever this was with Night.

As I poured a few beers and took orders for other drinks, I mulled over the fact that I wasn't human. I tended the bar for a living, and I wasn't human.

A shudder ran through me as another drunk guy called out to me. "Sugar tits, get it together!"

"I'm sorry. What did you say?" I put my hands on my hips and narrowed my gaze at him.

"You're off in la la land, but some of us are here trying to get our dick wet. Unless you want to volunteer?"

I blinked a few times. One of the security guards slid me a glance across the bar. We tried not to toss customers without reason, but if this guy said one more stupid thing, I might have to boot him out on his ass.

"If anyone should volunteer to worship someone's genitals, it should be you to her," a female Fae said from the other end of the bar. "Not that I would suggest such a crass thing. Unless you want me to dig a nice little hole to bury you in, you should apologize to the lady."

The man shifted his gaze between her and me. "Whatever. Fucking Fae Followers," he muttered, but drifted into the crowd.

"Thanks," I told her, approaching her spot. I cleaned the empty glasses left by another patron and wiped down the bar. "What would you like?"

"Whatever's good."

I snorted. "We sadly don't have any Faerie wine available to the public." Most Fae wanted it, but Finian kept it for the employees.

"Whatever's cold. Does that work?"

Nodding, I poured her a beer from the tap and slid it over. "It's a farmer's ale. Pretty decent, with a hint of nostalgia."

She brought the drink to her lips and some of the foam coated her skin. Her tongue flicked out as she licked herself clean. Her eyes pressed shut and shoulders relaxed. "Wonderful. It's been a long day of traveling, and I needed something cold."

My eyes widened. "Did you cross the wilds by yourself?" Most Fae and humans alike traveled in groups. There was safety in numbers, especially against the threat of hoswisps.

"Mother, no. I traveled with another male. He's run off on some business, leaving me to my wanderings tonight."

"Where are you from?"

She waved her hand in the air, taking another sip. She wore a cloak, one that blocked most of her face. Her eyes appeared dark underneath, and I couldn't see her features. "Around. A bit of everywhere and nowhere." Giving me a wink, she left over three times the cost of the beer on the bar. "Consider this an apology for the idiots in the world." Her smile sent something warm straight into my core, and as quickly as she had swooped into the bar, she was gone.

The rest of the night went by in a blur, and by the time I closed the bar, I realized Katie had been missing for more than an hour. Granted, she always disappeared close to the end of the shift, as she hated doing dishes. She hated cleaning out the grease trap inside the dishwasher more. While she was the better bartender and a decent manager, I got annoyed whenever I had to close by myself.

"You all set there, Jules?" Mathias, one of the bouncers, asked. We rarely worked the same shifts, as he only had one or two nights a week, spending most of his time with his kids. When he did, he always offered to walk me home, since we lived on the same side of town.

"I'm, uh, not going home this evening."

Mathias's eyebrow rose. "Oh? Finian finally convinced you to take him up on his offer?"

A blush crept across my cheeks.

Mathias ran his hand along the back of his short cropped blond hair. "Sorry, just meant… Well, we knew he liked you. Katie thinks he'd be good for you."

Of course she did. Katie thought *anything* with a dick would be good for me, but I wasn't about to pick apart my relationship with our boss to Mathias.

"Uh, we're… seeing how things go." Since I hadn't seen Finian tonight, I wasn't sure how things were going to be between us. Night seemed to think we could make everything work, but Finian's absence from the bar made me think of the pain on his face earlier. When Night claimed some supernatural bullshit on me, Finian seemed to shut down.

Besides, it didn't matter that I might have been the last of my kind. I had a say in my future and my life. I was my own person. If I wanted Finian and Night, and they were both comfortable with that arrangement, then why not?

"Good for you. You have a good head on your shoulders. I'm sure you'll figure it out. He's a great male."

"Yeah." I smiled. He was a great guy. My eyes darted to his office. "Anyway, I should probably…"

"Oh, yeah. I'll grab Katie, and we'll head out. She's in one of the back rooms."

"With a Fae?"

"Has there ever been a time where I've answered no to that question?"

I shook my head, waving Mathias goodbye, and went to Finian's office. My knuckles hovered above his door, ready to knock, but my heart was not ready for the possibility of disappointment.

The door swung inward, and I let out a yelp and jumped back. Finian stood tall. His hair was swept in a tidy bun away from his face, but as the light caught on his features, I realized how *wrong* they were. The area around his eye socket was swollen and mottled purple. His jaw held a nasty bruise as well.

I gasped. "What happened?"

"We have some things to talk about. Do you mind if we head to the apartment?"

"I was coming to get you, but… Finian." I placed my hands on either side of his cheeks, gently running over the bruises marring his skin. There was yellow mottling around the edges, which gave them the appearance that they had been here for days, not mere hours, but Fae healed faster than humans.

How fast did Dream Walkers heal?

My thumbs traced the marks. "Are you okay?"

His hand landed on top of mine, and he nuzzled into my touch with his eyes closed. When they opened again, his irises were glowing bright green. "I'm better now." Wrapping his fingers through mine, he nudged past me and walked toward his apartment, towing me along behind him.

When we were settled on his couch, he poured us two tall drinks and clinked his glass against mine. "I got a visit today, and you need to know about it, because my court could become dangerous."

I snorted. "Finian, *everywhere* is dangerous."

His gaze leveled with me, and I pressed my lips shut. "I owe some powerful Fae money. Night is going on some kind of heroic quest in my honor because he thinks he can fix everything. I have a feeling it's going to make it worse because of the parties involved. You can walk away now if you want."

"Do *you* want me to walk away?" I searched his gaze.

Color rose to his cheeks. "Do I think you would be safer? Yes. Do I want you to? No." One of the rings on his fingers clinked against the glass as he tapped it. "I can't promise your safety anymore. I can promise to try, but if a war breaks out between my court and the other court, I do not have the same amount of power as them."

"They have two Dream Walkers?"

He frowned. "Well, no, but you're not… until this afternoon, you had no idea you were a Dream Walker, Jules. No offense, but magic isn't something you can learn overnight. At least Fae magic isn't, and I bet it'll be the same for you."

"Well, Night can teach me. We'll have a few days at least, right?"

Finian let out a breath, considering me. His gaze darted toward the door, as if someone would burst through at any minute.

"I don't want to go anywhere," I said. I meant it in more ways than one.

"There's something else."

I narrowed my eyes, trying to assess exactly what passed through his expression. Desire, but also remorse? Excitement, but also fear? I wished I could put my supposed abilities to good use and fall into Finian's subconscious mind to peel him apart.

"What?"

He looked down and wrung his hands together. "Night kissed me."

I blinked.

"Jules?"

Downing the drink, I held my glass out to him. "Refill me?"

"Jules?" His voice felt smaller this time, nervous almost.

"I can't help but think that Night has played us exactly how he wanted to. Please refill me." I swallowed, focusing on the coolness of the glass.

Finian used his magic to get me another drink. His eyes crinkled. "What do you mean?"

"He seems to get what he wants. You told me he was the one who started the bet with you, thus creating a reason for you to keep chasing me at the same time as him. It gave him an outlet to taunt you."

His eyes flared.

"And he could have stayed with me this afternoon watching a movie, but instead he left to check on you. Where he kissed you, because *he* wants both of us. It isn't just me." I breathed out, lifting my gaze to my boss. "Tell me I'm wrong, Finian. Tell me Night didn't corral us together."

He pinched the bridge of his nose. His voice came out strained. "I think you're right, but the question is, what do we do about it?"

"Oh, no. There's no question. I know *exactly* what we do about it." I plucked the drink from Finian's hand and placed both of our glasses down on the coffee table. Letting out a breath, I straightened my spine. "We have sex."

His mouth dropped open.

"He got to have sex with me first in my subconscious, right? So, it's only fair you get the first real world sex."

"Is that how that works?"

"And also, he deserves to lose for manipulating us." I contemplated my sudden boldness as I pressed my lips into a thin line. Maybe it was from the harshness of Night in the dream, or perhaps this was from knowing I had another side to me now, but I felt confident. It warmed my body inside out. If I wanted Finian like I wanted Night, then I needed to make it happen.

The softer side of me also wanted Finian to know how much he *deserved*. I could fall for both of them and make them feel equally wanted.

Night thought he would bring out my darkness, but it was Finian who did. While the Dream Walker fed off my helplessness and submissiveness, Finian strived to make me more confident, make me feel powerful. He wanted me to state my desires, needed me to be sure of myself.

Finian snaked a hand behind my neck and brought me close to him. It was awkward on the couch, but I craved his warmth. "If Night planned this, then I'm going to have to thank the bastard."

"Thank him all you want, after you fuck me."

Eighteen

FINIAN RASKOS

When the word *fuck* escaped from Jules's lips, I was done for. Her voice made my dick hard. I closed the gap between us, bringing her lips to mine. I moved gently, partially because of my fading bruises, but also because I wanted to cater to the side of her Night could never touch. If I claimed this part of her, I was claiming a part for myself. My fingers kneaded the muscles on her neck until she relaxed. She gasped in a breath, parting for me and allowing me to deepen the kiss.

Heat coursed through me.

I ran my tongue along her lips, inching inside her to claim her as my own. I had no right, but Night had done the same to me. It had been an invasion, ownership. And Jules was mine as much as she belonged to him.

But did I also belong to him?

I pulled her tighter against me, nipping at her lower lip to coax a

149

moan from her mouth. My fingers trailed down her shirt, reaching for the hem. I grazed her delicate skin. "Jules, I meant it when I said I might not be able to control myself."

She climbed on top of my lap, parting her thighs so her middle met mine. Her teeth sunk into her lower lip, eyes flashing with a wicked sense of daring. "You can't compel me, Finian. At least, not into doing something I don't want. There's nothing to worry about."

That was true. I had been careful with her, holding my magic back to make sure it didn't flare out and cause her to do something she didn't truly want. It was hard to live with it confined in such a way, like I had to cork half of my being.

"If anything crosses a line—"

"It won't." As if to prove her point, she pressed her lips against mine. Her fingers trailed along my neck, and she was always so gentle.

My hands glided along her hips, rested there, and pulled her against me. I rocked her, feeling my cock harden against my pants. She let out a hum of approval as my tongue ran between her lips again, forcing her open. I explored her mouth, while keeping up a steady pace of her core against mine.

I would take my time with her because I wanted to savor every moment.

Her hands grasped my shoulders as her hips moved against me. A growl escaped my throat as one of my hands trailed around her waist, gripping the small of her back and pulling her down onto me. A surprised gasp escaped her lips as she realized how much I desired her. My other hand dived into her hair, tangling my fingers in it. I loosened her ponytail, shooting the elastic off, but rolling her locks around my fingers.

She smelled absolutely incredible.

Tugging on her hair, her lips left mine with a gasp. My tongue traveled down her cheek to her chin. I pressed my teeth against her neck and sucked. The noises escaping her were enough to keep me going. She writhed against me as I let her skin slide out from my grasp.

"Promise me this won't change anything."

"What?" I stilled, pulling on her hair so she'd face me.

Her eyes were open, searching mine with a watery film. "I don't want this to change anything between us."

"It will change things."

"No, I mean… I still want to work here. I don't want to lose this place. I feel like…" She sucked her lip between her teeth again as her brow furrowed. Jules leaned back, like she was going to open the distance between us.

My fingers left her hair and cupped her chin. "What do you feel, Jules?" I searched her eyes, because now was not the time for second-guessing. Whatever she needed, I would grant.

"I don't want to lose my semblance of normalcy. The world turned to shit, right? But you and Ceilidh made me feel normal again. With everything I've learned about myself, which I am not sure I fully believe, I don't want to lose this. Lose you." Her fingers ran along my skin, tracing patterns she had made while we kissed.

I brushed my thumb along her chin. "You won't lose me."

"Even if Night turns me into his—"

"If I'm not allowed to do things to you that you don't want, then neither is he." She glanced away from me, but I guided her face back toward mine. Her eyes blinked a few times, clearing the unformed tears. "And if that's something *you* want, I will figure it out." Especially now that I seemed to be involved with Night more than I had expected. "If anything changes, it likely would be for the better."

"For the better…"

I still wasn't sure how anything with Night could be for the better, but if it involved Jules straddling my lap, then I would take whatever came next. "Yes."

She nodded, gripping my arms with her hands as if she were trying to hold on to my certainty. We would figure this out.

"Come here." I brought her lips back to mine, sweeping my tongue along them. They were so soft, and when she let out another gasp, I couldn't wait any longer. Everything else in my life disappeared—nothing else mattered because I was obsessed with feeling everything there was to experience with her.

My fingers found the edge of her shirt and pulled it up over her head. The material drifted to the floor, and I almost died seeing my lingerie on her breasts. Her bra was a black delicate lace, and it offset her muscular shoulders. I lifted the strap and kissed the skin underneath the right side, then the left. Her eyes fluttered shut as my mouth roamed around her skin, barely tracing my tongue along her. Her fingers dug into my shoulder as one strap came down and I edged the bra down to expose her nipple.

I circled my tongue along the outside of the pebbled nub, and she moaned the moment my teeth grazed her. As I sucked her into my mouth, she gasped, and her fingernails bit into my skin. A growl escaped me. I would be gentle with her, but I also had to have her. There was no escaping this pull I had felt toward Jules. It had been here for years, resting below the surface, hoping something would change in our relationship to allow me this— allow her to be mine.

I rotated us so she was underneath me on the couch. Her eyes widened as I thrust against her. "Off. Now." I flicked my gaze at her pants. My magic rolled around us, no longer needing to be held back, and it was like a waterfall cascading down my skin. Relief flooded through me.

Her eyes widened, pupils dilating from my command, but she took a long moment to comply. She still had control. She was doing this because she wanted to, not because of my magic. Jules wanted this—wanted *me*.

I removed my shirt as she kicked off her pants. I stripped out of mine and smiled as her eyes trailed along my body.

"Why are all Fae so gorgeous?"

"All Fae?" I brought my lips back to hers, not allowing her to finish her thoughts. Her fingers sank into my hair, pulling at the elastic I had around it. She freed my locks, and it felt so damn nice to have someone touching me with this kind of intimacy.

It had been a long time since I felt desired for being me, instead of desired for what promises I could offer. A lot of Fae and humans tried to sleep with me as a Lord, because they thought I could provide protection or wealth. Jules never wanted any of that.

She parted her legs, showing me her glistening pussy. She was so wet for me, and we had barely begun. I lowered myself on top of her, using my hand to guide my cock over her clit. She gasped against my lips as I rotated myself against her. I enjoyed feeling her expectations rising to the surface, her readiness as her body squirmed underneath me, seeking more for herself with a lift of her hips. My other hand cupped her half-exposed breast, running my thumb over the peak.

"Finian." My name tumbled from her lips on a breathy moan.

My body tightened at the sound. I ran my cock along her drenched hole. Her back arched and legs wrapped around me, and she guided her hips onto my tip. I shuddered at the tightness, but also at how warm she was.

"Fuck me, please?" The words were so sweet; it was a miracle I didn't come right then.

I moved, pulling away completely before pushing forward. She moaned as I sank into her. Only an inch. Her hips writhed as I pulled back again, refusing to give her what she desired. As hard as it was for me not to take her completely, that wasn't what I wanted. I wanted to relish this feeling—her walls melding around me, accepting me without resistance, ready for me. How tight she got when I moved just right. I worked myself in and out as her fingernails scraped along my back.

"More," she said.

But I continued the slow entrance. I pulled out all the way and watched her pussy tremble. "You're perfect for me." I sank into her, this time all the way to the hilt. She sucked in a breath, clenching around me like a vise. My hand on her breast reached up to her jaw, grasping her chin and making Jules look at me. "How are you feeling?"

"Like I need you, need this, need more." She flexed her hips, bringing her flush against me. I sank deeper inside her.

I gasped as she pulsed against me. She would be the death of me, but what a wonderful way to go.

"Fuck me, Finian."

Who was I to deny her? I pulled out a few inches and thrust down hard. She tightened around me, so I did it again. My hips got into a steady rhythm as I pumped inside her, fucking her hard against the couch. Her legs and hips matched my rhythm, and while she was underneath me, she used everything in her ability to meet me thrust for thrust. I lost myself in her. I finally had her underneath me, and it had been everything I had hoped. Everything about her ignited my veins, making me go faster still.

She panted, and her body tensed. I reached between us and rolled my fingers over her clit as she inhaled another shaky breath. Her walls pressed around my dick, threatening to make me come entirely too early. I planned to drag this out, but perhaps the long wait had been too long. My rhythm became unsteady, and soon the sound of our gasps and movements filled the air around us. Her moans made something heady shoot through my body, going straight to my cock as she clamped around me.

She screamed as she let go, yelling my name. Every muscle I had tightened as I erupted inside her, filling her with me. Her pussy clamped down on me, milking every drop from me as I thrust a few more times, listening as the last of her heavy breaths became whimpers.

I held myself above her with unsteady arms as she gazed at me with half-closed lids. Her warm eyes flashed brightly, becoming the rich yellow-gold of honey. I blinked. It must have been a trick of the light because her eyes were brown with light accents. Dream Walkers only changed eye color if they fed. What Jules and I were doing was nowhere near the nightmares Night created. This was pleasurable, this had been joy. This had been everything I had ever hoped for.

She was mine, and I fully intended to take advantage of the fact that she was here with me.

Her teeth raked over her lower lip again, which was swollen from our kisses. Her eyes were glassed over and blissed out, and her skin was flushed. Despite how spent she looked, her voice came out low and husky. "What if I were to ask you to go again?"

I smirked, using a small amount of my magic to comply. She groaned as I hardened inside her. She was so wet with me, and a smile spread across my lips as I kissed her.

Nineteen

NIGHTMARE

It took me a night of traveling to get to Lady Burke's court. I had to stop at a tavern after Alpin's court to eat. The problem with shadow walking so much was how draining it was. In short spurts, I would barely feel the effects on my body, but I was skipping forward miles at a time, pushing myself through space like it was immaterial. It required my concentration and drained my energy.

By the time I arrived at Lady Burke's court, I was exhausted.

I roamed the exterior of her walls, waiting for the guards to relax their steady gaze over the walls of the court, then I shifted up next to one. He had a half-lidded stare, barely awake while protecting her court. I stepped out of the shadows behind him.

"I swear if you are afraid of clowns, I will kill you." I wrapped my hands around the male's throat, not giving him time to breathe. Consequently, that spurred his fear on, as his biggest fear was being strangled. *Excellent.* I latched onto his nightmares, breathing in the fuel I needed to survive.

After a few moments, I felt more like myself. Blood circled warmly through my veins and color washed over my skin. The world became sharper, my vision crisp and full of brightness. In these moments, it felt good to be alive.

I released the man, and he collapsed in a puddle of his own piss at my feet. Shaking my head, I stepped into the shadows, now on the hunt for Lady Burke. Her court was covered in white and gold, perfectly polished to reflect the colors of the blue seas. She had taken a page out of some Greek architecture book, even though we had never stepped foot into Europe. I had to thank human nightmares for my knowledge of the world, because people also feared their seventh-grade history teachers. Go figure.

It took little time to find her capitol building, as everything pointed to it. The streets, the alleys, the building facades, all of them headed straight toward where she resided.

Unlike other courts, Burke hadn't glamored a damn thing here, instead spending thousands of coin to make her court as lavish as she desired. And she did it by price gouging other places. I never had the need for coin, as there was no necessity for me to trade for food and I could step into the shadows to get anywhere I needed. But if Finian was getting punished over a few missing coin, I had feelings about that.

Strong feelings.

Thankfully, I was in a position to change something for him. Power was neither created nor destroyed, it simply was. I was lucky enough to have it, as was Burke, unfortunately.

I owned my abilities, and I was proud to be Dream Walker. Lady Burke, however, flaunted hers. She shamelessly made her court for the clout. She needed people and Fae to believe in her strength, so she shoved it in people's faces. And still, despite those knowing she held power, she continued to take more than she required.

I only took what I needed, and I didn't require such extravagant displays, not when my strength was so viciously real.

As I glided up the steps and into her foyer, I paused outside her office door before slipping through the cracks. She was nowhere to be found in the empty, vacuous room. I rifled through a few papers here and there to see what other deals she had in the works. The more information I had, the easier it would be to use this against her.

I found the list of courts that owed her money, some debts tremendously larger than Finian's. She had notes on planned escalation if she failed to collect. My eyes pored over it. She had her hands in the pockets of so many courts, it was a wonder no one had tried to kill her now that the curse was over. If the other courts banded together, they could easily overturn her and take her court for all it was worth. Sure, another Fae would rise to power and stake their claim, but it would be easy enough to pilfer her stores in the interim.

I, however, was not here to proposition the beginning of a revolution or call her out for her greed, because she was making about tenfold what she should have been from her factory work.

No, my goal was to get revenge for someone who mattered to me. And the rest of these Fae mattered none.

I shredded the book and threw the confetti remains into the garbage. At the very least, it would slow down her collection process. Walking out of her office door, her secretary bolted upright.

"You weren't supposed to be in there." Her eyes narrowed as they darted between me and the front door. Creases formed on her brows as realization dawned on her face. "How did you get in here?" An interesting choice for Burke to have a human working her front desk, but little surprised me.

"Through the front door."

"I would have seen you." She reached underneath her desk, probably to press a button for an alarm to alert security.

I smirked and stepped into the shadows as a couple Fae guards rushed into the building.

Blinking, she glanced around, frantic to figure out where I had gone. "Did you see him?" Her voice shook as she asked the two guards.

They exchanged a glance. "See who?"

"There was a male in here. He had gray hair, and he just—"

One of the Fae chuckled. "Did you have too much of an afternoon treat again, Frankie?"

"I told you the Faerie wine would go right to your head." The other one elbowed the first one in the ribs. "Did she believe us while she was enjoying herself the other night?"

A blush crept across the woman's features. "I will not have you shaming me for enjoying myself. I'm allowed to let off steam every once and awhile."

"It was a lot of steam."

"Fuck off, Jasper, before I cut you."

"I'm shaking in my boots, Frankie." The Fae winked and twirled on his feet, exiting with the other one in his wake.

Once the front door slid shut behind them, I stepped right up to the woman. "As I was saying, Frankie, I got in through the front door."

She had the audacity to yelp and slam her fist on the button again. With a sigh, I stepped back into the shadows. This was getting old fast.

The two guards rushed back into the room, eyes darting over

the empty space. They exchanged a long glance, eyebrows arching.

"He was here again. I swear!" Her eyes were large saucers, and the fear wafting off her tasted utterly divine on my tongue. "He spoke to me, and he was in Lady Burke's office." She nodded to the door.

Giving the guards space, I watched as they marched to the office door and flung it open wide. Both poked their heads in, and while they had their backs turned, I popped up on the other side of Frankie. My breath ran down the nape of her neck. "If you keep crying wolf, no one is going to believe you when the real monster comes out to play."

She screamed. The two guards turned, only to witness the hysterical woman crying. "I... I need to go home. I've been here for too long."

"Burke is going to—"

"Let her!" the woman shrieked, storming out of the building. I followed her, letting my instincts take over as she rushed through the streets. She took turn after turn, casting glances over her shoulder as goosebumps rose along her skin. Her eyes were wild, searching every angle and corner she could see. Sweat beaded on her brow as she glanced over her shoulder again, taking another turn. I stepped right in front of her path.

I didn't give her time to scream as I wrapped my fingers around her temples and dove into her dreams. I was searching for one in particular, and when humans hummed with this much fear, it helped me sort through their chaotic mind.

Show me Burke, I demanded her thoughts, coaxing the latest recollection to the surface. Burke had worn a ridiculously puffy orange dress, which matched her eyes with sickening likeness. Her heels had clicked along the polished tile floor as she leaned over Frankie's desk.

"It's time I make a personal visit to the guys at the new factory we have going up."

"Which one? The one on Center Street or the one on Main?"

Burke grinned wide; her white teeth too polished to be real. She was using glamor, even around her secretary. "The fact that you must ask, Frankie, is the best problem I could have. You know, I had my doubts about you when I started this empire, but you've proved to be a real asset when it comes to business management."

Frankie's memory preened at the compliment. "I do my best for you, Lady."

"One of these days, I'll give you what is due. I am headed to the Center Street property. It seems there have been some doubts about our operations in the mix, and I am going to squash them before they can manifest into anything. Wish me luck." Burke clipped her shoes all the way to the door before sending Frankie a wink over her shoulder. "Although, I don't need it."

Frankie practically sighed with envy as her boss breezed out of the building. Some people were too enamored with Fae for their own good.

To give Frankie some freedom from Burke, I morphed one of her memories into a nightmare, creating an impish version of her employer. The Fae grew gnarled hands, wickedly sharp teeth, and a vicious gleam in her eyes. I bent her elbows and knees backward, making Burke scuttle from place to place like a spider. Frankie's fear rose inside her as memory after memory turned sour, infected by this implant I fed her.

I let go of her temples, stepping back. "Take me to her."

"What are you going to do when you find her?" Her eyes were glossy, welled with tears.

"Do you care?"

Frankie's mouth turned down and her lips parted. Confusion

marred her face as she tried to parse through what was real and what belonged to her dreams. Her neck flushed as her nostrils flared. "I want to make sure the creepy bitch is dead."

If I could stay here for longer, I'd have a lot of fun messing with Burke's court. It would be my pleasure to warp the minds of her innermost circle, turning them against Burke without her realizing why.

Of course, I'd confess eventually, after I had a bit of fun. What good was creating nightmares if no one knew I was the cause?

But now was not the time, because I had two people to get back to. Specifically, a woman and a male who I needed to make obey my every command. The plans I had for them threatened to make my dick hard.

"Lead the way." I bowed and stepped back, opening the alley for Frankie to head off. This time, I followed her leisurely, as she led me through the gleaming streets of the court. It felt like the sun was shining brighter than before.

While King Balgair had issued edicts and missives banning the use of compulsion on humans, he had overlooked me. The only benefit of being the last of my kind was that the Fae often forgot about me until I was in their face. With all his laws for the Fae, he had never once mentioned manipulating someone's memories. Most Fae couldn't, so what would be the point?

I grinned as Frankie led me through the streets to a factory that still had scaffolding around it. The exterior wasn't finished with the same white polish that shone off the rest of the city, instead having gray tones and thick concrete walls. Smokestacks rose throughout the streets from the other industrial hubs she had constructed. Her court had become the center of exports. Judging by the stench coating the humans who worked here, it told me all I needed to know about the conditions she planned to run her factories.

This would have been the perfect feeding grounds, as humans dreaded the monotony of their day jobs almost as much as they feared falling.

While Raskos might not have had much inside his court, as most of it still lay in shambles in the wake of the invasion, the buildings he did have were clean, polished. His club smelled of pheromones and slightly stale beer. That, however, was typical of any tavern, let alone a club. He took great care of his people. He viewed himself as a weak leader because he couldn't get rid of me, but if anything, his self-depreciation made me want him more.

His modesty was attractive. He wasn't as vulnerable as he thought he was, but bending him so much to break him? That was a challenge I loved.

Frankie ducked inside, ignoring the raised brows from the people around us. She marched up two flights of stairs. The stairs hugged the far wall, wrapping up to an office that had already been finished. One wall of the smaller room was nothing but floor-to-ceiling windows, looking down over the factory floor that a future supervisor would lord over.

How insecure was Burke to need this much monitoring? It told me everything I needed to know about her court—if she were to let sleeping dogs lie, they would find ways to revolt against her rule. If she gave them no lead, they had nowhere to go except to stay under her control.

If we hadn't been on the opposite interests of Raskos's court, I might admire what she had created here. It was devious, like she had learned from the Dream Walkers.

She sat at a desk; long legs crossed under her full skirt. Her ankles peeked out from the hem of the fabric. The orange color matched her hair and eyes, but barely offset her skin. Burke's eyes pored over the paper, not looking up as Frankie entered the room.

I had disappeared into the shadows.

"Why are you here and not watching the office?"

The woman glanced behind her, realizing I was no longer with her. Her brows furrowed, but she straightened her spine and stared at her boss. "Because I quit."

One of Burke's eyebrows rose. Her eyes fluttered shut, as if this statement had been the most frustrating thing she had heard today. She folded the papers, placed them on the desk, and gazed at her employee with narrowed eyes. "I don't think I heard you correctly. You said you were quitting."

"Yes." An edge of fear wobbled the woman's voice, and I sucked it in.

"And why would you do that? I have treated you fairly, more fairly than humans typically deserve. Your pay has been better than others, and I have only compelled you upon occasion."

Frankie's brows lowered, and a frown crossed her features. The poor woman had no idea why she was quitting, just that her nightmares had taken every single moment and twisted them into a non-reality. She couldn't trust herself any more than she could trust the Fae sitting at the desk.

Burke's head tilted to the side. "Tell me." Her magic filled the room.

"There was a man with silver hair and eyes who made me think... Or made you... Or what are you?"

Burke's lips curled into a snarl as her eyes searched the room. "Come out, you fucking coward."

I sat on the desk in front of her, but didn't come out of the shadows.

Burke looked through me toward her employee. "We'll talk about this later. You are not quitting and forget whatever happened with that man earlier." Her magic bounced around the woman, settling until the frustration left the human's face.

Frankie shook her head. "Of course. I have no idea what came over me. I've always enjoyed our time together." She left the room, and as soon as the door shut, I appeared in front of Burke.

Her eyes swirled with magic, but I clamped my hand over her mouth.

"Oh, I wouldn't dare unless you want to spend the rest of your days trapped inside your own nightmares."

She said something behind my hand, but it came out muffled. Her magic quickly died, and her eyes shifted to a duller orange color.

"I'm going to tell you something very important, more important than you have ever heard from me. So, if I let go of your mouth, do you promise to listen?"

Her glower made me wish I was back with Jules, because I wanted to do dark things, none of which involved Burke.

"Great." I peeled my hand from her lips.

"Bastard."

"It seems you have an interesting fear, Lady. It's something I could exploit, turning your followers against you one by one."

She swallowed, nostrils flaring. Her lips turned down in a snarl.

"It was easy enough to do with Frankie. Her mind is malleable. Imagine how much havoc I could reap if I were to settle down and stay here?"

"What do you want, Night?" She pushed her chair back, as if giving herself distance could hide her innermost thoughts from me. All it took was a touch, and she knew she was at my mercy now.

"It seems we have something in common, much to my dismay."

Her eyes narrowed. "I have nothing in common with you."

"Ah, but you do. You have an interest in making Raskos's life hell." I snapped out my hand and latched it around her throat, pulling her and the chair back toward me. "But the problem is, that's *mine*. And I am quite possessive."

"Raskos?" She spoke the word through her clenched jaw. "Why the fuck would you—"

"You're not understanding. So, let me show you."

We fell into her dreams. I, however, didn't have a body to join her in this one, because her nightmares were not mine to influence. I wanted her to feel her worst fears coming to life, watch the possibility of this future unfurl before her. She needed to make some good and informed decisions next, otherwise I would bring her kingdom to its knees.

Burke stood alone. Her city was completely built with beautiful, luminous walls and gold accents reflecting the sun. The sky was full of birds fluttering and singing. The ocean crashed in the distance, but everything echoed off the cavernous, vacant spaces. Burke walked alone in a torn dress, one high heel broken, as she stumbled across the cobblestones.

"Anyone?" she screamed into the emptiness of the city. "Someone? Please?" Her arms wrapped around herself as fear coiled throughout her body. She had built everything to perfection, made everything exactly how she wanted it. Her hopes had been to build the court up so much that no one could avoid her. She wanted a city full of people and Fae to rule.

But in her heart of hearts, what she feared most was this: being alone. Having everyone realize that she was nothing and abandon her as so many had before. Burke had no attachments, and she had no real connections. She had never been in love.

That emptiness festered inside her, manifesting itself into outward darkness, spinning into the world as a virus. It seeped through her transactions with others. If she made herself irreplaceable, it would force others to need her. Despite her ruthlessness, no one could ignore the connections she had or the city she had created. She was the only one capable of producing goods on such a scale. She would never be alone, even if she were only surrounded by enemies.

One thing became certain—Raskos needed to get out from under her thumb as soon as possible. Maybe opening a brewery himself? I had seen breweries in nightmares, usually having someone drown in a vat, but such an undertaking shouldn't be *that* hard.

"Is anyone here?" She sank down in the middle of the street, her shredded dress fanning around her like vines. "Anyone?"

I spun out of her nightmare and shadow walked across the room, staring at her from the doorway.

"Get. Out." Her words were like whips, lashing out.

"I have to say, Burke, you surprise me."

She shook as she rose from her chair. Her nails curled into the wood on the desk. "Out!"

"Because I'm afraid I must tell you something. Something you won't like to hear."

Her magic swelled in the room and her body shimmered.

"You're already living your worst nightmare, because not even one of these people would care if you disappeared. They would carry on without you, like you never were. And if you touch Raskos again, you'll see what I am capable of."

She screamed, her magic whirling around her. When pushed, Burke was capable of more powerful magic than most. She flung her hand out, but I had disappeared before she had the chance to cast anything.

JULES

The words *honeymoon phase* had never made much sense to me before. My exes were mostly flings, never developing into anything further than a few nights at the most. While sleeping with Finian hadn't made me addicted to Fae sex, it had been *fun*, and I felt like an anxious kid on the last day of school waiting for my shift to be over so I could climb back into bed with the man for the third time.

Night had been gone for two days. A part of me worried about him, but the other part of me knew he was safe so long as he could disappear into the shadows. A man of nightmares, after all, was an apex predator.

His absence gave me time to focus on my relationship with Finian and what blossomed between us. Every time I thought about the Fae, I became giddy and excited. Tonight, because of my buoyant mood, I was getting more tips than ever before. Between the music, slinging drinks, and small talk, I couldn't stop smiling.

When Katie disappeared into the back room toward the end of our shift, I wasn't annoyed or upset.

That was because Finian came out of his office to help clean the bar.

We worked in perfect unison. He bussed tables while I polished the glasses. I sneaked glances at him out of the corner of my eye, and whenever his eyes flickered to me, I grinned.

I knew Night had herded us together because Night's end game had always been the both of us. I had figured it out when I proposed sleeping with Finian in the first place. But I had been attracted to my boss for a long time, even before I met the Dream Walker. I had never wanted to cross the line before, because it felt like dangerous territory, mixing work and pleasure.

Now that we had started a relationship, it excited me. It was new, fantastic. It was something we could build on toward a future I had never allowed myself to dream about. We needed to have a longer discussion about the three of us later, but right now, I admired his longer fingers, the way they curled around each glass. I had to hide my blush whenever I thought about those fingers inside me.

Watching him bend over to wipe down a table was becoming the sexiest thing on the planet, and perhaps Katie had been right all these years. Maybe I had been sex starved.

"What are you staring at?" Finian quirked an eyebrow as he piled the next load of dishes into the washer.

"Nothing." I shrugged and turned back toward the supply closet to grab the mop.

He tugged on my wrist, pulling me into him. "Nothing? You've been doing it all night."

Heat crossed my cheeks. "I need to mop."

"Tell me what's going through that head of yours."

"You're… hot." It still felt strange saying it to my boss. I had spent so much time distancing myself from him, but here he was, holding me. And I had spent the day having his cum inside me, sore, but in the best way possible. The thought made my skin warm.

"Hot, huh? That's all? Not drop dead gorgeous or sexy as sin? Just hot?" His eyes brightened, glowing slightly as his magic caressed my skin. The firmness of his hold made me forget how to breathe.

I bit my lower lip.

He kissed the tip of my nose and smiled. "Let's finish so we can go upstairs. I was thinking we could have dinner and watch a movie." The curl of his eyes and slight raise of his brows told me we would likely not *watch* the movie, which I was completely fine with.

In another few minutes, we finished the preparations for next shift. With all the employees sent home, we headed toward the apartment. In the stairwell, I couldn't take it any longer. I pulled him to me, crushing our lips together. He backed me against the wall, curled his fingers around my hips, and pressed into me with his hardened length. We had barely started touching, and already, my body ached for him.

"We need to eat something." He nipped at my jaw as I inhaled a breath. Finian always smelled sweet, which made me want to draw him into me more. "As much as I want to bury myself inside you, you're likely hungry, too."

"I feel great. Better than I have in most of my life, actually." It was true. I hadn't eaten much today, but my body felt electrified. I trailed my hand down his chest.

He threaded his fingers through mine. A coy smile played on his lips. "Come on." Pushing away from the wall, he led the way upstairs. Finian was an attentive partner, and it made me sad that I had kept him at arm's length for the past few years. We could have had more time together, but if what Night had said was true, I would stop aging as soon as I discovered how to feed.

Which meant we had plenty of time. My mind couldn't begin to fathom it, but I would take it one day at a time.

As Finian prepared dinner, I sank onto the stool by the island, contemplating what it would feel like to feed. I wasn't like Night. I didn't want to terrify people or scare them. If anything, I wanted that done to me, because I liked how he chased me. I wanted to feel the rush of getting caught, being prey. I wanted to be the bad girl who was taught a lesson and became the good girl only after my punishment.

Thinking about doing that to someone else? That wasn't me. Being a bartender was easy for me because I liked to make people happy. I tried to spread any semblance of joy I could. Once the portal had opened, everything had turned asunder, making the world a dark and dreary place. There were good people in the court who deserved a happy life, and I had to hope that things would get better over time.

That's who I was.

So how could I learn to terrify someone in order to stay alive another day, another week? Maybe it would get easier over time. Maybe I could find someone who liked to be scared.

Even so, the thought of becoming someone's nightmare unsettled me.

Finian must have noticed my mood shift as he placed a steaming plate of vegetables on the table. There was a small amount of jerky on the side, and he poured a hefty glass of regular white wine with it, chilled from the refrigerator.

"What's wrong?" He put two plates down and slid into the seat next to me. His fingers ran along my shoulders, soothing the stress from my back.

"I don't think I can do what Night does."

Finian winced. We hadn't spoken about it yet, but I knew Finian. The discovery of what I was made him uncomfortable, even if he wasn't showing it. He liked me—that much was clear—but denial about my lineage hung over us.

"You don't have to feed. If you are mostly human and only a bit Dream Walker, you could spend your entire life not feeding…" A frown crossed his lips as he loaded our plates up from the serving dish.

"But that means I would die sooner than both of you." My voice came out small. I was almost thirty, and in a world like ours, that was considered on the older side of things for humans.

Finian's frown deepened as he nodded. He stabbed a few stir-fried carrots and popped them into his mouth. After a few moments of chewing, he swallowed. He pulled the elastic out of his hair and tousled it around his ears. "I might regret saying this, but if it keeps you alive, I will let you feed on me."

My eyes widened, and I shook my head. "I wouldn't ask you to—"

His hand wrapped around my thigh, squeezing possessively. "I have to admit, one of the things I hated about trying to be with humans was how careful I had to be. I had to make sure they were on Faerie wine. That kind of caution… it made things complicated. It was worth it for their consent, but it required ample amount of double checking." He let out a breath, gazing at me as his eyes swirled to life. His magic was undeniably beautiful. "Jules, I don't have to do that with you. I can't compel you, even by accident. I don't want to lose you, so any number of nightmares would be worth it if I was able to keep you alive longer."

I stared down at my plate, using my fork to move the vegetables around. His declaration scared me because it was weighted. It meant more than simple words. He wanted me around for as long as possible. And I wanted the same. This was still new, which made it terrifying, but I wanted desperately to make this work.

His fingers dug into my thigh. "I want you to try it."

"What? Finian, no."

"Why not? The worst thing would be that you see my biggest fear, and you feed on it. You—"

"I don't want to." I shook my head and took in a forkful of vegetables.

He nodded as he waited for me to continue, but he took his hand back, giving me space. There really wasn't a more perfect man out there for me. Except... there was a strange twinge in my stomach. A heady feeling crept over my body. As much as I adored Finian's respect and his understanding, there *was* something missing.

It was a stitch inside me, a little quirk.

There were *two* perfect men, and if I was going to learn to feed, it had to be when Night was here. He would know if something went wrong. He would fix it. As much as he dominated the space he was in, he wanted me to awaken into my powers.

He'd make sure both Finian and I stayed safe.

"Sorry, I mean... We can try it, but I think we should have Night here for that. I feel like..." I paused as Finian looked down at his plate. His jaw ticked. "What if I mess it up? What if I go too deep into your dreams and ruin you somehow? What if I—"

Finian surprised me by pressing a soft kiss against my lips. "Breathe, Jules."

With his forehead against mine, I breathed.

He ran his thumb along my lower lip and hummed. "We don't

have to make any decisions tonight. I am up for watching a movie if you would like."

"Actually watching?" A smirk spread over my lips as he pulled back. His eyes were ignited.

"Sure."

"What if we..." I leaned over to him and whispered exactly what I was thinking in his ear.

Finian gazed at me. "Jules."

"Finian."

"I think I just fell in love with you."

"Shut up." I smacked him on the shoulder with the back of my hand.

"No, seriously. I'm screwed. Involved with two Dream Walkers." He shook his head, staring at his food with his brows furrowed. An amused smiled curled the corner of his lips, but his nose wrinkled.

"Do you want to be involved with Night?" I needed to know the answer to this, because our futures seemed to get more intertwined by the day.

"If you had asked me a few days ago, the answer would have been a resounding no. But now... things have changed, haven't they?" He glanced at me with his expression open.

"Yeah, but if I'm involved with him, you don't necessarily have to be. As much as you worry about making someone do something they don't want, I also worry about you."

He glanced at me, his eyes warming. "Why worry so much, Jules? Do you think you might end up being the jealous type?" A teasing smile curled his lips.

"Surprisingly, I don't think so. A part of me misses him, but I also like what we have now. He's kind of a possessive asshole, but there's something charming about him."

"It's the fact that he's attractive. There's no other explanation."

"Obviously, he is." His piercing eyes and intense gaze only added to the appeal of his chiseled muscles. I stabbed a few more vegetables on my plate. "But with your history, is that weird to admit?"

A laugh sputtered from his lips. "Weird doesn't begin to scratch the surface. Night and I have over a century behind us. He's part of the reason why my court fell into such disarray in Faerie in the first place."

"Really?"

Finian let out a breath and gave me a crash course history lesson. Typically, Dream Walkers traveled from court to court, never really settling in one place. Night, however, came back to Finian's court again and again, pillaging the minds of Finian's Fae so much that most started to abandon his court. As soon as the Fae door curse bound them to Faerie, the war between the Dream Walkers and Fae kicked up a notch. Night went into hiding, and Finian hadn't seen much of him except occasionally since the door opened.

It must have been heartbreaking, watching those he cared about having to leave his court due to the Dream Walker. One by one, being abandoned like that. It sent shivers down my spine.

"He told me the only reason he stayed was he felt like the court belonged to him—like *I* belonged to him."

"And how do you feel about it?"

Finian let out a breath and chewed for a moment. "I spent over a hundred years in his presence. It's hard to live through that and not feel *something*. But perhaps it's more like the cliche movies you have, where I'm falling for the villain or bully just because they showed me some affection."

"Well, I'm not a villain."

"No, you are not."

"And I know you both have history, but I see good in him too. I mean, he left to defend your court and your honor, right?"

His lips pressed together as he let out a slow nod. His muscles in his neck were tight with tension as he ran a hand through his hair. "He's likely talking to Lady Burke—well, threatening is more realistic for him. When I say things are going to get worse, not better, I mean it, Jules. Burke doesn't take kindly to threats, and that's all Night knows how to do. He means well for me right now, and heck, he might be trying his hardest to defend my honor, but Burke won't see it that way. There will be conflict. At this point, it's unavoidable."

"Conflict is always avoidable."

He gave me a sad smile. "Do me a favor and keep your hope strong. It makes me happy to see." His eyes searched mine, and he cupped my cheeks. "It's strange. Sometimes, I think your eyes change colors."

"It's probably what I'm wearing." I shrugged. "Some people said that they appear more honey colored when I wear certain colors."

"Can we put that to the test?"

"How?"

His lips hovered an inch from mine. "Let's see what they look like when you are wearing nothing at all."

❧ ✄ ❦

We didn't choose a movie. We barely made it to the couch before I undid Finian's pants, and they dropped around his ankles. He kicked them off onto the living room floor somewhere. My lips furiously pressed against his as he pulled me down onto the couch with him, but my wandering hands needed more. I knelt in front of him, pulling him into my mouth and finally fulfilling what I whispered to him—right before he had said he might be falling in love with me.

In love.

Two words I never thought I would hear. I was grateful, but I wasn't sure how I felt yet. I liked Finian a lot. He was kind, wonderful, and *hot*. Whenever he took care of me, butterflies danced in my stomach. I enjoyed being around him. I couldn't imagine leaving him now. And there was a deep well of desire, with enough depth to drown in.

But love?

Right now, however, I lost myself to the taste of him. He was sweet, which made me want to take him deeper. I swirled my tongue around him, taking in the salty bead that had formed. He groaned as I swallowed it down and lowered my mouth around his length. His hand went to the back of my head, resting there and letting me take the lead. His green eyes swirled as he watched me work my mouth around him.

Finian was a decent size, but I got a good rhythm going despite my jaw already starting to ache. As soon as Finian's eyes fluttered shut and his body shuddered, someone else cleared their throat from behind me.

My eyes snapped open—Night was back. My cheeks reddened as I realized I hadn't thought this through. While messing around with Finian without Night had originally felt exhilarating, watching the coldness creep into Night's blazing blue eyes now made me realize maybe I didn't have as much freedom as I thought. Night's gaze was steady on me, arms crossed over his chest from his position leaning against the wall. He looked bored, as if he were watching us have a conversation about the weather.

I pulled back, letting Finian drop from my mouth. I was still fully clothed, but Finian was undressed from the waist down.

"Oh, no. Don't stop on my account." Night shadow walked right behind me and grabbed hold of my hair. He got up in Finian's face. "I don't think he's done yet, tiger. Which means you have more work to do."

"Night—" I started, but he used the opportunity of my open mouth to shove me forward, all the way down on Finian's dick. I gagged as he hit the back of my throat.

Finian breathed out a gasp.

"Swallow," Night whispered in my ear, pulling me back enough so I could breathe through my nose. I swallowed, and it made it easier for Finian to slide back down into my throat. "Good girl."

"Don't be so rough with—" Finian's protest stopped when I ran my tongue hungrily along his cock.

"I leave to go save your court, and you repay me by... what? Fucking the entire time I was gone?" Night moved his hand in a steady rhythm, forcing me to take Finian down my throat again and again. Tears welled in my eyes, but wetness pooled in between my legs.

I was in so much trouble, in more ways than one. These men did things to me I didn't have words for. Desire spread through me as Night curled his other hand around Finian's throat. I wanted whatever punishment this man deemed to give me. I needed his praise, but I also craved his worst. I would happily take whatever came next.

"What do you have to say for yourself?"

Finian smiled. "I win."

Twenty-One

NIGHTMARE

Two words I hadn't expected tumbled out of Raskos's mouth. "I win."

I was surprised he had it in him—more surprised that he was capable of mocking *me*. A part of me felt viciously proud of him, and the other part of me wanted to punish him for being with Jules while I was off battling for his court.

I should have at least been invited to watch.

Jules chuckled around his cock. The sound came out muffled.

"You think this is funny?" I shoved her head down and held her there until she tapped my leg several times. I waited until her body shuddered with a retch before pulling her off him. "Stand up," I ordered.

Without waiting for her to get her feet steady, I pulled her into me, capturing her lips with mine and pinning her against me. My hand tightened in her hair until she shuddered. I ached to make her body come apart.

"Night, don't be such a—"

Letting Jules go, I hauled Raskos up to full height by his neck, my fingers digging into his skin. "I think you've forgotten who you are talking to." Staring at his moss green eyes, I licked the side of Jules's face. "And you've forgotten that she likes it. So, I'm going to do you a favor, *Finian.*" Releasing my hold on him, I nodded at Jules. "Turn around." She obeyed, and I wrapped my hand around her wrists, binding them behind her back. Pulling on her arms, I made her arch back, and a sweet whimper escaped her lips. With my other hand, I tugged the hem of her pants lower. "Reach in and see how wet our girl is for *us.*"

His gaze traveled up the length of her body as I nuzzled my chin into the hollow of Jules's neck. His cock twitched. Despite all his protests, he liked watching us—or specifically, watching me take control of her, presenting her to him.

This was why it had to be the three of us. Together.

"She's waiting."

"It's okay, Fin—"

I palmed her mouth shut, tightening my hold on her wrists so her back bowed against me, thrusting her tits out. "You don't get to tell him it's okay. He needs to learn for himself. You like it when someone else takes charge. You like it when *I* take charge. Touch her," I growled the last words at Raskos because he wasn't moving fast enough. Jules squirmed, rubbing her ass against my hard cock. If I wasn't having so much fun forcing Raskos out of his shell, I might have taken her with no consideration for his precious feelings.

But I wanted everyone to feel good.

"Touch. Her. Or I will." I left the last part hanging as a threat between us.

He swallowed and took a step forward. He undid the button on her pants and shimmied them farther down. I had no qualms about destroying the fabric. Raskos, however, did everything with such fucking care, I wanted to threaten him for going so slow.

But instead, I watched, letting Jules writhe against me as his fingers slid underneath her panties. Her shoulders pressed into my chest as she moaned into my hand. Raskos had barely passed her mound.

Oh, I was beginning to see why he was so careful. The anticipation swelled in the room as he slid farther down. Jules tried to suck in a breath through her lips. Her stifled breath on my palm made me ache. I dug my fingers into her jaw as Raskos pulled his hand free of her panties. They were drenched in her.

"How wet is she?"

His jaw had dropped open as he gazed at his fingers, as if not believing it. I knew Jules would love the sweet way Raskos took his time, but she also had the side that wanted demands. She would never just be satisfied by sweet nothings when she was both human and Dream Walker. She was the perfect woman for us.

"Why don't you see for yourself?" Raskos caught my eyes. His gaze softened in wonder as he held his fingers out for me. More hinged on this moment than he cared to admit.

My smirk grew. Damn, this Lord knew how to make things *fun*. Jules murmured incoherent nothing against my fingers as I opened my mouth. Raskos dared to bring his fingers to my lips, and I sucked them inside.

Her taste in real life was mind-blowing. Everything in my life clicked into place—this was what I had been meant to find my entire existence. I needed to be here, with Raskos's fingers sliding along my tongue and the swell of my cock pressing along her ass. The sight of him half-naked and proud in the middle of his living room, no longer shying away from the Dream Walker threat.

This moment and her on my tongue? I had never tasted anything sweeter.

"Get back on the couch."

"What are you going to do?"

"Taste her while she chokes on your cock." Jules sagged against me, breathing hard through her nose as she tried desperately to seek some relief by clenching her thighs together. "Sit down."

Finian had never listened to me before, but here he was, *listening.* As he sank back onto the couch, my erection became impossibly hard. I would take him the same as her someday, but not right now. Today was about teaching Jules a lesson for *giggling* at me. I needed payback. He had tasted her, savored her, and I had never gotten to.

Raskos wrapped his hand around his dick, giving a few lazy strokes as he watched me take off her pants. Jules stepped out of them and dutifully kicked them aside.

"Being a good girl now doesn't negate what you've already done wrong." I let my words lick the side of her neck. She practically melted into my shoulder. Lifting my hand from her mouth, I gripped her jaw, arching her backward so I could capture her lips in a bruising kiss. She opened for me, and I thrust my tongue into her mouth. The moans she made were so beautiful, like a concerto.

"Get on your hands and knees and give Finian the release he desperately craves."

She nodded underneath my touch, and I released my hold. Jules rubbed her wrists, which held red imprints from my fingers, but she licked her lips and complied, sinking in between Raskos's legs. He spread wider for her, giving her room. He guided himself in between her lips, and she rolled her tongue along his head. She licked a bead off him and swallowed.

Fuck, that was hot.

182

I sank behind Jules, rubbing her ass with my hands and spreading her wide. She was so focused on Raskos, but still her body sought my touch, trying to raise herself higher to take what she needed. Raskos's moss eyes were on me, watching as I lowered myself to her.

Jules was so wet a droplet of her arousal had fallen along her thighs. I kissed the space and trailed my tongue up to her slit. She clenched as I circled her, savoring the taste of her. Delicate and vicious.

"Jules." His voice came out raspy and heavy. Raskos rested his hand on the back of Jules's head, not applying pressure. He cupped her like something precious and fragile.

I ran a finger along her opening, right alongside my tongue and thrust it inside. She moaned, so I pushed another one in too, rotating until I found a good angle. As soon as she groaned along his cock, I shoved harder until I heard her choke.

"Fuck," Raskos breathed the word. "Jules, if you need a break, tap me, okay?" He swallowed at the end of his sentence, eyes hooded as he watched us.

"She doesn't need a break." I thrust my fingers in several more times, testing her. She quivered around me, walls getting more drenched every time I made her take Raskos deeper.

"Regardless, she needs the out."

"Do you need an out?" I cut him a sharp glance. He didn't get to respond, because I thrust so hard and deep, he ended up in the back of her throat. The noise that came out of her tasted as divine as her cunt did.

"Maybe at this rate." He rested his hands on her shoulders, helping support her.

She muttered something along him. Raskos glared at me as he lifted her up and off him. "What is it, Jules?"

"I want Night to fuck me." Her eyes were glassy as she glanced over her shoulder. She was still wearing her shirt, and I was completely dressed. Raskos also had too many clothes on him from the waist up. "I want him to fuck me so hard I choke on you."

"What have I gotten myself into?" Raskos's words came out on a stifled breath, but his eyes crinkled at the edges.

"Something incredible. Take off your shirts, both of you." I watched as they stripped dutifully. Jules had a few scars along her shoulders, but the rest of her skin was unmarred and sun-kissed. Finian was paler in comparison, but he still had more color to his complexion than me.

They were both stunning. I had seen them before, and I had seen all of Jules—the dream version of her but it had still been her. She had wider set hips, a soft middle, but shoulders that threatened to fuck any man up, not that she needed them once her Dream Walker abilities awakened. Raskos was slimmer with wider shoulders, but his body consisted of curves and grace. He moved languidly.

His lighter brown hair offset her dark brown hair. Both had enough to grab, which allowed my mind to run wild with possibilities. I was going to have so much fun with these two.

I cupped Jules's face with my hands and brought her lips to mine. She was wondrously nude, and I pulled her body flush against me. When I pulled back from the kiss, I searched her eyes. "I need you to hear something. I will not give you many choices in your relationship with me, because I like owning you. And I know you like it to." She whimpered against me. "But if I fuck you, I am not like the Fae. I don't have to infuse my magic into a coupling, which means—"

"There's a chance right from the beginning?"

Raskos stood and rested his hands on her shoulders. "I might

184

be able to form a shield. I know my magic isn't good for much, but—"

"But there will still be a risk." Jules chewed on her lower lip, eyes searching mine. Her pupils were blown, eyes widening as she realized what it meant. "So, your bet with Finian—"

I let out a breath. "I was never going to be the one to fuck you first."

Jules exchanged a glance with Finian, which likely meant they had figured this out while I was gone. It was a ruse, but it had worked gloriously. She turned her attention back to me. "You would have tried the first chance you got."

When I met Raskos's gaze, he shrugged.

"Look, I feed when I want, where I want," I said. "I know that makes me an asshole in the eyes of a lot of Fae and humans, but raising a youngling? That's... that's not something you spring on someone, even if you are my only chance at a future."

She pressed her lips together. Her jaw worked and red rose across her skin. Her eyes landed once again on Raskos. "How sure are you that it will work?"

"Well, maybe... sixty percent sure I can do it?"

That was a lot of risk to place on our first time together. She would be mine in every sense of the word. She would give me younglings someday, but once she was ready. "Jules, we can—"

"Let's do it." She looked at me with half-lidded eyes. The breath left my lungs, and I forgot how to exist. She shrugged. "And after, you can teach me whatever it is I need to know about this new... life I have found myself in."

Raskos's lips parted, tilting downward at the edges.

"You think you can, or you know?" I grabbed him by the back of the neck, pulling him into us. His forehead rested against mine, over Jules's shoulder. "Be more than sixty percent sure."

"I can." He swallowed. "I think." His gaze was piercing, but his chest puffed out as his forehead creased with determination.

I kissed him, pulling him into me with such force Jules let out a grunt between us. "Get back on the couch, Raskos."

"Yes, sir."

Hearing that shot straight to my groin. "On your knees, Jules."

She pressed a chaste kiss to the corner of my lips. It was too soft for me, too soft for the kind of man I was, and yet... She made me feel like I could be all aspects of myself. Wretched and wicked, soft and gentle, caring and nonchalant. And the chance she was taking for me—for *us*.

She was perfection.

Jules positioned herself back on her knees, hovered her mouth inches away from Raskos's cock. Fuck, she was gorgeous. Her dark hair cascaded on either side of her face as her plush lips waited for my command. I shed my shirt and pants, kneeling behind her.

"Are you ready?" I asked, directing my gaze to Raskos.

His eyes swirled to bright green. Magic prickled in the room around us. He nodded as he positioned himself. "Open up for me, Jules."

"And get ready to swallow, tiger." I notched myself at her entrance. She took Raskos deep into her mouth as I pushed inside her, just an inch. I wanted to savor this moment. This was the first time, but wouldn't be the last, because this woman was going to be mine for the rest of her life.

I enjoyed how her walls opened for me, letting me slide farther inside. Pulling out, I watched her quiver, wanting. I slapped her ass and caused both of them to jump. Without any further hesitation, I thrust all the way inside her. I groaned as she clamped down around me, making my cock twitch. She cried out around Raskos. Wrapping her hair around my hand, I rode her into him. His irises continued to swirl as his face blissed out. Her hands stayed on his knees, holding herself steady, but not tapping out.

"You're so fucking good to us. Letting us have our way with you." I pulled on her hair, and she let out a long moan against Raskos. His eyes rolled back in his head, and I enjoyed watching him get lost in her. "Do you see what you do to him?" She couldn't see what she was doing to me, but damn. Jules tightened around me as her watery eyes gazed up at Raskos. She must have done something with her tongue because his body shuddered.

I chuckled as I shoved her hard, forcing her flush against him. She gagged on him, but I pulled back just as fast. "Breathe." After I heard her suck in a breath, I thrust us both forward again. She found a good pace with me and was able to keep up when I pushed us faster. She had to keep swallowing, but even with her attempt at keeping herself clean, the corners of her mouth started to drool. Watching her let herself go on top of Finian's cock was almost enough to send me over the edge.

Her body shuddered and clenched around me. Her scream was muffled as I slammed into her. I didn't let up until her eyes rolled back inside her head.

"One more," I pulled on her hair. "Raskos."

He nodded, threading his hands through her hair. I wrapped my hands around her hips, bringing her back against me. Her tongue swirled lazily along the tip of him. He whispered something to her, kissing the top of her head. Whatever he said made her body shudder once more, clamping her down around me with another moan. He fucked into her mouth, taking a few more moments for his release. She swallowed, and that was enough.

I thrust in as far as I could and erupted inside her, rocking her hips slowly against me as she milked every last drop. My fingers dug into her skin as I breathed in the moment. I wanted to savor this, stay in this feeling of release for the rest of time. They were mine.

When I pulled out of her, I resisted the urge to push the mess back inside her—it would only make Raskos's job of shielding her more difficult. Raskos wrapped his hands around Jules, bringing her into his lap. She stared at both of us with half-lidded eyes and a boneless body.

"Sleep?"

"I'll get you cleaned up, and sure. Sleep." Raskos looked at me, as if surprised that I was still there. His eyes traveled the length of my body. While shaking his head, he stood up, clutching her to his chest. "We have a lot to talk about. Do you want to make us some tea?"

"Tea, Raskos, really? Do I look like a tea guy?"

His eyes glittered as he took in my length once more. "Everyone can be a tea guy. Put on a pot. Let me handle this part."

As he stepped toward his bedroom, Jules reached out her hand and wrapped it around my wrist. "Don't disappear. Whatever happens now. Please?"

I pressed my eyes shut. My habit was leaving, drifting into the shadows as soon as my business was over. Jules and Raskos were now my business, and they were so far from being over. This was where I needed to be, no matter how uncomfortable aftercare or these next conversations would be.

"I'll make some fucking tea."

Twenty-Two

FINIAN RASKOS

B y the time I got Jules cleaned up and myself washed, she was practically mewling for sleep in my arms. I laid her down on my bed after towel drying her hair. Her hands lazily searched for me, settled for bringing a pillow against herself. I would gladly join her as soon as Night and I discussed some unknowns about our new predicament. I had never seen him like this with anyone—possessive, craving, almost like he cared beyond the selfish desire to continue his species.

Almost like he cared about me.

Plus, I needed to know what happened with Lady Burke and the chaos he had invited into my court. She would be here in a few days; I was sure of it.

I clicked the door shut behind me as Night finished pouring a third cup of herbal tea—chamomile from the smell. His eyes darted to the door.

"Did she fall asleep?"

"Barely made it through the shower."

"Oxygen deprivation does that to a person." He leaned against the counter, staring at his mug.

"Is that… remorse I am seeing?" I slid onto a barstool and took both remaining mugs onto the counter with me. I could warm the second one up and see if Jules wanted any in a few minutes.

"I don't regret what just happened." His irises were still a deep shade of blue. Purple bags hung under his eyes. His skin had practically bleached white. I hadn't seen him this worn out since he first rolled into my court, before he fed on the Fae Slayer.

"You need to feed."

"No shit."

I frowned, staring at my mug. "Would it be better if I knew it was coming?"

"Raskos—"

"I heard what Alpin does for his court. If we're going to be involved, I can't have you feeding on my court."

"I don't want to feed on you."

"Why not?"

"Because I hate your fear as much as you do." His exhalation was long and drawn out. He grabbed the mug, but more out of needing something to do with his hands. "Seeing her dead under the rubble." He shook his head, locking his gaze with mine.

"So, you did realize it was about more than the club."

"Of course I fucking realized." His eyes blazed as he stared at me. The scowl spread down his face. "I don't want to experience that. I don't want *you* to experience that."

"I think you should feed." I held out my hand. "We can find a more permanent solution later. We could hire someone—"

"With what money?"

I flinched, pulling my hand back and wrapping it around my

mug.

"That was unfair."

"No, it was completely fair. Burke has me by the balls." I took a sip of tea as misery swept through my veins. Having Night acknowledge his behavior was something I wasn't ready to unpack yet.

"The only ones who should have you by the balls are me and Jules." His voice dipped into a growl.

"I'm sure that will go over well when she sends another one of her lackeys to collect."

"If she comes to collect, there's going to be hell to pay."

"How did it go with her anyway?"

Night took a sip of tea. It was so delicate that it made me want to laugh. Nothing Night did was ever delicate, but it seemed he was a different person when hungry and simultaneously sexually satiated. "Not great. I was hoping I could get her to agree to make some adjustments, but I might have poked a hornets' nest."

"Hornets?"

"An insect. Imagine... tiny flying hoswisps with less toxic venom and no tail, only a stinger."

"Kind of like bees? I saw a movie with bees."

"Yeah, like that."

I nodded. "So... I'm fucked."

"You're not fucked. We're in this together now. I'm going to work with Jules first thing in the morning. If we can get her trained before Lady Burke arrives, we'll be fine."

"I don't know if you realized yet, Night, but my powers aren't what they should be."

"Obviously, but Burke doesn't have two Dream Walkers on her side. With your shields and our abilities, we should have most of them incapacitated in minutes."

"And if she brings an army?"

His smile stretched across his face. "Then there's more to feed on."

I offered my hand again. "Please?"

"Are you... begging me?" Night arched an eyebrow, but he took a step forward. He placed the mug against the counter. The sound of it cracked through the room.

"You don't look good."

He snorted. "Your eyes told a different story earlier."

"You know what I mean." My hand hovered between us, waiting. He appeared to be waiting too—perhaps for me to change my mind, but whatever insanity had taken over wasn't letting this go. Night must have been starving after shadow walking for as long as he did, and while he likely made things worse with Lady Burke, he had tried.

He had attempted to fix my court.

His hand closed the gap between us. The coolness of his skin wrapped around mine as our fingers intertwined. "According to Alpin, who allows me to feed freely on him as needed, it never gets better. This is not a permanent solution."

"Take what you need."

His eyes softened at the corners, right before we stumbled through time and space into the aftermath of a battle. Bodies lined the streets, the club smoldering behind me.

I walked forward, sending ash swirling in my wake. It didn't take me long to find her. Her eyes were wide, staring off into space. A piece of steel had sliced straight through her core, making Jules's eyes empty shells. I swallowed, turning to the left. Using my magic, I lifted a large piece of concrete—one I had been too weak to prevent from coming down.

And revealed Night's twisted body. His silver eyes fluttered open as the weight lifted from his chest. "Not your fault…"

I clenched my eyes shut. This couldn't be happening. There was so much blue—so much blood. Jules was gone, and I couldn't—

I gasped as reality shaped around me. Night's hands curved along my jawline. His silver gaze searched mine. "Your nightmare changed." He stood in front of me, practically no gap between us, and we were back in the kitchen.

My heart hadn't stopped racing. It had felt so real. So fucking real. Jules was safe in her bed. Night was alive. Here and with me. I had allowed him to feed.

None of it had been real.

Everything was fine.

"That's partly why I allowed it. I wanted you to see."

"Why?" His thumbs traced the curve of my lips. "I've never been particularly nice to you, until I made Jules choke on your cock."

"Honestly, Night, I'm not sure. You kind of… became a part of my life." I slapped him off me and shoved him backward. "It's obnoxious. I should hate you."

He hummed as he picked up his mug. A flush crossed his cheeks, eyes back to their silver color. A smirk played on his lips. "It's an interesting conundrum you find yourself in. But there's something hugely wrong with your nightmare."

"Is this where you say something cocky and—"

"Absolutely. I'm not letting Lady fucking Burke take me out. Do you understand me, Finian?"

I took a few gulps of tea to calm my nerves. "Okay." Pressing my eyes shut, I said what had been on my mind for the entirety of this conversation, "What happens now?"

"Now?"

"With us?"

"Well, I train Jules, obviously. Then when Burke comes, we—"

"I mean long term, Night. What happens now? You need Jules to start a family, but what if I want—" *That too.* It felt too selfish to say the rest of the words. Night had lost everything and everyone he loved. Who was I to demand bringing more Fae into this world when he was one of the last two Dream Walkers left?

"We *become* family." As I gazed at the man, he shrugged and took another sip of his tea. "The bonding ritual for Dream Walkers is quite painful, but you can marry her same as me. We can be family."

"And younglings?"

"That's up to her, isn't it? You're running full speed ahead, Raskos, but we've barely started this thing. Yes, I want to fill her with my cum, and yes, I intend to make her pregnant with a youngling. Yes, I plan to bond with her, when the *time* is right."

"Time didn't seem to matter to you before."

His eyes flicked toward the doorway again. "It appears to have grown in importance."

"What about us?"

"What about us?" he shot back.

"What are... we?"

His lips quirked with a smirk.

"Fuck, Night, don't do that."

"Do what?"

"Act like you've put no thought into this. While you were gone, Jules and I talked. It was clear you put a lot of effort into this. In fact, it seemed like you aimed to get us together so that you could be with *both* of us. But what is it about me? Why me?"

Night picked up the mug again and tapped his fingers against the ceramic. He took a long sip before meeting my gaze again. "Because you've always cared so fucking much."

"What?"

He rolled his eyes. "Modest, too. Look, I've been to a lot of courts. I've seen a lot of Fae. Most of them are selfish and self-serving. You have only wanted what is best for your club, and sure, in a way that is self-serving because it's an extension of you, but you've done right by the community you've created here. I liked that you created a place people wanted to be not out of fear, but out of happiness. Plus, Jules was here."

"How did you figure it out about her, anyway? She's what was keeping you around, right?"

"Not entirely, but you already know that." His gaze hit me solemnly. "I had this sense from her. The dichotomy of being human and Dream Walker made almost a shadow of herself that I could feel whenever I shadow walked. Perhaps it's being the only two left of our kind that made her seem like a giant inferno, and I was nothing but a moth. Drawn to wherever she was. As I said, I confirmed it once I was in her dreams. No human or Fae can control their dreams like she can."

I sighed. "And she's going to have to feed exactly like you."

"To stay alive longer, yes. Though, we will find something more permanent. You cannot possibly be the food source for two Dream Walkers."

"And feeding on each other—"

"It works, but it's not always as satisfying. However, I was able to feed on Jules when I chased her down and took what was mine." His cocky smile was back.

"Mother, please tell me I didn't hear you right."

"What?"

"You did not chase our girl down and—"

He held up his hands. "She has a safe word."

A low growl stretched out of my throat as my protective

instincts took over.

His slender hands cupped the mug as he downed the rest of the liquid. His jaw worked. "See, you try to keep everyone safe. Which I appreciate about you, Raskos. It's admirable, but let me tell you one very specific thing about you *and* Jules." He leaned close, a snarl curling his lips. "It's the rest of the damn world that has to be careful, because if they so much as look at either of you wrong, I will fuck with their minds so much, they will not be able to do anything but piss and shit themselves for the rest of their pathetic existence." Night slammed the ceramic onto the table and shadow walked into nothing.

I pressed my eyes shut. "Night, I'm sorry."

Was I apologizing to the Dream Walker?

Yes, I was. And I had meant it. He would never intentionally harm Jules. I knew that with everything in my soul. And whatever messy relationship we had started, this felt big, as if we had begun the rest of our lives. It felt too soon, but it had been a slow build, a century in the making.

Waving my hand over the other mug of tea, I warmed the liquid until it steamed again and walked into my bedroom. Night was curled around Jules, having tucked her right up against him. His silver eyes gazed at me. He lowered the blankets on the other side of her as a peace offering. I placed the mug on the side table and crawled underneath the sheets.

What the fuck were we doing?

"Don't over think it, Finian." Night placed a kiss on Jules's exposed shoulder, and it made blood rush to my groin. "It's something beautiful."

A few hours later, Night and Jules were still nestled together under the covers in my bed. As they slept, I crept out of the apartment. I intended to take a few moments to crunch my numbers again. Perhaps I had missed something. Maybe there was another way out of this, a way to keep them safe. It was a few hours before noon, which was when Jules normally woke up. She might sleep later now that we had a long night.

As for Night, I didn't know his schedule. He looked so peaceful wrapped around her. His face was relaxed, muscles loose and languid, and I had never seen nonchalance like that before with him.

However, I didn't make it past the stairs. Evander leaned against the wall outside of my apartment with his arms crossed. His eyebrow shot up as the door closed behind me.

"Raskos."

"Evander. How did you get back here so quickly?"

"Oh, I never left. Burke has a real problem with you now. She discussed it with me this morning."

I swallowed, knowing full well what that meant. If Burke had sent a projection out, then it was only a matter of time before things escalated. "And?"

"It seems we're going to war." He pushed off the wall, running his hand through his black hair. "I'm not stupid enough to try to come in here with magic blazing against a Dream Walker. I am more on a... diplomatic mission."

"I am charmed, but I didn't tell Night to do any of that."

"But he's sided with your court."

"It seems." I kept my hand close to my chest. Evander didn't know how intertwined my life had become with his or about Jules.

"What were you planning to do now? Escaping?"

I snorted. If Evander thought I would run like a coward, he had a surprise coming. "To figure out how to pay Burke so I can keep my club going." I pushed past him and walked down a few steps. Evander's hand landed on my shoulder.

Snarling, I whirled toward him. "Look, I appreciate how little control you have in this situation, as you are locked in the same as me. You must follow Burke's orders, but I have to figure this out for my court. It doesn't matter what Night threatened her with, because if I can come up with the money—"

"That's my point, Raskos. She doesn't want money now."

I gritted my teeth. "What do you mean she doesn't want money? She always wants money."

"She's cutting off your supply. It seems she wants to piss off your patrons enough so they will revolt against you, then she can take Ceilidh for her own."

"What?" I spat the word out through my clenched jaw. She couldn't be the Lady over two courts. That wasn't how we did things.

"Without drinks to serve, she's convinced the club will go south. She wants to come in after that for a hostile takeover. She wants you to cave to her."

"Why are you telling me this?" I narrowed my eyes. He was on her side, and I couldn't trust anything he said.

Evander shrugged, hair falling over his purple eyes. "I might be employed by her, but I met some good people and Fae over the years at this club." A frown crested his lips. "I know how Burke works. She would tear Ceilidh apart. The prices would skyrocket, becoming so expensive that only higher Fae would be able to partake, just like what she did with the port city. You know her court is divided in half? There's a side for the Fae and a side for the humans. She makes them work endless hours for next to nothing in wages, even with the king's missives."

"So, what, I am supposed to believe you're telling me out of the goodness of your heart? Evander, I've known you for too long. What are you expecting in return?"

"Free drinks."

"What?"

"In the future, if you manage to retain power over Burke, I want free drinks for the rest of my patronage."

"One free drink per night."

Evander rolled his eyes, but magic spun around us. "Deal. You also have several others visiting from Burke's place. I am not the only Fae here, but the others won't admit it. Be on the lookout, as she is ready to do anything to make sure you fail."

"Names?"

He shrugged. "She makes us work separately. I've never met her other... *messengers*. Nor do I care to. I don't always like what I do, Raskos, but I like Ceilidh. For what it's worth, I hope—"

Evander's words choked off as Night appeared in front of him and thrust him against the wall by his throat. Evander's eyes glowed as he summoned magic around him. He pushed against Night, but as he did so, his eyes spun into vapidness, staring off in the distance. Night staggered back a step as Evander's pants darkened, but he held firm.

I shoved a shield between the two of them, not sure what else I could do. Night had already trapped Evander in a dream, as his eyes glowed bright silver. "Night, stop!"

He turned toward me, eyes practically hollow.

"Night," I eased his name from my lips.

The Dream Walker came back into himself, eyes pooling to liquid silver and bright as he gazed at me. "Are you defending him? He made a *deal* with you."

"Because he came to warn us about Burke."

"Information that left a lot to be desired." Night turned his attention back to the Fae, his glare as sharp as knives.

Evander backed up against the far wall. There was nothing but an emergency exit ladder on that side of the stairs. He glanced between Night and me, shifting his gaze back and forth as his eyes widened. "Burke's crazy to go against *it*. I had never experienced… Fucking, Dream Walkers."

I shoved my shield at him, and Evander slammed into the wall, blood bursting from his nose. The air wheezed out of his lungs as I squeezed my magic against him, pushing him hard against the concrete. "You listen to me, Evander. Night is a living being. And if you insult him ever again, our deal is off. I don't give a fuck what the magic does to me."

Dropping the shield, I pointed to the exit ladder. "Take it and get out. When you come back, you'll get your free drinks, but you'll be giving us an apology for your insolence."

Evander scampered up the ladder. The escape door to the roof slammed shut behind him. He'd figure out a way down because I was done with him. I sniffed, realizing how horrible the hallway smelled. I'd have to clean it up, because my manager likely wouldn't, and there was no way I'd make Jules do it by herself.

I really needed to do something about Katie's lackadaisical attitude. When she wanted to be a good bartender and manager, she was. Her special events for me always made us a lot of additional coin, but I also needed her to be a bit more compliant.

Night stepped toward me. "Why did you leave anyway?"

"How long were you watching?"

"Long enough to not be happy about the exchange."

I let out a breath. "I wanted to figure out if I could pay Burke, maybe buy us some time, but it seems she's going to cut off my supply regardless of any coin."

"How much time does that give you with your current supply?"

"Two days, tops. She'll likely be here in three or four days to scrape up the pieces of her club."

"Your club. We're not giving up Ceilidh."

I gazed at Night. "There might not be another way. I can't pay her, and whatever you did only made things worse."

"Then we fight."

"Have you seen me fight? Shields aren't really great for that."

"Except now. When you crushed Evander against the wall." Night's lips quirked up. "You can't fix this tonight, so come back to bed. There's no way to satisfy someone like Lady Burke. We'll beat her at her own game when she comes here." Night wrapped his hand around mine, closing the distance between us. Warmth emanated from him.

"Why do I get the feeling that if I say no, you are going to haul me over your shoulder and shove me back into bed regardless?"

"Because that's what I'm hoping to do."

"Can I clean up the piss first?"

Night wrinkled his nose. "I'll make Katie do it."

I glared at him. "She never cleans."

"She never had the right motivation."

"I don't want you using your powers on my employees."

"Only for disciplinary actions."

"Night."

"Fine. Your way, because I kind of like you, Raskos." Night wrinkled his nose. "Actually, let me do it. I can shadow walk myself clean afterward, and this smells foul. What does Evander eat? Hoswisp toxin?"

I snickered.

"Seriously. Go cuddle our girl."

I opened my mouth to ask if he knew where the cleaning

supplies were, but Night had already stepped into the shadows. Of course he knew where they were. He observed everything in my club. He probably stalked my employees too. With a sigh, I slipped back into the apartment and into the bedroom.

Jules's hair fanned out behind her. Her head moved restlessly back and forth. I climbed under the covers, and as soon as she was tucked against me, she breathed deep. "Finian." Her whisper was nothing more than a breath along my skin, but I pulled her close to me, savoring the time I had left before everything turned to hell.

Twenty-Three

JULES

Waking up next to two men felt strange. It felt like we barely knew each other, but I had never felt more alive in my life. I understood it now. Whenever people said they had sex with Fae and it was undeniably better than anything they had experienced before, I got it. I had never felt this with my previous Fae partner. With Finian and Night? It had been out of this world. My body ached pleasantly, reminding me of everything we had done and promising to have more things on the horizon.

In their arms, I was more myself, as if a part of me had been hidden behind a door. Night opened it, but Finian had been the one to guide me through to the other side.

My leg draped over Night's body, and Finian's arms were tucked around my chest. The amount of heat between them was so comforting, I wanted to fall back to sleep.

However, I desperately needed to use the bathroom. Both

Finian and Night looked so calm, but as soon as I inched my leg off Night, he grabbed onto my thigh.

"Good morning," he muttered.

"Hi," I squeaked.

Finian chuckled behind me, his voice low and raspy. "Coffee?"

"Does that need to be a question?"

He swept my hair away from my neck and placed a kiss on my skin. Goosebumps rose from the tenderness. "Coming up."

Night's eyes followed Finian as the Fae slipped out of bed and into the living room. His eyes were bright silver, and they hadn't been that way last night.

I narrowed my eyes, searching his. "What happened while I was asleep?"

A smirk played on his lips as he focused back on me. "I had a little fun in the stairwell with an unwanted visitor. We'll talk more about it at breakfast. I was thinking we could practice your magic. I am open to whatever you can throw at me, and Raskos said he would bear it, if it meant having two fully trained Dream Walkers on his side."

I nodded, trying again to slink out of bed.

Night wrapped himself around me. "Where are you going?"

"Bathroom."

"Mm... So, it would be horrible for me if I did this—"

We tumbled into a dream where I was surrounded by dripping faucets.

I curled my hands into fists. "Oh, clever." When I pushed him, the dream fell apart. I stumbled out of bed and away from him. "Remind me not to tell you anything anymore."

He frowned. "I don't like that."

"Well, I don't like being teased."

Night stared at me.

I blinked. "Okay, I don't like being teased about bathroom related things."

He folded his hands behind his head. His hair looked healthy and fully silver now. His body was flush with life, with a rosy hue to his skin. It must have been quite a night after I fell asleep. I tore my eyes away from gazing at the length of his body. His muscles all pointed straight to where the blankets had fallen, covering the part of himself that grew harder the longer I looked.

Shaking myself out of my reverie, I turned to the bathroom, quickly doing my business before Night got any other ideas. We settled down with coffee at the kitchen island. The guys gave me the summary of what happened last night with our visitor from Burke's court—Evander. His warning provided us with some idea of when we could expect the attack, but that also put the pressure on me to learn my powers.

If we were going to defend Finian's court, I needed to be able to tap into the Dream Walker side of me. If I was even Dream Walker. While Finian couldn't compel me like other humans, I wondered if Night was right. I didn't feel any different—so perhaps I wasn't what he thought. And what did it say that I felt disappointed by potentially not being what he needed me to be?

I had finished about half of my precious coffee by the time they were done talking about the events.

Night wrapped his hand around mine. "The easiest way to learn is for me to trap you in a dream and have you break it."

"Why do I feel like this is going to turn inherently sexual?"

A small smile flitted across his lips. "Well, that wouldn't be very fun for Finian, would it?" His eyes flickered to the other man. "Unless he wants to feel how wet you get when I have my way with you inside your head."

I pressed my eyes shut, sucking on my lower lip to stop my

heart from racing on without me. These men could do endless things to my body, and I'm not sure I would have a limit.

Maybe I would.

Probably not.

It was exciting to have someone challenge me like Night did, but also someone who would check on me and provide care like Finian. They were the perfect opposites, and I liked them so much.

It helped that they were both amazing at what they did.

"Do you want that?" Finian asked.

"I don't... not want that." I slid him a glance, taking in his earnest and open gaze. "But it will be easier if we don't get sidetracked. I want you to give me actual nightmares, ones I want to break out of."

"Why don't I give you nightmares of some of the humans I've been in? That way it isn't just your fears against you, but you can try to usurp them as your own."

"Scared of my fears?" I teased.

Night shook his head, looking at Finian. "I have been inside of Finian's, and I do not care for them. I imagine yours will have a similar effect."

I frowned at that. It seemed like an oddly personal moment, but if they were figuring out their relationship with each other and how we fit together, then I wasn't going to stand in their way. Honestly, I was glad about it.

"So, you want to feed me the nightmares of other people, and I will see them as my own. Then I have to break out of them or—"

"You already broke *out* of one this morning. I want you to take control of it. Command the dream, like you did to Finian's cock last night."

Finian choked on his coffee. "Do you have to be so crass this early in the morning?"

"It's past noon."

"Okay," I said. "Hit me with—"

I didn't get to finish as I fell into...

I was on a plane. I hadn't taken that many trips as a kid. My eyes stared out the window, watching the wing of the plane as we went into a cloud. The clouds grew so thick, the wing disappeared behind the sheet of white. I glanced around the cabin. This wasn't so bad. Was this someone's fear?

As soon as I thought it, bright orange burst in my peripheral vision with a loud pop and hiss. Flames erupted from one of the jet engines. The fire licked at the rest of the wing as a roar tore through the air. An explosion of sound threatened to rupture my eardrums as the plane shook violently, dropping in the sky and leaving me weightless. Screams sounded throughout the cabin as faceless people grabbed onto loved ones, picking up their phones with haste.

Smoke trickled in, whirled around the ceiling, and spread throughout the confined space.

"You want me to rip this apart?" I glanced around, feeling a tickle in my throat as more of the smoke filled my lungs. "I'm in charge of the dream, right? I can do whatever I want?" I looked down at my feet. What if I tore the plane in half, gave myself a parachute, and glided down to safety? I tried to imagine it, breaking the floor in two. I concentrated on the weight of the chute pressed against my back. I had never gone skydiving before, but I could imagine what it felt like.

Except the floor stayed solid, and more smoke filtered into the space. Coughing and sputtering sounded as the oxygen masks dropped. I put on mine, biding time to figure out how to change my surroundings. I had played with Night in my dreams before. I had changed my path, chosen a new story. I could decide how this would go, what this dream would become.

Calmness washed over me despite how hard it was becoming to breathe. This was a dream, and nothing would hurt me here. Maybe that's why I couldn't change anything—none of this was real. There were no stakes, even if nothing changed.

"You don't think it feels real?" Night's voice licked my ear. He was behind me, holding me instead of the seatbelt. "You're certain nothing in here can hurt you, tiger?"

"It's a dream. It can't be real."

Night beckoned the flames closer. They traveled up the wing as more people wailed. Horror filled their lungs as they spat rasping breaths of thick air. The fire crawled along the exterior of the plane, bursting through the window. The cabin pressure stayed the same, likely from Night's control, and the inferno brushed against my skin.

It *burned*.

I shrieked and tried to escape the chair, but Night's hands held me steady.

"Fuck, it's not supposed to hurt!" I yelled as the pain tore up my skin.

"Tell your dream that. Fight it."

The fire melted through the top layers of my arm. Burning flesh curled into my nose. Tears streamed down my face as the heat buried into my bones, ripping apart my body.

"Get us out of here. Allow yourself to escape," his voice commanded.

I thrashed under his grasp. I tried what I did earlier, to push Night's hold off me, but I couldn't force myself to wake up either. My skin melted off my arm as the flames coiled up my body. My breath left me as the smoke filled my lungs, hollowing out my insides and—

"Night, stop!" Finian's voice pulled me back into the real world.

I slapped my arm and my shoulder because the fire was still there. Still real. The barstool fell over as I scrambled backward, away from the memory. It took a few moments to orient myself.

Safe. In Finian's apartment. No plane, no flames. It was a dream. A dream I had no control over. Had Night been wrong? Were those other times a fluke? I let out a breath as I forced my racing heart to steady itself.

Finian had grabbed hold of Night's collar, fist clenched tightly around the material. His eyes were wide, pupils turned into pinpricks as he glanced at me. "You were screaming."

Night peeled Finian's fingers off his collar and stood. He knelt next to where I had fallen onto the floor. I had stumbled because of a dream I couldn't control. He offered his hand. "I'm sorry."

"You owe her more than an apology."

"No, I couldn't do it. It was my fault."

"You aren't going to gaslight yourself, Jules. Night took it too far."

"Finian's right." His lips pressed into a thin line as he swallowed. His eyes swept the length of my body as he tilted his head. "We can try again in a few hours—"

"No, we're trying now." I took Night's hand, and he pulled me to my feet. My hand stayed wrapped around his as he slid a glance at Finian. "I need to learn this. We don't have much time until Burke gets here with who knows what army."

"Perhaps we try another approach? Dream Walkers always learned this way, but... you are human too. Maybe you try to pull me into a dream first."

"That sounds manageable." I had done it before. Impatience reared inside me as I tapped my foot. "But I need to master everything, so if this doesn't work, we're going to try again the other way."

Finian and Night exchanged a long look.

I sighed, realizing I wasn't going to get anywhere without some kind of concession. "And Finian can stop us if anything goes too far before it gets out of hand, right?"

Finian didn't look happy about it, but he crossed his arms over his chest and nodded. His jaw ticked.

Night squeezed my hand in his. "Try it. Pull me somewhere I don't want to go."

I frowned and blinked a few times. "How will I know what you fear?"

"You should be able to sense it when you prod around my mind, see what makes me frightened, and then exploit it. Use it to your gain, take it into your body. It's your power."

"And if you're not scared of anything?"

His lips quirked with amusement, eyes half-lidded. "Everyone is scared of something, even I have things to be terrified of."

I licked my lips and squeezed his hand in mine. I focused on his brow, as if that would help me stumble my way into his brain. It should feel like falling asleep, except pushing him to do it instead. Drifting into the abyss, the unknown, and sensing that from him.

But instead of feeling any of that, I only felt the warmth in the palm of my hand. Finian's gaze stayed steady as he assessed us. Night calmly waited, entirely too patient for my liking.

And we waited some more.

I sighed, pulling back from him. "It's no use. I don't feel anything."

"Try me instead." Finian took a step toward me, offering his hand. "Night might be too used to this and on guard, but I have no such protections."

I shook my head. "This isn't going to work. The only time I had control of my dreams was when Night was chasing me."

"Try it," Night pressed, though doubt furrowed his brow.

I hated disappointing him, which was a new feeling for me. No one had ever relied on me in the past, not enough to matter anyway. I slipped my hand into Finian's. He cared about his club, about me, and now about Night. If any of us were torn away from him, it would break his heart. I tried to conjure that into reality, whirl the dream around us, and force it into being through his consciousness.

Except nothing happened. Images swirled in my brain. The emotions were there, but not a single thing transferred over to Finian. There was something preventing me from going farther than thinking about the unreality.

I turned back to Night, reaching toward him. "Again."

Night stared at my hand, as if he didn't want to take it.

"Finian will stop us. Right?"

"You were terrified, Jules," Night whispered the words. They sounded so sincere coming from his lips that it gave me pause. While he had scared me before in my dreams, it had been in the name of fun. This wasn't fun, it was work. I wouldn't shy away from it now.

"Well, I shouldn't be. I knew it was a dream. Again."

"I'll stop you," Finian promised.

With a sigh, Night latched onto my wrist, and we stumbled into another horrific nightmare.

Twenty-Four

NIGHTMARE

For once in my life, I had not enjoyed fear. Stubbornly, Jules refused to give up, which I admired and hated. Hated because she had already been through so much in her subconscious mind that witnessing her terror was hollowing me out emotionally. She had been picked apart and set ablaze, she had drowned, and so much more.

I didn't age, but I felt like I had.

"You look like shit."

"Helpful, Raskos, thank you." I sat in one of the chairs across from his desk in his office.

After Jules hadn't gotten the handle of her magic, he and I decided to hit the books while she prepared the bar for the night. The good-for-nothing Katie was running late, per usual. I would haunt her one of these days, regardless of what my two companions wanted. She deserved it. I understood she was valued when she was here.

It was the *when she was here* part that bothered me.

"It was horrible, wasn't it?"

I sighed. "I have never felt a part of my soul dissolve before."

Raskos pressed his lips together. He swallowed and let out a long breath. "She is determined to make this work."

"I admire it, but all the other times she did it, it seemed effortless. I wasn't expecting it to be so hard."

"Was this really how they raised you?" His soft moss eyes looked me over, searching.

"You mean to be able to conquer any fear? To be able to survive? Yes, that's how they raised me." My jaw worked.

"No, by forcing you to live nightmares until you could control them." Raskos tapped his fingers on his desk, but the glassiness crossing over his eyes made me angry.

I stared at him. "Yes, Finian. It's how Dream Walkers work. We are nothing without our powers. We are weak and able to be destroyed without them."

"Why didn't more of you go into hiding? When the portal closed with the curse, I would have thought—"

"We don't hide."

He stared at me.

"Not as a people. We didn't hide." I tore my gaze away from him, glancing toward the volumes of binders he had on one of his bowing shelves. "The only reason I survived is because of my sister. She told me to run."

"And you *listened* to someone?"

"Regardless of what you want to believe about me, there is one thing I am fearful of."

He tilted his head to the side. Eyes focused, hair done in a messy top knot. His lips parted as he considered his words, chewed on them. Raskos had a way of waiting in silence, endlessly coaxing out the truth. He was patient, able to stay still for long enough to wait me out.

I broke the silence with an admission. "Death. It claims us all someday, but it was never supposed to claim Dream Walkers. We can live fairly indefinitely, as long as no one outside interferes. But the Fae did, didn't they? I witnessed a lot of people I... cared for meet their untimely end. We aren't like you. We don't believe in the Mother. We don't have a version of the afterlife. We are, and then we are not. It is the absolute darkness that terrifies me, and I worry that is all nonexistence is."

I started as Raskos wrapped his slender fingers around my hand. Did he realize he touched me so easily now? If someone had suggested this future for myself, I wouldn't have fathomed it. Raskos and I were rivals. I teased him mercilessly because I could; I haunted his court because it pleased me.

Because watching his reaction thrilled me.

"Despite what other Fae believe, I have my doubts. My court used to be centered around the Mother, but that was from my own shortcomings. I didn't have the faith the others had. Because what if you are right and it is endless darkness? What if this is all we have until there's... nothing." Raskos swallowed, his throat bobbing. He ran his thumb over my knuckles, such a gentle gesture. "I do think that's what makes now worth fighting for because who knows what happens next? Perhaps the Mother, but perhaps not."

I squeezed his hand and nodded toward the book in front of him. "Let's figure out the damage."

"What do you think you are going to find that I haven't already combed through?"

"You'd be surprised by how many people are terrified of math." Letting go of his hand, I slid the booklet over to my side of the desk, leaning over it. A lot of Finian's notes were scrawled in the margins, and there were numerous cross outs and corrections along the way. I couldn't make much sense of most of it, but there was an overwhelming amount of negatives, most of those coming from Lady Burke's court.

"What about this?" I pointed out a few transactions that seemed less expensive than the others.

Finian sighed. "Alpin's court. He doesn't make enough to sustain the club, but I do buy some of the alcohol he makes whenever he is able to ship it. Mead, mostly. Not wildly popular, but we have some."

"Could we possibly support him in expanding his production?" The sooner Ceilidh got out from under Burke's thumb, the better.

He shrugged. "Not outside of having the capital to do it, but as you can see, I am lacking."

"And if I were able to get it for you?"

One of his eyebrows rose. "I don't want you doing anything that will put my court into further crossfire."

"Nothing of the sort. I can be rather persuasive when given the right motivation. With the amount of turnover within the royal courts, we should be able to get more humans here, if they were given the right kind of dream." After the Fae Slayer left the other courts in shambles, it would be an easy enough task.

Raskos gestured for me to keep going.

"I feed on nightmares, but I can give people the ability to dream for a better life, a better world. I could give them a dream of Ceilidh, make it seem like they belong here."

"And if more people defect from the other courts and come here, we'll have more coin and labor force to build up our court."

"Making it a better court, which brings in more people and more coin." I smirked. "Also, you called it *our* court."

Raskos winced, brows lowering. "Fuck, I did, didn't I?"

"I'll leave when we're done with Burke, while the other courts are still in turmoil. The more people we get here, the better it will be for us in the long run."

"I'll send a missive out to Alpin, to see if he is on board with more production. It would be a good alliance for both of our courts. I could kiss you."

"Do it."

Raskos climbed over his desk and grabbed hold of my shirt, pulling my lips against his. His teeth raked my skin, and I groaned as I yanked his hips into mine.

The door opened.

"Oh, uh… Good news then?"

With my hand fisted in Raskos's hair, I gestured with my other hand. "Come here, tiger."

Jules slipped the door shut and crossed the room like a good fucking girl. "Good news?"

"Night has some good ideas every once in a while," Raskos said.

"Good enough to be rewarded?" Oh, I liked the look crossing her lips as she sank onto her knees. Damn.

"Yes, good enough to be rewarded." Raskos laughed.

I tugged on his hair. "You get on your knees, Finian."

His body shuddered from the use of his first name. I was no longer spitting it out of my mouth, but saying it as a caress. He slid off my lap and sank down in front of me. The amount of restraint it took not to flip them both over the table and fuck them one after another was intense and heady. They watched me, waiting on my command like I was their god.

Which I was.

Raskos reached for my belt as Jules licked her lips. We had come a long way, him and I. For him to willingly be touching me, willingly sink below me. I had *plans* for the three of us, and none of them involved us folding to Lady fucking Burke.

"Jules, give our guy some attention." I widened my stance so she could fit between my legs. She crawled toward Raskos, and what a sight it was. He groaned as her fingers nimbly edged his pants down.

With my erection free, I wrapped my hand into Raskos's hair. "Open."

He, however, didn't listen, instead he wrapped his hand around the base of my cock, moving it enough to tease me. I groaned as Jules's swirled her tongue over the tip of his dick.

"Unless you want punishment, *Finian*, I suggest you swallow me down."

"What are you going to do about it, Night?"

I pulled on his hair, but still, his lips remained frustratingly shut. Fine. I could play dirty. I sent him a sharp image of him tongue fucking Jules while I was buried inside his ass. He gasped, and I used the opportunity to slide into his mouth.

His tongue ran along the underside of my cock, eyes widening as he toyed with my piercings, and fuck, it felt fantastic to finally be inside him. Decades of sexual frustration came out as I pushed myself to the back of his throat. He swallowed, staring at me with defiance in his eyes. His magic swirled around us, and I realized he was blocking me from going farther.

"Clever. Jules?"

She made the sweetest little hum from around his cock.

"Do me a favor and stop whatever you are doing. Finian's being bad."

Her lips made a pop as they came free from him.

"I need you to show him how to do it, since he apparently needs training." I pulled myself away from him. "Open up, like a good girl."

She got to her knees and slid a glance at Raskos. He glared at me as I ran my thumb along her lower lip, sliding my thumb inside.

"Night, this isn't—"

"You might be able to dom her, but you can't top me. Not even from the bottom." I grabbed the sides of her face. "Are you ready?" She nodded. I positioned myself and thrust inside her, not giving her any time to adjust. Tears prickled her eyes as she gagged around my cock, but she swallowed just the same, allowing me down her throat.

Fuck, I loved watching her lips take me in. Loved how her tongue pressed against my skin, rolling over me in her eagerness to please.

"That is how you do it, Finian." I slid my gaze over to him. He watched our girl with swirling green eyes. Jules ran her tongue along me, pressing against each piece of metal. I shuddered. "Maybe she should ride your face instead. This kind of treatment deserves a reward."

His eyes flicked up to mine. "Fine. But only if I get to bend her over the desk once you're finished."

I gazed at him with half-lidded interest. "What makes you think I am ever going to be done with her?"

Jules whimpered and tried to rub her thighs together.

"Come on. Don't leave her wanting." Jules kept working her mouth along my length as Raskos slid onto the floor. He took both of their pants off and positioned himself below her.

He grasped his own cock with one hand, while his other slid along her opening. Raskos brought his fingers back out. The light reflected on her arousal coating him.

"So wet for us. Tell me, Jules, do you want Finian to eat you out until you come so hard you see stars?"

She nodded, making another whimpering noise that sent shivers into my dick.

I ran my thumb underneath her eye and caught the tear trying to escape. I sucked the saltiness off my finger as Raskos guided her body down on top of him. Jules jolted against me as her eyes closed with bliss.

"Open your eyes." I pulled her off me and forced her to look down at Raskos. He rolled his tongue along her as she breathed out, moaning.

"Fuck," she said.

"Does he feel good?"

"So good."

I plucked one of her nipples in between my fingers and rolled the sensitive nub. She bucked against Raskos's face. He used the movement to slide a finger inside her, and she nearly came apart right then and there.

"Open for me, tiger."

She licked her lips, then swirled her tongue around the tip of my cock. She showed me the bead she collected and brought it back into her mouth. She swallowed. I wanted to be inside her, buried in her cunt, but I also didn't want to risk making her pregnant before the time was right. Each time we fucked, there would be a risk, even with Finian's shield.

And while I wanted to see her swell with my youngling, I needed her to want it. Until then, she had other holes for me to fill.

I grabbed the back of her head and guided myself in between her lips once more. She hollowed out her cheeks and pressed on every part of me that made my nerves ignite. Without pushing her, Jules brought herself down hard on my cock, choking herself for me.

"Raskos."

"Kind of busy, Night."

"Fuck our girl for me." I wasn't going to last much longer, and I desperately wanted her to come while my cock was in her mouth.

Raskos smirked. "Jules, I need you to sit up." She listened to him instantly, still keeping the steady rhythm over my dick. I blinked slowly as Raskos maneuvered himself. He sat behind her, pulling her onto his lap so quickly that my dick swung free of her mouth.

Jules, in all her perfection, reached for me. Holy shit, the sheer desperation on her face was enough to set my blood on fire.

Raskos positioned himself at her entrance, toying with her as he so often did.

"You ready?"

"Please, Finian," she mewled. Hearing her beg for it made my cock twitch.

He inched her down, thrusting his head into her entrance. She stretched around him and bucked her hips, but Raskos held her firm, only allowing her to sink onto him with agonizing slowness. Jules tried to seat herself, but he chuckled, drawing it out.

"Tease," she murmured, breathless. She gazed up at me. "You wouldn't tease me, would you?"

"Not a fucking chance. That's his job." Though, I enjoyed watching it happen.

Jules moaned as Raskos grabbed the end of her ponytail and pulled the elastic out from it. Damn, I had liked wrapping my fist around that too. His teeth grazed the skin of her neck.

"You're so perfect." He worked into her as his tongue ran along her skin. Once he was flush against her, he brushed the hair away from her face. "Now, open for Night." The words came out commanding, but holding the gentleness that only Finian could muster.

Jules turned her head, bringing her mouth to his and kissing him with a ferocity I hadn't witnessed before. The bruising way she pressed against him was hot. When she had her fill, she turned toward me, dutifully opening her mouth wide. She curled her tongue as I entered again.

Her warmth enveloped me. She made everything feel so *good.* The way her tongue circled me, the teasing way she flattened it against the bottom of my shaft and slowly pulled her lips back. And when she looked at me, her gorgeous brown eyes met mine, and she had a look of confidence I wanted to steal.

"You enjoy feeling in control, tiger?" I wrapped my hand around the back of her head, thrusting myself deep into her throat. Her eyes watered, but her gaze stayed locked with mine as she swallowed me down.

Fuck, this woman.

Raskos ran his fingers along her neck. "You sure you can take it?"

With her defiant eyes narrowing, she let out a hum of assent that wrapped around my erection. It took everything in me not to lose it right then. She tried to pull back, but I refused to let her mouth go.

"Raskos, she's focusing too much on me. Pick up the pace."

He snickered. One of his hands snaked up to her breast, cupping it gently. His other traced over her hips and toyed with her clit. She bucked against him, groaning as he pressed on her nerves. He buried himself so deep inside her, but still moved gently with his hips, seeking the perfect angle and rhythm.

"Come for me, Jules. Let Night know how much you love it when I am sweet to you." He swirled his fingers around her, and she moaned around my cock.

Her nostrils flared, breathing rapid fire as her jaw slackened.

Her pupils were blown wide. I pushed myself into the back of her throat, feeling my release as her eyes watered and she came apart beautifully between us. Watching her fall to pieces was a wonder.

I pulled out of her mouth, and she let out a contented sigh.

Raskos gave me a smile, still fully inside her. "It was so nice of you to come for Night, sweetie, but I need you to do me a favor." He swept her hair away from her neck and kissed her, pulling her close and running his thumb over her nipple.

"Anything," she breathed.

"Give me one more." He ran his hand up her chest, grasping onto her neck as he gauged my reaction. She moaned under his hold as he continued the steady circles on her clit. Raskos pumped inside her, still not finished.

I bent down, watching her eyes glitter as Raskos toyed with her. "Can you, tiger?"

She swallowed. "I think—"

I didn't care what she wanted to say next, because her ability to think meant we weren't doing enough. I grabbed onto both of her nipples and twisted them. She screamed, panting against Raskos and unable to catch her breath.

"Choke her, Raskos."

He applied the slightest amount of pressure to her neck. I growled as I cupped one of her breasts.

"Choke her, or I fucking will."

Raskos shook his head, but clamped down on her throat. Jules stopped breathing, cutting off all the pretty words she thought she needed to say. She became writhing want and need, and as Raskos thrust inside her over and over, Jules orgasmed again, a silent scream tearing out of her throat. Raskos bit down on her shoulder as he came, filling her.

Fuck, what I wanted for that to be me.

As he lifted her up, I scooped her in my arms, placed her on the desk, and inspected the mess Raskos had made. I swiped my fingers through it and pushed it back inside her. She moaned, eyes half-lidded and blissed out.

"You might need Katie to cover tonight." I pumped my fingers into her a few more times, ignoring how much she thrashed.

Finian snorted. "I would have better luck with Mathias."

I frowned. "Then we have to cover. She's not able to work after that."

Jules tried sitting up, looking deliciously boneless. "Of course I can work."

I pushed her chest down and pulled my fingers out of her, bringing them up to her lips. "Correction, I don't want you working tonight. Clean them."

"Fuck, Night, we can't have sex all the time," Finian protested, but when I glanced over my shoulder, his wide pupils said everything he wasn't.

Jules opened her mouth for me.

"Tell me how delicious Finian tastes."

She did. Like my good fucking girl.

Twenty-Five

JULES

As soon as I got back to the bar, an angry patron shouted, "It took you long enough."

I sighed, settling in for the night.

Night and Finian would have let me go home, but Finian needed the coin, and frankly, Katie was getting worse as time went on. I regretted my choice, because tonight, it was difficult to keep a brave face with the grumpy wave of customers not getting their drinks in a timely manner.

When the supply ran low in two days, what would they do then? I suppressed a shudder as I leaned over the bar. "What can I get you?" My voice went chipper and cheerful, forced, and full of bullshit.

That was the thing about customer service: you learned how to forget yourself when dealing with the public.

I filled the guy's order, and he was no less surly by the time the alcohol was in front of him. I fell into the rhythm of serving the rest of the bar, then tidied up after.

Katie leaned over a table as she flirted with another Fae. The girl had it bad for any who came through the door. She was on Faerie wine, just like the rest of the human staff, but Katie *liked* Fae. She once told me that she felt like her life had been completed the moment she slept with one of them. She had been on Faerie wine then too.

She was arguably the better bartender, as I was slightly more accident prone than her and sometimes made the wrong drink. But she was a terrible coworker. But as the number of disgruntled patrons complained about the slow service, her continued trips out onto the floor and ditching the bar got me thoroughly annoyed.

A woman said she'd get better customer service from a bunch of rocks, and I gave her a venomous smile. "If you told my coworker your complaints over there—" I nodded in Katie's direction as she ran her fingers down the Fae's forearm. "—I'm sure she would help you out."

The woman scoffed, as if I had told her to go fuck a hoswisp.

The night continued to get worse. Exhaustion crept into my bones. A few hours into service, a gentle smile greeted me from the opposite corner of the bar. She was the same Fae from a few nights earlier.

"Seems to be a rough night tonight, huh?"

"You have no idea." I cleared the drinks, shoved them into the dishwasher, and pressed the button to start another cycle. If Katie were helping me bus—heck, if she was helping me do *anything*—we'd be in much better shape. At least I wouldn't have to split my tips with her tonight.

No way would I give her any of the coin.

"What would you like?"

"Any kind of whiskey?"

I reached for the bottle behind the bar but came up empty. Leaning down underneath the counter, I looked at our stock of liquor—no whiskey. Pressing my eyes shut, I let out another breath. I should let Finian know. If we were starting to run out already...

I stood back up, ready to face whatever this Fae threw at me. "Fresh out, I'm afraid. But I am happy to get you whatever else."

A light smile curved her lips. "Oh, not a problem. What about some kind of vodka?"

That was getting low too. "Sure, coming right up." I tossed some ice in the glass and made her a martini.

She took a sip, wrapping her lips around the glass. "Not bad."

"Thanks. You seem to be showing up at the worst times of the night."

Reaching her hand underneath her hood, she adjusted it, so her face stayed in shadow. "I have a habit of being in too many places at once."

I snorted. "That's sometimes how I feel at the bar."

"Yo! Service, bitch!"

I whirled around, fully prepared to yell at the patron who had the audacity to scream at me from across the bar, but Night was already there. His fingers clenched around the man's throat, eyes burning with molten silver.

"Say it again," he growled.

The man's eyes drifted, unfocused. I had been trapped in those nightmares willingly, so I knew the kind of hell the human now found himself in.

Night wrenched on the man's neck, dragging him close. Several patrons backed up, giving the bar a wide berth of space. "Say it again."

"Is that Nightmare?" The Fae woman's voice rose an octave.

"Defending… you?" Her eyes slid over to me. "What have you done to get on the Dream Walker's radar, I wonder?"

I shrugged, not feeling comfortable enough to admit the truth. Without having full access to my power, confessing I might be Dream Walker could be dangerous. They were hated among the Fae with a history that stretched eons. Night had told me about it after one of my particularly horrible nightmares. His eyes had glowed, full from my fear, as he calmly walked down his horrible memory lane.

While he told me about the demise of his race, he had glossed over the details of what happened to his sister. I imagined it was too painful, and I wasn't going to pry into his past until he was ready to tell me about it. Being the last of your kind was daunting and terrifying, even if Night would never admit it.

"I asked you to say it again," Night growled.

The man swallowed as his body sagged against Night's grip. "I called her bitch." His voice choked out from his throat. The man's fingernails clawed into Night's skin as he tried to tear free. Blue blood blossomed out as a sinister smile curled up Night's face.

"Did you now?" His eyes blazed bright silver as the man slumped more underneath his hold.

"Please, man, I have kids."

"No, you don't. But you have used that excuse before, haven't you? When you've been caught doing other things you shouldn't have been. *Please, don't. I have kids.* There are so many delicious things in your history, but I have one thing to show you."

The man's eyes rolled back inside his head.

And then blood poured out of his ears.

Night let go of the man's neck, and he slammed against the floor. Lifeless.

I stared, mouth gaping. I dimly registered the screams from

227

people around us and barely noticed as Finian came out of the back room and cussed out Night. Finian's irises whirled as he shielded the three of us from everyone else. His influence washed over the people in the club, instantly calming them down. He used his magic to squelch all surrounding sounds, leaving us in a bubble.

"What in the Mother did you do, Night?"

"Cleaning the world of one more useless man."

Finian's mouth dropped open as he ran his hand through his hair, destroying the top knot. He ripped out the elastic and stared at the dead body.

Dead. Just like that. Blood leaking from his ears with flecks of gray matter in them. No wonder people were terrified of Dream Walkers.

"How did you do it?" I asked, mesmerized.

"What?! Now is not the time for a training session." Finian rubbed his temples.

"Imagine being so scared that your brain wants to implode. I did that. I made that happen."

I shook my head. "That doesn't make sense."

"Magic rarely does." He shrugged, as if it were that simple. His eyes looked like an electric silver sign, glowing viciously in the dark club. "I had to." The last words almost came out like a plea.

"Why?"

Finian pressed his fingers against the man's neck. "Fuck! In my club, Night. This is supposed to be a—"

"He stole Faerie wine from your club, used it to make women compliant, and—"

"He stole from my club." Finian stood up, fingers clenching at his sides. "And then used it against women?"

"Some people are just as bad as the worst Fae."

"We need to get rid of the body."

"Oh, that?" Night bent down and placed a hand on the man's face. One second, they were there, and the next neither was. Night reappeared standing next to me and the beer tap. He poured himself a drink.

"Where did you put him?"

"Into the shadows. He's still there." Night gestured to the empty spot on the ground. "But no one else can see him unless they shadow walk."

"But people will feel like something is wrong." Finian curled his fingers against the side of the bar, glaring at Night. "Please take him out once we're closed."

"I am feeling particularly satisfied right now, so I'll do whatever you want, Finian."

Finian's eyes narrowed. "If you keep pissing me off—"

Night must have shadow walked because it looked like he moved through the bar. He stood in front of Finian and grabbed the sides of his face. "You'll what? Beg for me to tell you what a good boy you've been?"

If we weren't in the middle of a busy bar with folks jostling for space and my attention now that the body was forgotten, I would have torn off my own clothes to let them have at me. Because watching the two of them together was like fireworks.

Night licked Finian's upper lip. "I'll do that and more. All you have to do is ask."

"I hate you."

Night's nose wrinkled as he chuckled. "No, you don't."

"Can you drop the shield?" I gestured to the unruly patrons at the bar. "I have drinks to serve."

"I'll join you," Night said. "You look lonely."

"No more killing people, Night," Finian ordered.

"Only if they deserve it."

"Night."

"Raskos." Night offered him the beer. "Care to join us behind the bar? I think we could have a lot of fun."

His lips twitched, and my boss made his way onto my side of the bar. He dropped the veil, and the sound of the club rushed back around us, along with annoyed comments shouting from every angle. Night brushed his hand along my ass as he reached for a pint glass, pouring another tall brew.

"What do you think, Raskos? Will this be fun?" Night pressed against me in the tight space.

As a blush crept across Finian's cheeks, I stifled a laugh. I should have been horrified. I should have felt terrified. Somewhere inside me, my self-preservation was begging for me to run. But no, I didn't want to escape this. I wanted them, wanted whatever future was coming next, regardless of Lady Burke and her threats.

I might not be ready to fight, but I was ready to stand by my men. That was a promise.

It wasn't until I was mixing my fifth drink that I realized the Fae woman was gone. She had breezed in and out of here like last time, but the way she assessed me had the hair on the back of my neck rising. But just as the foreboding feeling swept over me, Night spanked my ass.

"Keep daydreaming like that, and there's more where that came from."

"Is that a promise?" I slid him a smirk as his eyes narrowed on me with conviction. Yes, it was definitely a promise.

Twenty-Six

FINIAN RASKOS

I was beginning to question my existence. Perhaps Night had trapped me inside an endless dream. Perhaps I never quantified what it meant to feel *more*. But here I was, making coffee again while Night and Jules were curled up, still naked, in my bed.

We had one day left before Burke's arrival, and Jules was nowhere closer to finding whatever power she was supposed to have. Night had worked her hard last night, to the point where she began screaming incessantly. I had to blast a shield between them to separate them. Night's eyes glowed wickedly, like a full moon on a cloudless winter sky. He wore an apologetic look, one that never graced his face before Jules came into our lives. Jules, meanwhile, kept her furrowed brows of determination, until I declared the time over and lulled her to sleep with multiple orgasms.

Night and I had stayed up late, gazing at each other over her resting form, watching as her bare shoulders rose and fell. We eventually slept too, and now I had coffee on for us.

I sighed staring at the half-full bag of beans because it was another thing I would have to cut from my life once it ran out. Coffee was a luxury item, expensive, but it was a great way to start the morning.

Plus, being able to dote on Jules and watch the satisfaction part her lips made my stomach flip every time.

Night was still a mystery to me. My emotions were jumbled up with how he made me feel. Sometimes, I'd get aggravated, but the charged tension between us was like a fire pauldrin, quick to ignite. I still wasn't sure how we fit together, but both of us being with Jules felt right.

If we survived whatever Lady Burke planned, the rest would be figured out with time.

It was strange to see how much had shifted in such a short amount of time. I had previously thought that Dream Walkers weren't capable of gentleness or caresses. As much as Night claimed he wasn't good at it, his instincts to protect Jules and care for her came rather naturally. He was like the rest of us, but he didn't need food to survive.

Jules stumbled out of the bedroom with her t-shirt hanging loosely off her shoulder. She had nothing but panties on underneath, and it was enough to make me stiff. Her dark brown hair cascaded around her shoulders, looking ruffled from sleep and sex. Night slapped her ass so hard she leaped across the threshold into the living room. His eyes swirled silver, and she giggled.

As her laughter filled the room and I poured the mugs of coffee, I caught a glint of yellow honey hue in her eyes. I frowned as she bounded up to me, hair flying behind her.

"I could kiss you." Her eyes glittered, but the color was warm brown. Her usual. Nothing new, nothing changed. It must have been the morning light.

"Please do."

Jules leaned into me, pressing her lips to mine. They were slightly swollen, likely from Night ravishing her in the bedroom as a good morning wake up. A smile threatened to part my lips. Our dynamic was something I never expected, as I always had previously been the dominating force in a relationship. However, having Night be the one more in charge was almost a relief.

She pulled back, grabbing the mug from the counter and breathing in the aroma as if it were her lifeblood. The bliss spreading up her cheeks from her quirky smile made my cock go rock hard.

"Night and I decided to take a break from training."

"Really?"

She nodded, looking grim. "Everything he's telling me makes sense logically, but in the dream, none of it's happening the way it should."

"And I haven't seen the other side of her since... well, since I chased her."

I arched an eyebrow as Night slid onto one of the barstools. I handed his mug over to him. He had told me, of course, and it had previously been a point of contention, but the blush rising to Jules's cheeks told me she liked whatever they had done together. Seeing the confirmation on her face was all I needed to know.

"Jules has some dark fantasies," Night added.

"Only because those fantasies involve you." Her eyes flicked to mine, and she chewed on her lower lip. "And sometimes you."

"Oh?" I took a sip and looked between the two of them. "Did you fantasize about me before we actually—"

She waved her hand. "Of course I did, but you're my *boss*. It's like... off limits for so many reasons."

"And yet." Night chuckled, letting that sentence speak for itself.

"And yet," she agreed, grinning. Her eyes flashed brightly. I leaned forward. Jules placed her hand on my chest. "What?"

"Nothing, it's…" I searched her irises again, swearing I saw something different every time she seemed… happy? At peace? "You seem happy," I added, not knowing how else to explain it.

Night stared at me, head tilting to the side. "What is it?"

"I'm not sure, but maybe we're thinking about this all wrong. What if it's not fear, but something else?"

"Dream Walkers operate on fear. We feed on it."

"But Jules isn't *only* Dream Walker. She's also human."

Night shrugged. "I don't see how that would change anything. If she's going to activate the side of her that is Dream Walker, it stands to reason it would resonate the same as mine."

I turned to Jules. "When you were in that dream with Night, what were you feeling?"

Red deepened across her cheeks. "Well, I mean… I was…"

"You're going to act shy now?" Night pinched her arm.

She shook him off and rolled her eyes. "I'm only not shy because you make me."

"Make you? I bet I wouldn't be able to make you do anything if you didn't want to do it."

"I was shy. I never really talked about this stuff with anyone, but you do make me open up." The color spread farther up her cheeks.

This was going to get us nowhere fast if he kept directing the conversation. "Night, you said you confirmed she was a Dream Walker based on her having the two sides of herself in that dream, yes?"

He nodded, taking a sip of his coffee. His eyes flicked between both of us, as if searching for where my thoughts were going.

"Okay, so Jules, when Night was in that dream with you, what were you thinking? I'm not going to be upset. I know how attracted you are to both of us. There's no jealousy here."

She swallowed. "It feels weird to admit it, you know? It's one of those things that should feel wrong or something that society tells me I should feel ashamed about. I don't feel shame, but that in a way makes me feel shame? The lack of embarrassment makes me think there's something wrong with me."

I cupped her face, running my fingers along her jaw. I tilted her head, so she had to look at me. "There's nothing wrong with you, but I want to know what you were feeling. It might help us figure this out."

She let out a breath and reached up for my hand. Her fingers curled through mine, and she brought it between us. Her thumb ran along my knuckles. "When I saw him, I was excited. There was this anticipation, where I had no idea what was going to happen next. There was fear too, but more than that, there was hope that I was finally going to experience something truly life changing."

"And was it?" Night asked.

"My life is changed, so yes." She wrinkled her nose and squeezed my hand before dropping it. Hers curled back around her mug.

"You have a bite today. I like it." Night snapped his teeth at her.

"Night."

"Finian."

I shook my head, refocusing on Jules. "So, you felt hope or happiness, or at least some kind of... uplifting feeling?"

"Yeah, I guess. I mean, I knew Night could have been bad news from what you told me, but I also kind of... wanted that."

"But she had fear in her too, I felt it. I fed off it."

"Yeah, but that was sexually charged fear. That was fear because she has a kink for it. You said it yourself."

Jules buried her head in her hands and muttered incoherent words.

"No, don't do that, tiger." Night wrapped his fingers gently around her, prying her apart. "You don't need to be ashamed of any of it. It was hot. I enjoyed the chase."

"It sounds dirtier when Finian says it for some reason."

"You don't think I can talk dirty?" I arched my eyebrow but frowned. "You both are very distracting. Night, I think you need to try it again."

"Chase her?"

"No, the dreams. But this time, give her something... uplifting."

"I'm going to be honest here. I am not sure this will change anything, but I am willing to try if you are." Night offered his hand to Jules.

She stared at his open palm for a moment, swallowed, placed her mug down, and slipped her hand into his. "I'm not—" Her voice ceased as her eyes shut. Her brow furrowed, and her eyes moved rapidly behind her lids.

I turned toward the fridge, pulling out some items for breakfast. As long as they were busy, I could at least do something for the three of us. Jealousy wasn't quite what I felt toward Night and Jules because their connection was due to them being the same. They made me feel included in their lives, but this was part of their relationship I couldn't touch.

As I cut off a slab of meat and prepared it for the frying pan, Jules's hand wrapped around my wrist. I stilled, glancing up at the two of them. They were in another world, but neither looked horrified. Night's brow was relaxed, something that never happened when he placed her into his plethora of nightmares.

And I—

Stumbled into the other world.

"Holy shit!" Jules jumped, wrapping her arms around me.

We were on a hilltop with an array of picnic items out in front of us. The sheer amount of food was mouthwatering, and we were overlooking a lake with a sunset.

"Hi, *Finian*," Night said, elongating my name like he usually did. "Welcome to this reality."

"You were right!" Her voice rose an octave as she kissed me on the cheek. "I realized as soon as Night started kissing me that I could control it."

"And instead of continuing to kiss me, she brought us here." Night plucked something purple from a vine and popped the round object into his mouth. He sounded bored, but his face relaxed as he chewed. "I can't say I mind, because this food is better than what we have." He tossed one at me.

I stared at it. "What is it?"

"You know our wine? We made wine from these. Well, not these, but a variety of these. They are grapes. But this is like… everything I miss about before." Jules gestured to the red and white checkered mat behind her. Some of the items I recognized from the films I had watched, but a lot of the food I didn't have a name for. It looked interesting, with a melange of colors and variety of shapes and smells.

"And you pulled me in?"

"I asked her to reach for you to see if she could." Night chewed slowly, pressing his eyes closed. "And you were right." His eyes shot open, narrowing at me. "Don't get used to it."

"I'm not sure if I can do it whenever, but it's a step in the right direction." She frowned. "Though, I am not sure how creating joyous dreams helps us in a battle. I am not sure I can turn someone's brain to mush."

I kissed her, pressing my lips gently against hers and smoothing my thumbs over her cheeks. She opened her mouth, moaning softly against me. I peeked at Night, who adjusted his pants as he watched us.

"Who cares how you can use it in a battle when we have right now?" I didn't want to think of the inevitable. The horizon loomed with danger, and I didn't know what tomorrow would bring.

But this was nice. This was perfect.

"What should I try first?"

Jules folded her legs underneath her as she took up a corner of the blanket. Night lounged on his side, taking up an entire length. I sat in the corner opposite Jules. She picked up a small butter knife, smeared a spread across a cracker, and held it out for me.

"It's brie. A cheese, but a soft one."

I wrapped my fingers around her wrist and brought it up to my mouth. Curling my lips over the cracker, I licked her fingers clean as I drew the bite into my mouth. That delicious blush was back on her cheeks, and her irises churned with a honey hued color.

"Right there," I said, looking over at Night. "See it?"

Jules glanced between the two of us, shrinking back as Night's scrutiny fell on her. He closed the gap between them, grabbed the back of her neck, and slammed his lips onto her. It was so fast and sudden that she fell back onto the grass with an exhale as he thrust his tongue into her mouth.

They were going to be the death of me.

"What?" she squealed as she got out from under his bruising rapture. "What's going on?"

Night licked her lower lip. "Your eyes changed color."

Her eyes widened. She sat up, and Night gave her space. "What do they look like?"

"Make yourself a mirror." Night's gaze pierced into her.

Jules tried to conjure something up, but her eyes faded back to brown.

"Hey." I crossed over to her and grabbed onto her hand. I pressed it over my heart. "Feel this. This is real." My heartbeat was strong and steady against her hand. "You brought me here. You can do this."

Her expression softened, the furrow disappearing from her brow. A mirror appeared out of thin air as her eyes changed hues again.

"It seems you are good for more than you know, Raskos."

Jules gazed at her reflection.

"You make her more comfortable than I do." Night's jaw ticked.

"Night, don't pout," she said. "Finian makes me feel like I can never do anything wrong. You make me feel like I am about to jump off a cliff. Both things are intoxicating in their own way, but yes, if we're talking comfort, Finian is more like a warm blanket, and you're like a cold shower."

"Ouch," both of us said at the same time.

Night met my gaze, a small smile playing on his lips.

I laughed. Night joined in, and Jules frowned, eyes darting between us. In another moment, a smile spread across her lips and a chuckle escaped her.

"Wow, I am sorry. That was a terrible metaphor."

Night shook his head, amusement still crinkling his eyes. "No, it was perfect. And any time you want to feel ice cold, I am here for you." He brushed another kiss against her lips.

Jules turned toward me. "And you're okay being a blanket?"

I shrugged, pulling on her arm until she got within kissing

distance. "It's not like I have a choice, but no. I don't mind *covering you in me*."

"It should be illegal for you to say dirty things." She swallowed, turning her attention back toward the food. "You know, I can almost forget how this isn't real."

"It's the benefit of being us. We can exist here forever. Though, I am not sure how you are feeding on… happiness." Night leaned back, considering her. "I've never heard of anything like it. At least with full-blooded Dream Walkers."

"Have you met half-blooded Dream Walkers before?"

Night shrugged. "No, but in comparison to the rest of my kind, I was considered young when the massacres happened. I don't remember a lot of our history, but some of them came over here, otherwise you wouldn't be you. Besides, most Dream Walkers become independent as soon as we reached maturity. We were wanderers."

"Wanderers until you found a place to claim." I glowered at him, not forgetting what he told me before he kissed me that first time. According to him, my territory had always been his because he had deemed it so.

"Exactly, most of us never stayed in one place. You were special, Raskos. Still are. Can't you tell?" Night snatched up another piece of food I had never seen before.

"Okay, introduce me to all of this," I told Jules, gesturing to the array of items in front of us.

Her face lit up. "I am so excited that I can tell you guys about this. Okay, so—"

I watched her as she spoke, explaining every item with care. Night watched too, curiosity crossing his features, probably wondering how such a thing was possible. Dream Walkers and humans weren't supposed to be able to have children, that's why

Night had been the sole survivor.

But here was a woman who was raised as a human by other people she thought were human. She was, however, part Dream Walker, absolutely confirmed now.

And she was everything I desired in a person. Her kindness and patience topped my own. Her frustration simmered under the surface, but only came out when necessary to defend those she cared for. She was a bridge between me and the other male.

The food she introduced me to didn't matter, because she had given me the one thing I never thought I could have: a chance at happiness.

Twenty-Seven

NIGHTMARE

We had bought ourselves a few hours by living inside dream sequences Jules created. Her eyes were the color of golden honey by the time we were done. We had real world needs to attend to, and a Lady who needed to be taught a lesson. Dreams could last lifetimes, even if they were minutes long, but we still had the inevitable horizon creeping toward us. Burke would face us down, and we had to win because I refused to lose what we had created.

Raskos had finally sucked my cock.

Jules had opened up to me.

I had a chance at a future. I had a chance to continue my race with a *family* in place. Burke's threats loomed overhead, wanting to unravel my new reality. I wouldn't stand for it. She had to be stopped.

Plus, as the alcohol dwindled, the club grew boring. Without the drinking, there were less fights on the dance floor. Whenever chaos happened inside Ceilidh, I could sneak a nightmare or two to feed. I didn't want to place Raskos's club at risk anymore, so I couldn't terrorize his patrons any longer.

Attachments were making my life complicated. Mostly, the complications arose from Lady Burke's pending arrival.

On the last night before she was likely due, I worked behind the bar with Jules. I refused to let her out of my sight for a minute. If a patron so much as looked at her wrong, I would step up and serve them.

They learned fast who she belonged to.

Raskos asked me to cut it out, but honestly, there was no way I was letting the peasants leer at our girl. They weren't deserving of her service, let alone allowing wandering eyes to travel the length of her. She was *mine,* and the sooner people learned that the better.

As more varieties of alcohol ran out, most patrons remained respectful. Likely, this was from my threats. As the tap dried, I charged a guy half for his drink, as most of it was foam. He grumbled about it but left the coin on the table and didn't argue. Smart man.

"That was the last keg," Jules said, coming from the stockroom. "We're down to moonshine and the makeshift alcohol from the local vendors."

"Better than nothing."

She let out a breath. "My tips are going to suck tonight."

"Do you need coin when you are married to the Lord?"

"Finian and I aren't married."

"You could be."

She stared at me, mouth slightly ajar. I loved making her feel off-center, though I'd rather be doing it with my cock shoved inside her. "And what about you?" Her eyes narrowed the slightest amount, that crease of defiance marring her lips.

243

"We could too, but it's a different ceremony."

"You would want to marry me?" She blinked.

Some guy yelled at us to get him something, but I cut him a glare. He clamped his jaw shut with a click so loud I heard it over the music.

"I want to fuck you until you are full of my babies. Of course I want to marry you."

"Babies and marriage are not synonymous."

"Well, now you know." I poured a glass of moonshine over ice and slammed it down in front of the guy, leaning close to him. "You're going to drink this while smiling, and if you so much as flinch one time from the taste, I will skin you alive in your dreams for the rest of your life and smile while I do it." I pressed my hands against his as I pushed the glass into his grip.

He swallowed and left too much coin behind as he took the drink onto the dance floor.

I fucking loved my life.

"You don't have to terrify everyone you come across." Jules nudged me with her elbow.

"But it's so delicious when I do." I flashed her a smile. "Marry me."

"I'm sorry. Did you just ask me to marry you while I am putting dirty glasses into a dishwasher?"

"Demanded, actually."

"You barely know me, Night."

I shrugged. "What's there to know? We're the last two of our kind. Marry Finian, too."

Jules let out a breath. "This is not the kind of thing that should be—" She slammed the door to the dishwasher shut and pressed the button to start the machine. "—discussed while working behind a bar. Where's the romance?"

"You want romance?" I latched onto her arm.

We stood on a tropical beach during sunset. Seagulls flew above us. Salt filled the air as I got down on one knee in the sand. Oranges and pinks cascaded over the sky. Clouds reflected yellows and reds, casting a warm hue onto Jules's skin.

"Marry me."

"That's still not a question. You don't know me, Night. Marriage isn't—"

I sighed and pulled her down on top of me. We collapsed back into the sand, but it got her to stop talking at least. I pressed my lips to hers. "I demand it because you are mine, regardless of the ceremony. I refuse to let anyone near you or Finian. And the Lord certainly will not be convinced to marry me. So, you have to marry both of us."

"What if Finian wants to marry you instead?"

I nipped her lower lip. She sucked in a breath that went straight to my cock. "Then he marries me. Regardless, neither of you are leaving. You're mine. He's mine. You're his."

"And me? What do I have?"

"Both of us. We're yours." Grabbing the back of her neck, I pressed our foreheads together. "Marry me."

She chewed on her lower lip, then pulled us both back into reality. The bar bustled with several people demanding drinks we didn't have to offer. "Only if Finian agrees, too." Jules shook her head, uncorking a bottle of alcohol and pouring three drinks for a few women at the bar. "This is crazy."

"Nothing crazy about it." I opened the dishwasher, now done after the quick sanitizing cycle, and placed the glasses away. "You know as well as I do nothing is going to change this."

"I barely know you. And I... I know Finian. But I just met you."

"And?"

"And—" Her eyes assessed me. They were honey-hued, and it made me want to pull her right back into a dream. "Isn't it too… fast?"

"You could argue that about everything." After putting the final glass away, I turned to the next set of patrons who were watching me with tight lips. The Fae didn't dare make snide comments toward Jules when I was behind the bar. I preferred them this way, subdued. I filled up glasses for them, and they scurried off after leaving a decent amount of coin behind. "For example, wasn't it too fast for you to grow up and get a job? Wasn't it too fast for you to lose your family? Wasn't it too fast for the Fae to invade? Wasn't it too fast for you and Finian to move in together?"

Jules frowned.

"Life is too fast, but it has to be that way. Finite things need to be cherished."

"You said I wouldn't be finite if I started feeding."

I let out a breath. "That is my theory, which has been incorrect one time already. I hope it's true, Jules, because I want lifetimes with you. I will not be satisfied with just one. But if we do have just one human lifetime together, then do you want to embrace the chaos or live in fear?"

Her eyes narrowed as she cleared off the next set of glasses. "When you put it that way…"

"You'll marry me?"

"Fine."

"Tonight. After work."

"Tonight?"

"Yes." I tugged on her ponytail and kissed her shoulder. "I'm going to tell Finian the good news and get him something so he can propose to you properly."

A blush crept across her cheeks again. "What would you have done if I said no?"

"Fucked you mercilessly until you said yes." I brushed my lips down the length of her neck as she leaned into me. "I can still do it, if you want."

"I think I prefer being your bad girl over your good one."

I chuckled. "I'll be back soon."

Stepping into the shadows, I traveled to the door to Faerie. It had been a while since I had been back here. Not much was left on the other side, save for the wild creatures that had stayed behind to forage through the remains.

It was a shame, really. The Fae had no idea that while they were over here, creating chaos on Earth, Faerie started to right itself. Without the royal line destroying the delicate ecosystem, it had begun to heal. With a smile, I stepped through the portal, going home for the first time in years.

I had a woman to marry but I needed one more thing to make sure Finian could marry her too. I had meant what I said to Jules. I wouldn't be satisfied with just one lifetime with her. While I hoped my theory was true, I needed to solidify a contingency plan.

Twenty-Eight

JULES

Katie tried to escape into one of the back rooms with a Fae, but I latched onto her wrist. "Not this time."

She turned toward me, red hair flaring around her. A scowl marred her pink done up lips. She had used charcoal to highlight her eyes and had applied something to emphasize the freckles on her face. Katie didn't need to try so hard, as most Fae here were open to sexual experiences. With a flick of her wrist, she could have had several dropping to their knees.

It was the kind of Fae and humans Ceilidh attracted. Everyone who walked through those doors was looking for a fun night, something to make them forget the woes of their reality. And since the Fae had to keep their magic in check while here, it was even ground for both.

"What's gotten into you?" Katie glowered, staring at where my hand latched onto hers.

"I am sick of cleaning this bar by myself. You need to help

instead of disappearing with the patrons."

She put her hands on her hips. "Do you ever think that maybe this is something clients want? Maybe they don't just come here to get some cheap booze and dance the night away, but to fuck me."

"Are you getting paid?"

"Are you judging?"

I blinked, never expecting for the Fae to pay a human for sex. They seemed to ooze pleasure, and I never thought one would need to pay for it. But no, I was not judging—just surprised.

It did make more sense why she disappeared so often.

"I really need help with the bar tonight," I said, voice dripping into a plea. "There's some things going down with—"

"The supply chain, I know. I've been getting a lot of news from the Fae I've been with tonight. Look, I think Finian needs to expand revenue services."

"By becoming a brothel?"

Katie shrugged. "If he can't get booze from Burke anymore, there might be other services he can offer. He treats us well, which is the only reason I felt comfortable starting this."

"Does Finian know?"

"Nope," she popped the p in the word. "Not officially, anyway. He might suspect, but he's never asked. I don't imagine he'd be happy if he knew, but I have a couple of regular Fae who enjoy role playing. It's sometimes extreme stuff—things not every human is into."

"Interesting…"

"There was a need, and I filled it. It's not hurting anyone." Her green eyes softened. "Are you going to tell him? I kind of need the coin."

"I won't tell him *yet*, but I'm not going to hide things from him either. I do need something from you, because you gave me an idea."

Folding her arms across her chest, she arched an eyebrow. "What?"

"People come here for an escape, right? They want a break from what is happening outside those walls. They want to forget the politics and the brewing civil war. This is a haven for them, a place they can let their guard down."

"Yeah, and?"

"And it's about to be ripped out from under them. It's about to become whatever Lady Burke wants it to be. It's about to be destroyed. The way you are making coin now? It might not be *optional* under Burke's rule. You understand?"

A scowl parted her lips. She rubbed her elbows with her fingers as she stared at me. "What can I do about it? I can't give you any of the coin I've earned. I need that for—"

"I am not asking for money. I am asking for your support. Talk to your clients. You know more people around town than I do. The court needs to show up for Finian. We might not have an army like Burke or the fire power, but if we don't do anything, Ceilidh is doomed."

Katie licked her lips. "I'm not sure I am ready to put my life on the line for a nightclub."

"But would you put your life on the line for freedom?"

She rolled her eyes. "You're being melodramatic. I'll talk to Finian tomorrow, depending on how everything shakes out. Okay?"

I sighed. It had been a long shot to get someone who had such a selfish history as Katie to join a cause for someone else's benefit. I hoped to appeal to the selfish side of her, but that had fallen flat too. I thought maybe she cared about this place enough to fight for it.

"Listen, Katie, if we don't make it out of whatever happens tomorrow, I have to tell you that working with you has been awful."

She gave me a full on grin. "Oh, I know. I am literally the worst coworker and manager. I have no idea why Finian hasn't fired me yet." Katie winked, spun on her heels, and strode off to one of the back rooms.

With a sigh, I went back behind the bar. The patrons who were left were drunk off their asses on moonshine, but most had filtered out. The Fae woman was back, sitting at the end of the bar in the same seat she had been in last time.

"If I were you, I wouldn't let her get away with that. I would storm in there, pull her off whatever dick she's trying to ride, and make her get back to work."

I shrugged, uncorking a bottle of moonshine and gesturing to it. The woman nodded from underneath her hood. I slid her a glass. "If she doesn't tell Finian tomorrow, I will."

"And what will he do about it, I wonder? Do you think he would turn this place into a sex house?"

I shook my head. "Not his style." The back rooms were for encounters and were cleaned regularly, but he had never charged anyone for using them. If we were thinking about expanding avenues for coin, perhaps charging folks for renting a space would be worthwhile.

It was worth thinking about more, when my brain wasn't consumed with worry over Burke's looming arrival. In just a few hours.

After I apparently married Night.

And Finian? Had Night even asked Finian about this? What the hell had I been thinking agreeing to that earlier?

"You look distraught." The woman ran her fingers along the

edge of her glass.

A wave of emotions washed over me coming from the Fae, but I couldn't place them other than a definitive coldness. Had I felt those because I was a Dream Walker?

"What's going on in that pretty little head of yours?" she asked.

"How do you know if you are in love?"

She chuckled. "A loaded question to have when there's nothing better than moonshine to drink. I am not sure I have been in love."

"You're not sure? Most Fae have been, though. I mean, you've been alive long enough." I sucked in a breath. "Sorry, that was so presumptuous. I have a lot on my mind."

She chuckled. "No need to be sorry, but this is less about me and more about you. Why don't we look at how you feel?"

One guy collapsed onto the counter, his drink spilling in front of him. I sighed and grabbed a rag, cleaning up the mess. "Right now, I feel annoyed."

"I meant about the feeling you suspect to be love."

I shrugged. "Who is to say what it is? I have never dated, let alone felt... this."

"And what does *this* feel like?"

As soon as the rag became a slopping, dripping mess, I switched it out for another one. What a waste. The guy had paid for the drink, but he only took one sip. The rest of it was now on my bar and floor.

"It feels good. I feel... excited and safe at the same time. I know I'll be taken care of. I get the butterflies people talk about in films." I let out a breath as I put the other rag into the bin. Rinsing my hands off, I poured the next couple of drinks for those who lingered. We were only a few minutes until close, but some people grabbed last call drinks from the bar.

"But when you look at the men, what do they make you feel?"

"I never said there was more than one." Eying her, the hair on my neck rose. I launched myself across the bar, trying to grab onto her to do what Night had taught me and see inside her, but the Fae disappeared in front of me, as if she had never existed.

I turned toward the nearest patron. "You saw her, right? She was real?"

He looked at me. "If I say yes, can I buy a drink before you close the bar?"

Growling, I slammed a glass on the counter and passed it to him. "Did you see a Fae sitting there?"

"I wasn't paying attention. I was..." He cast his eyes down. "Look, that guy with you is terrifying, okay? So I wasn't, like, checking you out or anything. I swear." The man took his drink and disappeared back into the throng of dancers.

"Where the hell have you been?" Finian's voice rumbled behind me. I turned around, about to say how I had been here the entire time, but saw he was yelling at Night. Night who had shadow walked back into the bar.

"I had to get something for tonight."

"Yeah?" Finian crossed behind the bar, thrust out his finger, and poked it into Night's chest. "Imagine my surprise just now. Walking out of my office expecting to see you and Jules behind the bar. Instead, I see her alone with a mirage of Lady Burke sitting right *fucking* there." He pointed to the now vacant seat, the one I had launched myself at to try to grab hold of the Fae.

Mirage? My mind spun. What had I said to her? Was she going to use it against us? Terror seized me. "Don't be upset with Night, because I think we have bigger problems." Somehow, she knew I was with both of them, and a part of me knew she would use that against us.

Twenty-Nine

FINIAN RASKOS

My eyes hurt. Everything hurt. I had spent the evening staring endlessly at numbers, realizing I could only come up with less than half of the coin she had requested. No matter what, when they arrived the next day, we would be at war with Burke. There was no way around it, no clever opportunities. My finances had run dry, favors called in, and still, I came up short.

I had hoped to pull together enough funds to throw a sack at her. Maybe have her call off her troops and stall her hostile takeover. But just over nine thousand coin wouldn't get me anything, especially after losing whatever good graces I had from Nightmare's interference. I appreciated that he had tried for me. It was more than most had ever done.

Still, I tied the coin bag together and prepared it for whatever confrontation happened later this morning. I wasn't sure how much sleep I would get between now and then, but with the alcohol almost drained in the club, my income had slowed. If Burke decided to wait me out, it'd be even worse tomorrow.

Knowing her style, Burke would likely invade later today—perhaps just after sunrise. My desperation could be felt for miles. With a sigh, I packed up the office and glanced around. This space had become my second home. It was comfortable. I had plans to fix the court, but now they were never coming to fruition.

When I started this club and rebuilt my court, I had every intention of creating a vacation from the wilds, a getaway. A place where Fae and humans could be together. But the humans had that saying about the road to hell.

I shut off my lights and stepped into the club, ready to help Jules with closing duties for the night. Ushering the patrons out today would take more effort than previous nights, as the air held a somber weight.

As I approached the bar, I stopped in my tracks, frozen at the sight of someone who was too early. Here too soon. In a blink, she was gone.

A mirage. *Her* mirage.

How long had she been scoping us out?

My heart sped up without my permission. As the Fae vanished, Night reappeared behind the bar, stepping out of the shadows. He wore a grin on his face. A smudge was on his pale skin, and his hair appeared windswept.

Anger rose inside me as I charged toward him. "Where the hell have you been?" Jules whirled around, and I regretted my word choice instantly when her eyes widened.

Night's brows slammed down. "I had to get something for tonight."

"Yeah?" I stepped behind the bar and thrust my finger against Night's chest. "Imagine my surprise just now. Walking out of my office expecting to see you and Jules behind the bar. Instead, I see her alone with a mirage of Lady Burke sitting right fucking there." I pointed to the now vacant seat.

I hadn't seen her face, as she had a cloak on and had been looking away from my office. However, I would recognize her ridiculous dresses anywhere. She had worn all black as if trying to blend in, but there was a lacy flare to her skirts, like that of a giant cake. I didn't have the words to describe her fashion choices, but her style was not flattering on her.

"Don't be upset with Night, because I think we have bigger problems," Jules squeaked.

I turned to look at her as Night wrapped his hand around mine, lowering my finger away from his chest.

Jules continued, "She's been asking me questions for a few days, and I'm not sure if I told her anything... important."

"Fuck!" I yelled.

Night placed his hands on my shoulders. "It's fine. Burke can't do worse to us than I can do to her."

Jules wrapped her arms around herself. "I felt something emanating from her earlier tonight. Like a wave... it was... cold?" Her lips pressed together. "Do you know what that could mean?" She looked at Night.

He shook his head.

Using my magic, I thrust up my shields, nudging the remaining patrons toward the door. It took a few minutes for them to trickle out, but once they were gone, I called my bouncers back.

"Listen, I'm not sure what is going to happen tomorrow, but I wanted to give you a week's pay in advance just in case." It was the best I could do under the circumstances. After that, they had to figure something out if Lady Burke took over.

Mathias grunted while Jersey looked grim. Both men took off, not waiting around to see what would happen next. I couldn't blame them. Safety was important, and there wouldn't be any to find here.

While I still had vague hopes of paying Burke off, if she had been spying on my court, things would get messier before they got better. Whatever chaos she brought, I would deal with the consequences. My employees didn't have to suffer the fallout.

For the thousandth time in my existence, I wished I had better magic than shields to defend my court.

"Finian." Jules's voice was gentle as she wrapped her hand through mine. Her warmth spread up my arm. "We're going to fight this. You'll see. We'll take it one step at a time in the morning, and we'll go from there."

In the morning. I sure as hell wasn't going to be sleeping tonight. My energy level was through the roof. I shut my eyes and focused my magic around the court's barrier, adding a layer of protection that would notify me the moment Burke or any of her court crossed into mine.

When I opened my eyes, Night had curled his hand around Jules's shoulder. His gaze pierced into me. "I didn't know she sent a mirage here."

I shook my head. "You had no way of knowing. Where did you disappear to?"

A small smile curled on the corner of Night's lips. "How would you like to be married before Burke tries to destroy everything you've built?" He reached into his pocket and pulled out a small stone that contained multitudes of jagged edges and had the color of an earthen rainbow.

"Pretty. It looks like pyrite." Jules's eyes sparkled. We both looked at her. "What? I was really into rocks as a kid. Thought I was going to become a geologist or something.

"So, you left to find… a stone for the band?" I searched Night's gaze, my brain not catching up to the first part of what he said. *Married.*

"It's not pyrite," Night said, but held out the stone to me. "What do you think, Raskos? Want to start a family with me?"

I blinked. "I'm not marrying you, Night."

"You would have answered differently when you were on your knees in your office, but no. This is for us to marry our girl. Tonight, before shit happens with Burke."

Picking up the rock, I held it up to the lights in the bar. We hadn't shut off the music or the dance floor cascading beams. Each colored light brought a different hue to the surface of the stone. It was stunning, and there was power inside it.

"What is it?"

"It's a family heirloom. I retrieved it from Faerie. I figured if she was going to be stuck wearing a wedding band for the rest of her life, it might as well be something important."

"What if I have my own?"

"Do you?" A gray eyebrow arched.

"No." I turned my attention to Jules. "Are you prepared for this? Has Night talked to you about—"

"I'm not prepared, nor do I think I will be. But Burke might be coming to destroy us tomorrow, and there's only one thing I want for tonight. You. Both of you. Inside me."

I let out a shaking breath. "We don't have to be married for that."

She shrugged. Her shoulders looked so well defined in her tank top. "Yeah, but what if this is our last chance to do it? We might never get another moment. And… I don't know. I guess I am tired of being scared. There are so many things that could happen next, but you both make me feel…" Her eyes swept to Night. "Well, *you* make me feel safe, Finian."

Night narrowed his gaze.

"You make me feel terrified for everyone else who looks at me wrong."

"I could make you feel good tonight, Jules, or I could punish you. Your choice." He crossed his arms over his chest.

"You make me feel protected. There's a difference."

"Good save."

I pulled Jules into my arms, wrapping mine around her shoulders. "You really want to do this? If we survive what happens with Burke, this is forever. You understand?"

She nodded into my chest.

"And you know the pain that comes from the Dream Walker ceremony?"

"What?"

"Night," I glowered.

"I have a way to combat that. It's called a distraction. She won't feel the pain as bad if she's also feeling something else."

I narrowed my gaze. "What are you proposing? And Jules, you have the right to refuse anything."

She pushed gently away from me and gazed at me with warm, honey-hued eyes. "Of course I know that."

"You'll need your magic for the marriage bond and for tomorrow, so I don't want you shielding her," Night said.

I opened my mouth to protest.

"But I'm going to make it so you don't have to shield her. While you fuck her, I'm going to be the first one to claim her last hole."

Jules pressed her lips together, but her pupils dilated as she looked at Night. "How do you know I haven't—"

"I've been inside your mind. It's a fun fantasy, tiger, but that's all it's ever been. I won't lie—Finian is right. The marriage bond for Dream Walkers is not pleasant for the female. It never has been, but if I give you something to distract you, it might be... tolerable."

Jules set her jaw, brows furrowing. We stayed quiet for a beat, watching her. "I already said I would marry you—both of you. And sure, why the fuck not? It might be the end of the world as we know it tomorrow, so let's do everything."

Night's lips twitched.

"I don't think you should give him an open invitation."

"Nope, she already did." Night wrapped his arms around her waist and hauled her over his shoulder. He spanked her ass so hard the slap echoed over the music. She squealed and thrashed in his grip, but her laughter bounced off the walls.

I used my magic to shut off the lights and extraneous sounds. "We're feeding her first."

"She's fine. Haven't you seen her eyes?" Night was already halfway toward the stairwell. "She's been feeding, and she'll continue to feed. We'll eat real food after. Promise."

With a sigh, I followed behind them, staring at the stone in my hand. Married. To Jules. Tonight. A family. The words wrapped around my head, circling but not settling into place. I wanted desperately to have something go well in my life, and this felt like it could be the start of something beautiful.

Unless it was the beginning of the end.

"Finian, you coming?" Jules had lifted her head up from the position over Night's shoulder, clearly having forced him to stop at the threshold to the stairs. Her warm smile ran through me, forcing back my doubts and fears.

"Yeah, I'm coming." But not before she did.

JULES

Whenever Night got an idea in his head, there was no stopping him. By the time he hauled my ass up the stairs—literally—and dropped me onto the bed, he was beaming. It was the kind of grin a child might get after waking up on Christmas morning.

I wrapped my arms over my chest, fighting back a shudder from his intense gaze. He wasn't usually this happy. The air about him tended to be serious and brooding, but his eyes were curled at the edges.

Excitement coursed through him.

"Becoming shy all of a sudden, Jules?"

I was, yes. Because it wasn't every day a girl got married. Sex was sex, but this was a commitment. This was exclaiming to the world that... well, it felt too soon to be love. But I did care for Finian, and Night brought out a different side of me I never imagined seeing. I felt something more than lust, and it felt *right*.

For the first time in my life, I belonged somewhere.

Night's eyes blazed silver as he stared down at me, licking his lips. He climbed over me, using his arms and body to cage me against the bed.

Finian leaned against the threshold, watching us. His arms were crossed, looking more amused by how Night was treating me than his usual scoffing. His eyes were half-lidded, but there was still a fire behind them that was like a wick to my candle.

I was drawn to him. Both of them.

"I'm going to tell you how this is going to go, tiger. Are you ready?"

Shifting my gaze back to Night, I nodded.

"Raskos and I are going to make you nice and wet. He's going to fuck you until you feel so good you can't help but squirm. Once you're relaxed, I'm going to claim your ass." Night ran his fingers along my cheek, down to my neck, and added the slightest amount of pressure around my throat. "As I'm pushing in, I'll perform the bonding ceremony."

"The one that might be... unpleasant." I swallowed against him.

"Tell me, Jules. Have you been fucked by two men before?"

I shook my head.

"Then we'll provide plenty of distraction from the ceremony itself." Night flicked his eyes at Raskos. "And then he will marry you. His bond is the easy one for you, but hard for him. And you'll have to reward him, right? You'll let him come in your sweet cunt."

My pussy tightened at the thought.

Night pressed his lips to mine with fiery intensity. He claimed me, pushing me into the bed. The weight of him, the pressure of his lips on mine, the way he growled as his hands found my wrists and held them against the mattress. I peeked a glance at Finian, and his hand was around the bulge in his pants, adjusting himself.

I moaned, because I loved how he watched us with burning, liquid desire. The way they both displayed their passion and arousal matched what I needed—Night's alpha personality and Finian's quieter coaxing.

"Are you looking at him?" Night sank his teeth into my lower lip, drawing it into his mouth. I wrapped my legs around his hips and pulled him into me. I gasped with some relief as soon as he hit my core. "Looking at Raskos, but thinking about my cock?" He pulled back, glancing over at Finian. "That sounds like she's being a rather naughty girl. What do you think we should do with her, Finian?"

Finian arched an eyebrow, and his lips parted. His gaze caressed my body. "She's wearing too many clothes. Maybe we remove those as the first punishment."

"Gladly." Night smirked and grabbed hold of my shirt. "I hope you didn't particularly like this one." He tore straight down the middle. With an arched eyebrow, he asked, "No bra today, tiger? Naughty. I wonder…" Slipping his fingers underneath the hem of my pants, I panted as he teased me. "No panties either."

Finian approached the bed. "Were you looking for Night to punish you, Jules?"

I swallowed. "No, I—"

He cupped his fingers under my chin, forcing me to look at his intense, green stare. His cheekbones were so defined, I wanted to lick them. "You?"

Night slowly undid the zipper on my pants, hooking his thumbs around the waistband and grazing my skin.

"I, uh—"

"Use your words, Jules."

Finian's words were stern. They didn't hold the wicked

promises that Night's did, but his voice still cut straight to my core, making me desperate to please him.

"I thought you might like it."

"Like how vulnerable you were underneath just a thin layer of clothes?" Night arched a brow as he pulled my pants down, ripping them off my body in one fluid motion.

Both men were still clothed as their eyes trailed along the length of me. I bit my lower lip, allowing them to take in the sight of me.

"That I was doing it for you…"

"It only helps us if you tell us ahead of time, Jules," Finian cooed, running his fingers along my jaw. His touch was featherlight against my skin, making goosebumps rise on my exposed chest and neck. "So sensitive. It's one of the many things I love about you."

He said the word so easily. I sucked in a breath, chasing his touch by arching into him.

Night chuckled as I tried to close my legs to get friction there. Tutting, he grabbed the insides of my thighs and forced me open. "And wet," he said, staring at me. "Move back farther on the bed, tiger. Your guys need more space."

I scrambled backward, head hitting the pillows.

Finian barked out a laugh. "And so eager."

"What did I tell you, Finian? We are the perfect counterparts for her." Night's eyes flashed blue. "Open your fucking legs, tiger. I didn't give you permission to close them."

I opened instantly, and Night grasped my foot. We stumbled into a dream, where Night was chasing me on a beach. As I ran away, I glanced over my shoulder. But I instantly hit a wall—or rather… Finian's open arms.

"Night," Finian warned, bringing us both back into reality. "She's trembling."

"With anticipation. See for yourself."

Finian eased onto the bed, gazing at my body. I wiggled my hips, trying to free myself from his scrutiny, but Night's fingers tightened around my ankles.

"You're about to be our wife. There's no hiding from us."

I crossed my arms over my chest. "Maybe I am second guessing that."

"Finian," Night's voice dripped with command.

Finian smiled and latched onto my wrists, pulling each of my arms away from my breasts. The men held me open as Finian climbed on top of me. His hard length pressed against me. "You aren't actually second guessing, are you?" The words curled out of his lips with curiosity, but his eyes held concern.

I shook my head. "No." I sucked in a breath as Night's hands climbed up my legs and reached my inner thighs. His fingers brushed over my nerves, barely touching me. It was enough to make me shudder under Finian. "I'm not," I gasped as Night traced his fingers along my entrance. "I want to marry you, both of you." Especially if it came with the perk of these two touching me as much as they wanted.

"And why is that, tiger?" Night's voice demanded.

I stared at Finian as his eyes drank me in. One of his hands released my wrist and traced long lines down to my breast. He arched along my curves, circling until his fingers brushed the hardened nub. I bucked against them. With my free hand, I took advantage, pressing my palm underneath Finian's shirt and running my fingers along his stomach.

Night chuckled as he thrust a finger inside me. "I didn't hear your answer." I moaned as he pushed a second finger in.

Finian's lips met mine, capturing my breath. His tongue traced my lips and licked inside me. I opened my mouth and deepened our kiss as Night curled his fingers. My hips rolled, trying to get

Night into the perfect spot, but I didn't have much room as Finian's weight kept me pressed against the mattress. Leaving my lips behind, Finian trailed his tongue along my skin, finding a sensitive spot on my neck. He sucked.

"Answer Night, baby."

I always thought I would hate hearing that pet name on a man's tongue, but from Finian, spoken with a dark rasp as he grazed my neck with his teeth, I loved it.

"Because of how you make me feel. I'm not sure what this is, exactly, because it's early, but I want this for the rest of my life. I want however long I have left to be spent with both of you. This is right. I feel... whole." The last words came out as a whisper. Night pulled his fingers out of me. I whined at the sudden emptiness. He crawled up to my other side and placed his fingers on Finian's lips.

"Taste our girl."

Finian flicked his tongue out, eyes glittering as he closed his mouth around Night's fingers and sucked off my arousal. This was really happening. The noises coming out of my mouth were purely feral. There was so much *want* inside me, I felt ready to explode.

"Hold her, Night."

Night's smile was wicked as he shadow stepped behind me— losing his clothes in the process. He hauled me back against him, using the pillows to prop us in a sitting position. Wrapping his legs around mine, he kicked my thighs open wide for Finian.

My body clenched, dripping with need. The movement itself was so hot, I panted from the way Night had me pinned on display.

Finian's eyes swirled with magic. "I want you to scream my name as I make you come, and then I want you to beg for us to fuck you." His magic whirled around us but didn't do anything other than caress my skin. He could let go with me, not needing to worry about holding anything back. Finian was careful with his employees and other people. He made sure everyone was taken care of and happy, never overstepping with his powers. I loved watching his caution fall apart.

He knelt between my legs, running his cheek along my inner thigh until his breath tickled my nerves. His eyes shot up to mine as he blew out a steady breath against me. It was cold, making my body prickle with goosebumps and anticipation.

I squirmed against Night, feeling his hard length pressed against my ass. Night kept a firm grip on my arms, pinning me open and helpless to whatever teasing Finian wanted to do.

"You know what's great about this angle?" Night bit my earlobe.

Finian flicked his tongue out, running it against my clit. My toes curled.

"What?" I asked, breathless, waiting for him to touch me some more. Finian took his time. He lavished in the things undone. I was close to the edge already, and he had barely touched me.

"I get to watch Finian's reaction to your taste."

The lord flattened his tongue along my entrance and gave a long, languid lick. My nerves exploded, cascading up my body and making Night tighten his hold around me. Finian sucked my arousal down and swallowed. His eyes blissed out, expression serene, pupils dilated.

"Looks like you taste good, tiger." Night's voice purred next to my ear, breath kissing my skin. "How many orgasms do you think we can get out of you tonight?"

I gasped as Finian trailed his tongue lower, licking my pussy. He pushed his tongue inside me. His lips curled in a wicked grin as I wiggled underneath him. Every part of my body wanted release, especially when Night shifted his hold, so my wrists were in one hand behind my back. My chest pushed forward as Finian hooked a finger inside me. Night trailed up my side, over my ribs, and cupped his hand on the underside of my breast.

Finian played with me, only pushing in his first knuckle. I groaned as his tongue circled my clit. Night ran his fingers over my nipple, pinching the hardened nub. I bucked in his arms, against his hold, whimpering as Finian still fooled around with my pleasure.

"Please," I gasped. An orgasm welled under my skin, igniting me. I wanted desperately to come, to feel the relief cascading across my body. I needed it more than the air in my lungs.

"Please, what?" Night said, voice husky. His teeth wrapped around the shell of my ear as Finian pushed his finger all the way inside me. He sucked the most sensitive part of me into his mouth and lightly grazed his teeth over my nerves as he hooked his finger.

And I came undone. I pushed against Night as he grabbed my chest, pulling me into him as I bucked. I screamed Finian's name as the Fae pushed a second finger into me as his tongue chased my orgasm to completion. I breathed hard as they both let me come down off my high. Night slowly released me, and Finian sat up, gazing at me as if I was the best thing he had ever seen.

I blushed. "What?"

"You're stunning, Jules. Absolutely stunning." He pressed a kiss to my lips, and I tasted myself on him. I melted into Night, who chuckled.

Night trailed his hands lower on my body, swiping a finger through the wetness Finian and I had created. He brought it to his lips, and the sound of him sucking it down next to my ear made me quiver against him. "You're so sweet when you come apart. Ready for round two?"

I nodded, beginning to bite my lower lip, but Finian captured it in between his teeth instead, drawing my lip into his mouth and letting it go with a pop. These men were making me forget that our lives might be on the line tomorrow, and I was going to savor every second of it.

"Finian, lie down. Jules, climb on top of him."

"What are you going to—" As I started rising, he spanked my ass—hard—and I yelped.

"I'm going to take this and make you my wife."

A shiver went down my spine at the pure possession in his voice. Finian stripped out of his shirt and kicked off his pants. As he laid back, I crawled on top of him. He looked at me with a half-lidded gaze, still intense despite letting Night give out the orders. His hard cock pressed against me, and I rotated my hips a few times. He groaned as his hands found my waist, stilling me against him.

I pouted as Night came up behind me, wrapping his hands around my chest.

"If she wants to rub your cock on her clit, who are you to deny her, Finian?" Night bent me forward so my breasts grazed against Finian's firm chest. He ran his hand down my back, running a finger along my spine to my hole. Applying some pressure, he tested my entrance. "Fuck, you are so tight."

A moan escaped my lips as Finian brought my nerves right against his cock. He moved me gently back and forth, setting the pace for us, going mind numbingly slow.

"You have lube?" Night asked Finian.

Finian gestured to his end table.

Oh fuck, we were really going to do this.

Night opened the top drawer, grabbed the tube, and slammed it shut.

Finian wrapped a hand around my chin. "Eyes on me." He lifted my hips and positioned himself at my entrance. "I want you to watch me as I fill you." Slowly, I dropped down onto his tip, but

Finian controlled the pace with a wicked grip on my hips. I tried thrusting down to feel him stretching me, but he worked me onto him, teasing me.

When I was about halfway down and moaning for more, Night scoffed. "Any hour now, Finian."

The green-eyed Fae grinned wickedly as he brought me down the rest of the way, inch by inch. Once I was fully seated, Night thrust me forward again, bringing my ass into the air. His finger reached my other entrance, this time covered in lube.

"Breathe for me." Night pushed his finger in, working it in and out. I clenched around Finian, feeling the stretch of both of them. A single finger would be nothing compared to Night's cock, and I was already feeling it. I wiggled, trying to get myself adjusted, and I did as he asked—I breathed.

It was a new feeling—pleasant almost, but a curve of pain was there too. My nerves had never been touched like this, and my body wanted more and less at the same time.

Night slapped my ass, and I yelped.

The Fae pulled me in for a kiss, searching my mouth with his. Finian languidly explored my lips with his tongue, then inside me as he slowly rocked into me. Sensations ran through my body as another wave of pleasure built inside me again.

Night worked in a second finger, and my body clamped up. I sucked in a breath.

"Relax, tiger," he said, slowing his pace.

The stretch of both his fingers was unreal. It felt like too much, but I loved the ownership he had over me. I wanted to give this to him—to be *consumed* by him. As Finian made gentle thrusts inside me, I focused on that instead, the pleasure building in my core. Night worked me slowly, taking a page from Finian's book. I relaxed into the feeling, but as soon as I did, Night pushed in a third finger. I dug my fingernails into Finian's shoulder as my nerves fried and pain built on top of the thrill.

Finian's eyes swirled green and the pain subsided. I let out a long breath as his gaze narrowed. "Careful, Night. I had to heal her. Go slower."

"If you wanted me to go slow, you should be the one taking her ass."

"I'm okay," I said on the edge of a breath. Cupping the side of Finian's face, I ran my thumb over his cheek. "Thank you, that helped." His skin was warm under mine.

Finian captured my lips again, and I relaxed into the feeling of being filled by them.

"Okay, Jules. Remember to breathe because this is the hard part." Night notched himself at my entrance, smearing lube over both of us. I shuddered from the cold, and Finian cursed under his breath as I tightened around him. "And it's not me fucking your ass."

"What?"

Night pressed his hand over my right bicep. "Is this place good for the marriage band?"

I glanced at him over my shoulder. "Is that where it normally goes?" He's hovering right at my entrance, and my body is aching for him, barely allowing me to gasp out the words.

"Traditionally, yes, but we're not traditional here, tiger."

I swallowed. Even if I was mostly human, I felt like we should keep part of the Dream Walker spirit alive. Nodding, I said, "Yes, let's get married."

Night smirked and kissed my shoulder. "Finian, get ready to distract her."

Doing as he was told, the Lord dipped his fingers in between us and pressed down on my clit. "Ready."

"You are acting like——" I stopped breathing.

As Night pushed into me, creating a wealth of pleasure, an overload of feeling from my nerves being teased, he also clamped his hand down on my arm. I had thought anal would hurt more, but the stretch and pull as he worked into me was nothing compared to what my arm felt.

It was like my cells were rearranging, setting themselves on fire and spreading throughout my skin with a vengeance. Something inside me tore through the surface. It was worse than breaking my forearm in the second grade. It was worse than my bicycle accident that left me with road rash all over my back a few weeks before Homecoming in high school. Fire spread through me.

And even as that built, the sensation of both of them working me brought me back to the present. Night thrust slowly, like Finian had asked. The Fae rolled his fingers over my nerves, and there were so many sensations, because he began to drive into me again. I was being invaded, my mind scrambling to connect with what was happening to my body.

Night pushed farther inside, and I gasped as his piercings entered me. I dug my nails into Finian's shoulders. It kept me grounded as everything threatened to spin me off into space.

"Halfway done, tiger." His fingers pressed into my skin—his hand glowed blue. I had never seen anything like it. My body willed my arm to detach so the pain would ebb, but the pleasure built at the same time from having them push inside me. I was going to pass out.

"Breathe." Night's voice, clear and commanding.

"You're doing great, Jules." Finian's voice, quiet and coaxing.

Hell, maybe I did love these men.

I gasped as Night pressed farther still inside me. He was so fucking big. My body felt pushed to the limit adjusting to them inside me, and my arm…

Finian's eyes whirled, and the pain ebbed, allowing the pleasure of them to invade my senses. "That's it, Jules. You can take us. You're so perfect." He increased the pressure on my clit and thrust faster. I was going to fall apart.

Night pushed the rest of the way inside me as the pain in my arm disappeared as quickly as it had come. I panted, trying to catch my breath now that the only thing left was both of them with me. "Fuck, Jules. You're so tight. I almost…"

Finian smirked. "Not able to handle yourself, Night?"

"If you want to be next, Finian, I'll be ready soon after this."

He chuckled and shifted his attention back to me. "Are you okay?"

Blinking a few times, I tested a thrust back against my two men. They cursed in unison. I looked down at my arm and sucked in a breath. It resembled scarification. Two long ovals wrapped around my arm, interlocking at each end. My skin was angry and red, but I felt this pull toward Night.

"You could have warned me," I murmured.

"Yes, but…" He pumped in and out of me, and my body screamed out in pleasure. "I think you wouldn't have been distracted enough for me to take you this way."

"You feel so big." I gasped. "Both of you." They stretched me, filled me, and now, I wanted them to fuck me. "Make me come?"

"Finian, if you set a slow pace, I will kill you."

He chuckled but followed Night's lead. They found a rhythm, working in and out of me. Their pace sped up, and Finian swirled his fingers once again over my nerves. My body was pushed to the limits, but I felt so alive. I loved feeling this full.

And I wanted this to be my forever. We had to survive tomorrow. This was what I wanted every day for the rest of my life.

Night bit down on my shoulder, and I cried out as I came. Finian thrust deep inside me and followed me over the edge. Night worked in and out of me a few more times, as Finian gave him a teasing half-lidded smile.

"Who is teasing now?"

Night thrust hard and deep, filling me with him, and I cried out again, a third orgasm causing Finian to buckle underneath me. Night let out a dark chuckle as he held himself on trembling arms above us. He pulled out of me and growled at the sight of me. It made heat rise to my cheeks.

I eased off Finian as Night wrapped his arms around me, pulling me into him.

"Finian, marry our girl."

The stone seemingly appeared out of nowhere. Finian's magic swirled around us. He placed the stone against my right wrist, the same arm Night had used. I shuddered at the coolness of the stone.

"Will it hurt?"

Finian shook his head as Night licked the shell of my ear. "No, Jules, our marriage bond will be painless for you. I, however, might need some rest afterward. It uses a lot of magic." He gazed at me with hope filling his moss green eyes. "This is forever, Jules. Once this goes on—"

"I want to be your wife."

Night ran his hands underneath my breasts, making goosebumps rise across my skin. "If you are second guessing, Finian, I can keep her to myself."

With an eye roll, Finian grabbed my wrist and placed the stone in the center. He pressed his eyes closed and focused on his magic. Coils of steel spiraled out from the stone, the edges of the metal darkening. It became a thick band, wrapping around my wrist and connecting at the other end. It looked like a...

"Wine barrel steel?"

Finian let out a breath. "Yes. I felt it was fitting, considering you've been a bartender here for so long." His face was flush. Sweat beaded along his brow. "That was hard." He laid back, popping open an eye to look at me. "But worth it, wife."

My pussy clenched at hearing the words.

We were officially married—I was married to both of them. I marveled at my arm, from the red, angry welt of Night's bond to the metal around the intricate stone.

Night kissed my back, inching down my spine again. His kisses were possessive, consuming, but I also was raw. I needed time to recover, and I needed to sleep.

"Night, I can't."

He hummed to himself, as if my protest didn't matter, and he opened my legs. Everything was sore. My arm, my pussy, my ass. These two had done a number on me, and despite that, my body still somehow quivered, wanting more. This *was* going to be forever. I refused to settle for anything less.

Night rolled me toward him, despite Finian's sleepy protest. He pushed my legs open, and for a minute, I worried he was going for a second round. Instead, he brought his mouth down on my pussy and licked. He crawled back up my body and pressed his fingers into my jaw, forcing my mouth open.

He spat the mixture of Finian's and my cum into my mouth. "Swallow like a good girl." He clamped his hand over my lips, not giving me another choice. It was sinful, such a way of claiming me—claiming us as his own. My traitorous body wished he had tried for round two.

I swallowed the salty combination of flavors.

"That should not have been as hot as it was," Finian muttered, managing to stay awake, but just barely.

"Correction," Night said, "it was as hot as it should have been, and I will definitely be doing it again." He removed his hand and kissed me. He still tasted like us. I moaned against his lips. "Kiss our wife goodnight, Finian." Night brushed the hair away from my face.

I fought unconsciousness as Finian pressed a chaste kiss to the outside of my lips. And as Night grabbed the back of Finian's neck and kissed him hard enough so he could taste us too, I fell asleep.

FINIAN RASKOS

Jules's arm draped over my chest. I absently traced my hands along her skin. Night pressed against her other side. Her dark brown hair sprawled out behind her, and her breathing was even and steady. It was a marvel she lasted as long as she had. Her wrist held the stone that Night had retrieved from Faerie. The band was imbued with my magic, making her a part of my life for the rest of it. His brand was on her upper arm, still red and irritated.

We were hers for life, and she was ours.

"I never thought I would see you married, Night." My voice escaped in a whisper, and Night chuckled softly in response.

"To be honest, I never thought I would be, either. But being the last one alive…" He shrugged, running his hand through her hair, pulling the strands back to expose her neck. Her skin was mottled from our kisses and biting. We had gotten a little carried away.

Jules shifted, curling her hand into my chest before easing back into her relaxed dream.

"It made you want to connect."

"Fuck, Finian, I've always *wanted* to connect. I never... really knew how." When he said my name with no harshness around the word, it made my cock stiffen. I wasn't sure how that was possible, considering how hard I came earlier.

I glanced at him. The sharpness of his features seemed softer now. His skin held a light rosy hue. His eyes gleamed brightly. The expression held awe and wonder; jaw relaxed as he gazed at the woman in between us.

Sunlight streamed into the room, and despite how late in the morning it was, no alarms had gone off from my wards or shields. For now, we had time. We could steal this moment and keep it for all it was worth. No matter what happened next, I would cherish everything that had happened between us over the past two weeks.

"What do you mean you didn't know how to connect? You could have *said* something, Night."

"Said what, exactly? 'Hi, Finian, while I need to haunt your nightmares and feed on the Fae inside your court, I also want to bury my cock inside you. Is that okay?'" He pressed a kiss to Jules's neck, sweeping his thumb against her skin when he was done. "You know as well as I do, prejudices ran deep in Faerie."

I opened my mouth, wanting to contradict him and tell him he was wrong. But the words to disprove him never came—they would have been a lie. A lot had changed in both of our lives, and I regretted not talking to him sooner, hearing him out, listening to him.

Although Night hadn't made it easy to speak with him either, since he always played into his persona as a villain. And perhaps a nightmare bringer would always be seen as such by most people, but I knew better.

"You have a valid point."

He snorted. "Of course I do." His fingers trailed along her bare shoulder to her arm, lingering on the raised mark he created. "Whatever happens, she needs to stay safe." His eyes locked on mine, gaze thick with meaning. We would keep her safe, even if it meant keeping her hidden. "And we have to survive whatever happens today, Finian, because I want to fuck her until she is pregnant."

"You raising younglings terrifies me."

His silvery blue eyes flashed to mine, a wicked grin curling his lips. "What? You don't think I could teach them how to survive this world?"

I shook my head. "Survival you can teach. It's the softness I worry about. The empathy."

Night pressed his eyes shut. "They'd be your younglings too." When he opened his lids again, his gaze settled on mine with intensity.

I blinked several times, not knowing if I had heard him correctly. "Seriously?"

"Yes." The corners of his lips turned down. "Did you think the marriage was just for show? Finian, I want Jules to have *our* younglings. I want to continue my race, but I also want you to continue your line. If we beat Lady Burke, we'll have plenty of time."

I swallowed, doubt edging in. Even if we won against the Lady, there was so much up in the air. "How can you be sure that her feeding is going to keep her young?"

"I'm not. But that is the contingency plan." He nodded at the wedding stone. The one he got from Faerie, his family heirloom.

I blinked, picking up her wrist and inspecting the iridescent material again. And at that moment, I wanted to kill him. I could have ripped out his heart right then and there. "What the—"

He pressed his finger to my lips. "It's just a backup if we need it, Finian." His voice was so soft, his eyes wide as he pleaded with me to understand. "It would work if she doesn't stay young from feeding."

"But do you know how fucking dangerous it is to have that on her *wrist*?!"

"Well, a few other things occurred to me. No Fae has an eternal gem because *my* people hid them all. Which means if anyone wants to get one, I need to stay alive. We could use this as leverage against Burke, if we need it, or we can use my knowledge to get the rest of the gems and sell them once things have settled in the Fae kingdom."

"The Dream Walkers stole them all?" My mouth dropped open. They had become impossibly rare, with only a few lucky Fae having them in their possession as the war with the Dream Walkers broke out. I hadn't given it much thought—most Fae never spoke about them.

Now I knew why.

"Stole or took back what originally was ours?"

I let out a breath. "Okay, fine. But this could create a target on her back."

"It took you long enough to notice it, and you married her with it. We can say it's... what did she call it? Pyrite? Whatever that is. If it matches something logistically human, no one will question it. They would have to touch the gem in order to feel the power, and no one will risk touching a Dream Walker. It's the perfect disguise, keeping it in plain sight if we need it." A small growl rose from his throat. His hands curled around Jules possessively. "But I'll be honest, Finian, I hope we don't need it."

Vulnerability crept into his irises, and I caught the meaning.

"Because if you do, it means she dies when I do."

And then he'd be alone.

The eternal gems weren't perfect. They didn't make humans live for an eternity but tied their life to their Fae partner's. Before the curse of the Fae door, most Fae used these gems for the humans who crossed over into Faerie and found a partner. The humans would still be *human*, but they would age slower, matching the pace of the Fae. The history of the gem before that was lost to the ages, but it was true—before they belonged to the Fae, they belonged to the Dream Walkers.

What they used them for was anyone's guess. Bartering, perhaps?

As far as I knew, the gem held no magical properties for Dream Walkers. It had to be used with a Fae's magic—an old magic I wasn't sure how to wield—but if Night had access to the gems, he could help me figure out how to use it if we needed it. It would buy me a lifetime with Jules if her Dream Walker side didn't keep her young. It would buy Night more time with both of us.

"Thank you," I said finally. Because as dangerous as it might be, there was no way anyone could steal it. It was permanently attached to Jules now. We had a guarantee at a future—so long as Lady Burke didn't kill us first.

"Oh, come on, Raskos. I was beginning to enjoy your yelling."

Jules grumbled something incoherent against my chest. She rolled over, wrapped her limbs around Night, and pulled him close.

"How is it possible for her to smell this good?" He buried his nose in her hair. "I can't stand it. It makes me want to strangle her."

"Strange way of showing affection."

"Would it be better if I said I wanted to choke her with my cock?"

"Not really." Though my body heated at the thought.

Night grinned. "We should try to get some sleep."

I shook my head. "You should feed. I need to stay awake in case any of my alarms go off."

"Are you giving me permission to feed on your subjects?"

"Can you do small nightmares on a bunch of people instead of creating one horribly traumatic one? People have bad dreams all the time. Could you make it mild?"

He thought about that, pulsing his jaw. "For you, Finian, I will. But it's easier when I feed on one person. But sure. I'll make some people think they are naked in front of a classroom. That seems to be a thing most adults hate dreaming about."

When he shadow stepped, Jules groaned and rolled onto her back. "What time is it?"

"Early enough that you can continue to sleep." I kissed her forehead.

She rubbed her eyes. "Where's Night?"

"Feeding."

"Mm…" Her eyes were a deep shade of brown again. "I think I need to do that, too. What should we make for breakfast?" Her hand traced along my jaw, cupping my cheek.

"No breakfast yet." I pulled her close, a smile climbing up my lips. "I just want you."

Her eyes softened as she pressed her lips to mine.

Thirty-Two

NIGHTMARE

It took far too long to glean the energy I needed feeding the way Raskos requested, but it was his court—*our* court. With the imminent attack, the least I could do was respect his wishes. At least for now, until I could disrespect him in another way.

Respectfully, of course.

Once I finished my twenty-third small meal, I shadow walked back to the apartment. Finian and Jules were at the kitchen island, sipping cups of coffee. The bag of it had gotten dangerously low, and I was becoming fond of the taste. Honestly, I had expected the two of them to still be in bed, with Finian hopelessly wrapped around Jules, but a part of me was glad to see they hadn't spent the entire time in bed without me.

I appeared behind her, enjoying how she jumped as my arms came around her. "Hello, wife." I ran my tongue along her ear. "And husband." I gave Raskos a wink. He sipped his coffee, not leaning into my antics.

He was learning how to stop my pestering, and that wouldn't do. After Burke was dealt with, I would have to find a way to keep him on his toes. He'd understand soon enough that I would always get a rise out of him.

"Night," Jules whispered as I squeezed her. "It feels strange calling you my husband."

I sat next to her, grabbing her mug and drinking several gulps before passing it back to her. She scowled at me, which was absolutely adorable with her mussed brown hair, plush lips, and loose-fitting pajamas.

She had to dress like that more often. There was something sexy about her clothes practically falling off her, with plenty of space for me to play underneath them.

"Why? We're married."

"Yeah, but I've known you for like…" She grimaced and ran her fingers along the t-shirt, which covered the scarification from the wedding. "Not that long."

I rolled up her sleeve and kissed her arm. The mark was still viciously red, but it was only around the scar now. She had healed a decent amount—not as quickly as a pure-blooded Dream Walker, but faster than a human. "Want to know what I love about you, Jules? You jump in headfirst. You're impulsive, but always with self-preservation. You take calculated risks. And you aren't afraid to challenge me."

"What is there to be afraid of?" she sassed back.

Tempering the desire to punish her for her mouth, I stood and snatched a mug. I poured in coffee and gazed at Jules. "Remind me to teach—" As soon as I started speaking, Raskos startled.

"I don't think we have time for that, Night." He pressed his eyes shut, jaw clenching. "They've crossed."

"How many?"

"I'm not sure. It feels like an army, but with Burke's power to manipulate herself, it might only be ten people." He pinched the bridge of his nose, brows lowering over his eyes. "We can handle ten."

"We can," I nodded. Ten wasn't a problem. I could melt a few of their brains before they had time to react. The problem was the strategy behind it. If we killed Burke, another head would appear on the snake. We had to get this right to remove her court as a threat once and for all. Raskos's court couldn't withstand the constant barrage of increased prices and inflation.

"How do you want to play this?"

Raskos frowned. His jaw pulsed a few times. "Jules, go get dressed." He used his magic to change his clothes instantly. "Choose something you can move in if it comes to it." As she got up, he grabbed her wrist and dragged her in for a vicious kiss. It was claiming and dominating, so unlike him, but tension wafted off him in waves.

"We'll be fine," Jules said. The concern on her face didn't bolster her words. She scampered off to the bedroom.

I watched as the bedroom door swung shut behind her and leveled a gaze at Raskos. We were on the same page about Jules— no matter what, we would keep her safe.

I swallowed. "Want me to kill as many as I can? Mess with Burke's moral compass?"

Raskos shook his head. "I will attempt to negotiate with the coin I have. It's not what she wanted, but it's something. I want to show a good faith effort to get back into her good graces."

I scoffed. "She's been abusing your club for months, and you are going to... what, roll over and accept it?"

"She wasn't *abusing* my club."

"Don't defend her." I crossed my arms over my chest. "She was taking advantage of the fact that she owns every industry in the new world."

"Fine. Yes. And when the missives went out to pay the humans, her prices skyrocketed. She definitely used her position as leverage to gouge me. But it doesn't change the fact that Ceilidh needs her trade route."

"I can make her confront everything she's terrified of, but I think she's already there."

"What is it? Maybe we can use—"

"She's terrified of being alone."

Raskos let out a breath, face turning paler. He ran his hands through his hair, grabbed an elastic off his wrist, and pulled it into a messy top knot. "A self-fulfilling fear if I've ever heard of one."

"Many people are scared about being alone." Jules came out of the bedroom, dressed in a tank top and skinny jeans that hugged her hips fiercely. She wore heavy boots, and the stone on her wrist gleamed under the lights. Part of me believed she had chosen that shirt for me—so everyone could see our marriage bond.

I wanted to kiss her until she forgot how to breathe.

"We could offer her something she doesn't have—having all the coin in the world doesn't bring you friends."

"Friends? With Burke?" I snorted.

Raskos covered his mouth to smother a grin.

Jules crossed her arms indignantly over her chest. "Yes, you can propose something other than money. If it is more worthwhile than coin, perhaps she will listen. If she fears being alone, then offer to make her *not* alone."

"The reason she's alone is that no one can stand to be around her."

"Except the receptionist, who I… messed with a bit."

"Night!" Raskos groaned, dragging his hand over his face. "No wonder why she's so peeved."

I shrugged. "She deserved it."

Jules scowled at us. "If we continue bickering like this, she's going to get the drop on us. So, I ask both of you, what do we want to do?"

"Defend the club," Raskos said, but as the words left his mouth, he flinched.

"What is it?"

"More alarms. There's… I am picking up hundreds now."

My eyes widened. "What the fuck. Isn't she spending more paying them than she's getting out of you?"

Raskos shook his head. "I don't think she's listening to the missives. At least, not with this. Perhaps she's found a loophole I haven't seen. She's pretty good at weaseling her way out of situations. Her mirages and manipulations have always served her well." He shuddered.

I crossed the space between us in a second and tipped his head up, forcing him to look at me. "Stop doubting us. We've got this. Ceilidh is the best thing to happen in the new world—trust me, I've seen a lot. It's one of the few places where Fae and human treat each other equally, and next to Alpin's court, it really is unmatched. We might not have the financial power of Alpin's trading hub, but we have something better than that."

"And that is?"

I arched an eyebrow. "Do you doubt my abilities?"

Jules snorted. "I doubt mine." She placed her fingers on top of my free hand, searching for a moment. "See? It comes and goes. It's like having the most finicky superpower on the planet."

"What I mean is… we have heart. Alpin might care for his people, but his place still has a coldness to it. Ceilidh has *life*. This place oozes with it."

With a sigh, Jules said, "I tried to get Katie to recruit people to stand up with us, but she didn't want to risk her life on it. What good is a place so teeming with fans when none of them will come to our aid?"

I clenched my jaw, fighting back the urge to scream at them. Seriously, they were going to wallow now when we were so close to the big confrontation?

"Well, I won't sit here and wait for her to make the first move." I walked toward the door.

"Where are you going?"

"To the battle neither of you seem interested in attending." I hooked my fingers around the knob. "Unless you care to join me?" Glancing between them, Jules was the first one to come to me.

Finian took his sweet ass time standing up and crossing the room. Jules reached for him, and he wrapped his fingers through hers. She let out a little sigh, and it was enough to awaken every protective instinct inside me.

Dream Walkers were the most dangerous when their mates were threatened—same for Fae. It was part of why I wanted us to get married.

Because now she was fucking mine. And if a hair on her body so much as moved during our confrontation with that good-for-nothing Lady, I was going to scramble all their brains. To hell with the consequences.

I had to hope that my partners were ready for this, because their grim looks spoke of nothing but fear.

"Listen," I said to them. "You were the best part of my life. No matter what occurs next, that's never changing. If things don't go our way today... No, fuck that. We're getting out of this. I refuse anything less. I don't finally get the world to have it yanked away."

With that, I slipped out of the door. They came after me, and this time, Jules stood straighter and Finian's irises swirled to life with his magic.

We were as ready as we ever would be.

Thirty-Three

JULES

It took us a few minutes to get outside of the club, but once we opened the doors, we stopped in shock. Tons of people and Fae stood around the exterior of Ceilidh. I bristled, expecting someone to throw a bolt of magic or a punch, but nothing happened for a breath.

Then I realized why. These people had shown up because of Ceilidh—not to overthrow it. They were defenders, not attackers. A cheer rose from the crowd, and I stared in awe, wondering where they had come from. Night grabbed onto my shoulders as Finian took several steps forward.

Lord Finian Raskos never acted like a typical Lord. He didn't have a reputation like the other courts, which was why it surprised me when Katie was so vehemently against turning up for him today. We could have had it worse, because Finian paid us from the beginning. He respected humans.

But looking at the crowd in front of us, Katie must have told people. Here they were, ready and willing to lay their lives down for the court.

The court consisted mostly of rubble. It had never been much to look at, but the streets directly surrounding the club were clear and free of debris. The disarray stretched far beyond what the eye could see. Today, people took up most of the cleared area, silencing me with astonishment.

Finian held out his hands in front of him. Slowly, the crowd quieted, waiting.

"We're here for you, Finian!" someone called out.

"Lord Raskos for life!" Another voice.

"Ceilidh let me lose my virginity!" A few chuckles came from the crowd with that.

A smile crept up Finian's lips. "Well, that likely would have happened regardless of my club, for someone as beautiful as you." He winked into the crowd, but I hadn't been able to place who he was egging on. A few people whistled. I stifled a smile.

"Friends, it means a lot to see you here today. We are defending our club against corruption, standing up against overpriced goods, and making our voices heard. Lady Burke never plays fair. She will use her powers to manipulate you and trick you. If at any point you feel you can no longer handle the magic being thrown at you, please leave. I do not want any of you to die for me or Ceilidh. It's not what this place is about."

A burly man stepped forward, his hands resting protectively over a Fae woman. "This club is the only thing that gave me hope after the world went to shit. It showed me that not all of you are half bad."

The woman smacked his arm.

He chuckled, rubbing his muscles. "And the wife told me if I didn't show my support, she would make me anyway."

She rolled her eyes. "I told him we had to because we met here. Raskos, there are so many of us who have stories like this—where Fae and humans got to meet on common ground. I might not have a lot in common with Garrett, but he's a *good* man. Our personalities match, which is more important than interests, in my opinion. And it's because of *you*. What you built here, this place." The woman gestured to the club. "We'd be stupid to run away now, not after you spent so much time building something better than Lady Burke could ever create."

"And what's that?"

"A community." Katie shoved her way to the front of the crowd. "You created a home inside the craziness that is our new society. We feel safe here—safe enough to explore things we never thought we would." Her eyes shifted to me, glittering under the late afternoon sun. "We won't get a second chance. Not like this."

"So, we need to protect it!" a voice rang out over the crowd.

Shouts of agreement surged around us.

Finian raised his hands again. "Thank you. But my statement still stands. We're not warriors. If you need to, please save yourself. We built this once, and we can build it again."

"Fuck that."

"I like this club."

Night stepped up to Finian's side, bringing me right along with him. "Most of you will not call me friend. In fact, most of you are prepared to write me off as a monster, but I will defend this club."

"While feeding on us?"

Night's serpentine smile widened. It practically gave me shivers, and he was on my side. "Not today. Only if you side with Lady Burke are you in trouble." His hand wrapped through mine. "Plus, Finian is being modest. He wants to defend the club at all costs, because his wife is here too."

"You got married?" someone shrieked—it sounded distinctly feminine. "And you weren't going to tell us?"

Finian glared at Night and ignored the question. "We have a long history with the Dream Walkers."

A few confused murmurs rose from the humans in the crowd.

"And I have to say that a lot of what we believed was wrong. Or specifically, what I believed about one Dream Walker in particular." Finian wrapped his fingers through mine and raised our hands. "And now we have one fighting on our side, and we have something worth defending. Family."

They were keeping my status secret, which was probably smart, considering Lady Burke didn't know I could defend myself—if I figured out how to use my magic. We still barely scratched the surface of what I should be able to do, but now it was sink or swim.

"I ask you, friends, are you prepared to defend this court?"

A few magic sparks shot into the air and the roar of the crowd grew to deafening levels. My eardrums rumbled, and it took me a moment to realize the ground was shaking, too.

"We're going to win this defensively. The rubble provides great cover. Find places to hide. Take out the soldiers toward the back and make it quiet. Get as many of them incapacitated as possible before they reach the club." Lord Finian Raskos let out a long, low whistle. Magic sparked around us, and the people dispersed, eager to listen to the man they had followed into a new life on earth.

"That was beautiful," I said.

"Don't compliment me yet." He brought my hand up to his lips and pressed a kiss against my skin. With his moss eyes glowing brightly, he dropped my hand, fixed his hair, and focused on the long street leading away from the club.

"Thank you," Night added.

"If you get sentimental on me now, Night, I swear to the Mother. You know what I need from you?" Raskos stepped up to him, sizing up the man. I had only seen this side of him when they fought over me. "Your worst. Get out there and do it and fall back to us before they get here."

Night smirked. His gloriously white teeth and deep silver eyes glowed under the sun. He wasn't hungry, but that would never stop him from enjoying a good meal. And Lady Burke had led in an all-you-can-eat buffet. "I thought you'd never understand me, but Finian, you are speaking my language." Night wrapped his hand around the back of Finian's neck and pulled him in for a bruising kiss. He winked at me, then shadow walked away.

How did that man make a wink seem sexier than being kissed by him? It made no sense.

"I hate how much I like him."

"No, you don't," I chuckled.

Finian smiled. "I don't."

"What are we going to do?"

"Well, I am going to prepare some shields. I have something inside my desk, top drawer. Want to grab it?"

I nodded as Finian's magic flared around us. Rushing up the stairs, I burst into his office. Pulling the top drawer open, I frowned. There was nothing inside but papers. I shifted them aside as the door slammed shut, and I nearly jumped out of my skin.

"No," I growled the word, rushing back to the door. Pounding my fist against it, I realized exactly what Finian Raskos had done. There wasn't anything in his office. He had lured me up here so he could trap me in here—away from the fighting.

"Sorry, tiger." Night popped up next to the bookcase. The set of his jaw made his angles look harder. "We talked it over, and we'd both feel better if you sat this one out."

I crossed the room and tried to slap Night across the face, but he caught my wrist easily. His eyes flickered with amusement.

"That fuel you are feeling right now?" He towered over me. "Use it to figure out how to wield your power, then join us on the battlefield. We want you out there, but more than that, we *need* you safe. We can't have both if you don't have your powers yet."

"So, you're just *leaving* me here?"

"It won't be for long." Night frowned. "The magic will die if Finian does, or if we win, we'll come and let you out."

"If Finian *dies?!*" The words were a shriek on my lips.

"I don't plan to let that happen." Night wrapped his arms around me, pinning my arms to my sides, not allowing me to beat his ass like I wanted. His muscles tightened, holding me close. "It'll be fine. You'll see." He pressed his lips to my forehead. I curled my fists as he shadow walked out of the room.

Prowling the length of the office, I pressed my eyes shut. I had fed before, because Finian and Night saw my eyes change. There was power inside me, but I needed to find it. I had seen Night feed and shadow walk. I had felt what it was like for him to control my dreams. Staring at the door, I wondered how hard it would be to emulate that same feeling for myself. I had time to figure this out. I could still help them.

Then, the first explosion sounded.

Thirty-Four

NIGHTMARE

The look of disappointment on Jules's face after I spoke with her practically broke my heart. After all this time of searching for another Dream Walker, there was no way in hell I was letting her get involved in a battle without being able to use her powers. Raskos hadn't been the biggest fan of the plan, but when I pointed out how Jules had no training in physical combat, he agreed.

Neither of us wanted to risk losing her.

What likely hurt her more than me was the deception from Raskos, which was why I had made the appearance. If we were a united front, she'd forgive us. Eventually.

At least she'd be alive long enough to be livid. And if she figured out how to use her powers to get out of that room, she could join us on the battlefield.

"How pissed is she?" Raskos asked the moment I shadow walked back outside.

"On a scale of one to ten, probably a twenty-five."

Raskos shook his head. "I should apologize or explain, because if she—"

I cupped his chin. "You should get your head in the game. The reason we forced her to sit this one out was for her safety and you know it. We wouldn't be—"

An explosion cracked through the air, and a giant mushroom cloud erupted from the earth, spiraling straight into the sky. Debris and shrapnel rained down from the smoke, and a few people shouted. There were plenty of Fae in the mix, and I was confident they could heal a few casual wounds. This was nothing compared to what was to come.

My nostrils flared as I breathed through my memories. This was like when the Fae destroyed my home. While most siblings never stayed together after they were done with being a youngling, my sister and I had a bond. We were always within reach. It was late in the day that they attacked, and through her sacrifice that even in my weakened state, I escaped.

It was a guilt I swore never to bear again.

I finished my earlier thought. "We wouldn't be able to focus if we were worried about Jules getting killed in this mess. Come on. We need to kick Lady Burke's ass."

Finian's brows creased with determination. He nodded but took one last sweeping gaze back at Ceilidh. His eyes swirled as another whirlwind of magic went around us—a shield for the perimeter. After all this time, I could understand parts of his powers. He was creating an alert if anyone got through his defenses and was attempting to keep the building safe and standing, despite whatever magic was thrown at it.

"Ready," he said.

We headed straight toward the sounds of chaos.

"Good luck," Raskos said, frowning. "And stay safe."

"It's adorable that you think I need either of those things." I stepped into the shadows and prowled to the back of the line of soldiers. Lady Burke stood in the middle, surrounded by mirages. I couldn't tell which one was the real one. Figured.

Her eyes whirled bright orange as she used her influence over her subjects. I felt her magic cascade along my skin. She wasn't using compulsion, no. She was toying with their emotions. On top of her ability to duplicate herself, she manipulated people around her. All the Fae and humans thought they were in danger by being here—that *we* were a threat. It wasn't like the king's power, where he could compel Fae and humans alike. It was something more subtle, winding its way into the bones of those around her.

It was influence, and it was insanely powerful.

Thankfully, none of that worked on me.

Hanging at the back of the unruly mob, I picked stragglers off one by one. As soon as someone stumbled behind because of a bunch of steel rebar sticking up at odd angles, I stepped out and grabbed hold of the side of their face. I drank their nightmares down until I found one that would make their brain melt.

Literally.

One by one, slowly but steadily, the Fae and humans at the end of her pack dropped. She had hundreds, but it felt like I had all the time in the world. Especially as more of Finian's court copied my lead, taking down one after another. We waited in the shadows for opportune moments to remove the threat piece by piece, and they corralled themselves straight toward the club.

It was a beautiful sight, watching so many of them fall. One after another silently.

There were some who were terrified of Burke herself. Instead of killing them, those who were not here by choice, but by force, I removed her influence. I gave them a dream of a better life, of Ceilidh, and I let them scamper off like scared rabbits. Maybe they could come back. Maybe the dream, as Finian said, would live on.

Normally, I wouldn't have blinked at a slaughter, but it seemed my partners were having a good influence on me.

By the time the massive crowd came to an abrupt halt, we had removed about a third of her army.

"I see we're doing this the hard way, Finian Raskos."

"What makes you say that?" Finian's voice arched out as he stood on top of a hollowed-out building. The few loose strands of brown hair drifted in the breeze. His eyes held such depths of green they looked out of place among the dusty browns and oranges of his dilapidated court.

"Siccing your Dream Walker on me before we've reached your front door?" Lady Burke yelled. Her voice came from every version of her, making it impossible for me to determine which one of her was real. If I could figure it out, I could sneak up on her and crush her under my influence. If I was wrong... well, absorbing the nightmares of a duplicate would not be pleasant.

I had only met one other Fae like Lady Burke before, and the encounter had not ended well.

I kicked myself for not doing more damage to her court when I was there. I had hoped the warning would serve as enough of a reason for her to cut down her prices, but instead, she amassed this army to fight us. There was no denying my involvement in this, but I refused to take the blame for Burke's toxic response.

"That's twice now that he's been involved in a disagreement that was distinctly ours."

"The disagreement is no longer just between us, seeing as how you came unannounced, uninvited, and with an army. Take your leave while you still can, Lady. We can walk away from this."

I had to hand it to Finian. He sounded like a Lord.

She smirked; the wicked smile curled on every version of her lips. "From what I hear, you have little *court* without the alcohol. Must be a shame, losing your followers to other courts that should be lesser than yours."

"Who says they are lost?"

Lady Burke gestured to the empty streets. "Do you not stand alone? And without that pretty woman I saw either. What's the problem, Finian? She leave you for Alpin?"

Raskos's jaw worked. "You know what your problem is, Burke?" He cast a glance at me. "You talk too much without saying much of anything." His magic shifted, giving his followers a signal.

Humans ran out from underneath their cover. Fae flung their magic into the mass of people. Weapons were drawn, and Burke's army screamed as they were surrounded.

Smiling, I strolled into the chaos, grabbing one of her soldiers here or there, leaving collapsed bodies and broken dreams behind me. It was an absolutely beautiful day. A human scream broke off as a Fae spell sliced them down. Blood splattered my shirt as another bolt of magic hit its mark. Still, I walked, eyes set on the woman with flaming orange hair and equally bright eyes.

The twenty versions stood in the middle of the throng, scowling at her surroundings like they disgusted her. Her arms crossed over her chest. She at least wore something for the occasion—tight cargo pants with a desert camouflage print and crop top.

It was better than seeing those hideous dresses.

I grabbed the first mirage and felt nothing but emptiness as it broke apart in my fingers. The first pang slid behind my defenses, jolting straight into my brain. Absorbing her duplicate was like shooting ice water straight into my veins.

Burke's smile split her face in two. "Ah, Nightmare. I was

hoping to see you. Keep choosing wrong, and you know what happens next. But please, have fun in the meantime. I'll try to keep it interesting."

I refused to give up on this chase. She was here, threatening our court, my wife, and Finian. No matter what happened to me, the sacrifice would be worth it to watch her fall apart under my hands.

But I knew the risk. If I took in too much of her power, I could die before I guessed correctly.

I glanced at the copies, thinking the one to the right had a tick in her jaw. I reached for it and shuddered as it broke apart under my fingers.

Fuck.

"It will be fun to watch you fail. What was it? The last of your kind? Pity there aren't more of you to kill."

If only she knew.

I snapped the neck of another one, but the magic was too fast, pooling into my skin with a black stain, stretching out into my veins. My muscles convulsed, fingers curling painfully into my palms. I stumbled back.

Her replicate army stepped toward me; their hands outstretched. Any attack I performed incorrectly could be the reason I died. I swallowed, forcing my spine to straighten as I studied their advance. Something needed to show the difference. As the five closest got within spitting distance, they shuddered to a stop, almost like they had hit a wall.

Finian. His brow furrowed with concentration as sweat beaded on his skin. He had a shield in between us, preventing the monster from getting closer to me. "Focus on someone else. I'll handle her."

Fuck that. I wasn't letting him fight her alone. Not anymore. We were in this together. I did, however, take a moment to pull in two quick nightmares from her soldiers, refueling me after her drain in my power.

It still felt like something was crawling under my skin. There had been a nightmare I once witnessed. It had been about alien creatures, ones that could burst forth from the skin. Her magic felt like that.

"Raskos." Burke's face turned red as she looked up at him. "Are you going to come down and play?"

His eyes continued churning as the sounds of the fight rose around us. Weapons clashed, screams and grunts filled the air, and the smell of dirt and copper surrounded us. Raskos took a step down, landing on a shield he created. It looked as if he were walking on air as he lowered himself to the ground.

He held his hands out wide. "I was going to ask if nine thousand coin would stop you from attacking my court, but I see we're well past that."

"Because you started this, Finian. This could have been a diplomatic mission, but you started taking my men out before I reached your club."

Finian laughed, and it was the first time I heard him sound like that—cold and cruel. "Make no mistake about this, Burke. *You* started this. You created this problem when you raised the prices to unreasonable amounts. Your personality breeds toxicity because you're too scared to let anyone see the real you. And because you've never been honest or real with anyone, you will never know love. You will never know what it is like to be accepted for everything you are—and everything you are not."

A gut-curdling scream pierced the air, coming from her. She rushed toward Finian. As the first blow knocked him off balance, the shield between me and the other Burkes dissolved. A sickening crack sounded as her flesh hit his and he fell backward. I stepped into the fray, no longer caring what her magic did to me as long as I got to end her once and for all.

Thirty-Five

JULES

As soon as the explosion sounded, I yanked on the knob. My fist pounded on the door. The magic would dissolve if he died, but fuck, I didn't want that. I wanted to be out there—doing… what? It wasn't like I could be useful to them. Not without my power.

I banged my head on the wood, feeling helpless. My men were out there, fighting a battle that should belong to all of us. Together until the end.

But this couldn't be the end.

It couldn't.

Endless, weighted moments went by. Anger ripped through me, followed by hopelessness at how useless I was. I was at the mercy of my powers that didn't want to come. This was not how our future was supposed to begin.

I screamed against the wood, pulling again. My arm ached where Night had bonded with me, so much so that I winced.

I glanced down at my skin. It had been raw around the edges, but this morning, it had become scar tissue. Now, however, it had risen, becoming an angry shade of deep red. I watched in horror as the welts got bigger and then burst open. Blood ran down my arm, not the red of other people, but blue.

My blood had never been blue before.

I snarled. I was a Dream Walker. And I wouldn't let a single door stop me from getting what I wanted—*vengeance*. This woman had no right to walk inside my court, badgering my husbands because of her greed. Screw her. This ended today, and not with any of my partners dying.

Wrenching on the door, I remained unsurprised when nothing happened. I pressed my eyes shut, focusing on the emotions welling inside me. Something screamed below the surface, wanting to break through. My body flared to life from the inside out.

I tried the knob again, and finally, the door opened. So fast that the wood smashed against the wall, causing pieces to splinter off.

It was like the magic had disappeared. *No.*

I sprinted out of the room, darting down the stairs, and hit the exit door running at full speed. When I got outside, I gasped. The afternoon light was so bright compared to the inside of the club. There were bodies and blood layering the already broken ground. My eyes traveled over the Fae and humans, trying to make sense of the remains.

There were no words for it. It was senseless, and all of this was because of a debt. Money. Greed. Power corrupting.

Curling my fists at my sides, I tore off toward the sounds of fighting. My arm throbbed as more blood burst forth, and I staggered. Once I saw the chaos, I understood what was happening to me.

Night battled with Burke—or at least *copies* of her. Every time he touched one of them, the duplicate disappeared into his skin. It was like he was absorbing poison. His fingers were already black, and with each new replicate he took in, the darkness spread up his arms. Pain furrowed his brows, and his eyes were blazing bright blue.

Lady Burke's magic filled the air as she continued to duplicate herself. Several versions of her were fighting Finian, who had sweat beaded along his brow. Every time he flung up another shield, Burke would tear through it like tissue paper. The back of Finian's skull was already bleeding, and whenever the veil dropped between them, Burke would get in a punch or two. Blood trickled from his nose, his cheek, his ear.

All this chaos because of one heartless woman.

"Hey!" I screamed. My vocal cords fried from the sheer volume of it. Burke's heads snapped up, all her orange eyes staring at me. "Why don't we leave them out of this?" I dug my fingernails so hard into my skin that they cut crescent moons in my palms. "You and me. That's what you wanted when you tried to manipulate me at the bar, wasn't it?"

"Jules, no." Night pressed his hands against another version of her. The magic seeped into his body, spreading up his veins, reaching his shoulders. He gasped. "We have this." He staggered forward as one copy shoved her hands out, sending him flying over the rubble and destruction. His body slammed against the ground, and he let out a cough. Sheer determination settled over his features, but I would not let him sacrifice himself for me.

The battle raged on around us, but the four of us were in what seemed to be a bubble. Perhaps it was from Finian's shields, but likely it was from Burke. She held more power than most Fae, and I wasn't sure why or how, but it ended *now*.

I straightened. "Come on, Lady Burke. Or are you terrified of a simple human?"

"There's nothing simple about you." Multiple voices threaded through each other, creating an odd harmony to the cadence of her words. "Is there?"

Finian lurched to his feet, casting out a shield around me. I could see his magic swirling, his eyes erupting with color. Burke slammed a fist against his chest. Blood sprayed from his mouth as he toppled backward, landing hard on the concrete remains of the old town. His dazed blinking was the only thing to tell me he was still alive.

Anger lashed through me. I took a few steps forward, my lips curling in a snarl. "I'm about as human as they come, since I don't know how to use any of my powers."

Night's eyes had gone dark blue as his head lazily rolled toward me, watching me with a somber, pleading gaze. I had seen this expression earlier, when he told me why they were making me sit this out. He needed me more than he needed himself.

But that was too bad because I needed both of them. I wouldn't leave them, and she wasn't scary.

For once in my life, I had people worth defending. I had people worth fighting for. That was enough to stand against her. Whatever it took.

"Maybe we can come up with another agreement." The throng of Lady Burkes stepped forward. "I wouldn't mind having a Dream Walker inside my court. If you leave these two behind, perhaps I will let them live. Maybe give you visitation rights?" Her magic swirled around me, and I could feel the deal pressing in. I wasn't sure if it would work on me.

"There's a huge problem with your proposal."

"And that is?"

"It sucks."

She laughed. "It's comical that you think you can stand against me. How brave you are, not even trembling the slightest. Honestly, I didn't think you would have it in you. Such an innocent little thing behind the bar—so worried about her life and future. So worried about feeling love and making roots grow. Tell me, how is that treating you?"

The wave of sorrow washed over me, and I pulled on it, bringing it into me. My eyes flicked to a Lady Burke near the back, one that looked a little less intense than the rest.

Her. She was the real one. Because that hurt, that pain, it stained her soul. There was nothing anyone could do about it, except…

"I have a counterproposal."

"And that is?"

"If I can choose the right Burke, you give me five minutes to change your mind about this war."

"And if you choose wrong?"

"I'll take your first proposal."

Finian coughed, blood trickling from his mouth. "Jules…" His voice barely broke over a whisper, and it shattered my heart to hear his voice so strained.

"Interesting. I can't make deals with Dream Walkers, but if you break this deal, whatever happens next is on you."

"Ditto."

The sea of Burke's faces blinked. She raised their arms, and she invited me to step forward. "As you wish. You have one chance to guess correctly."

"I don't need to guess." I walked through the crowd, feeling Night's eyes trace my every move. Wandering through the copies, I found the real one. I stared at the Lady, or more specifically, at the pain spilling out of her. It coated the world around her, tainting the ground. The sorrow choked the air, making it impossible to breathe.

This was the right one.

"You," I said.

Burke scowled and crossed her arms. Her duplicates remained immobile. "Well, now starts your clock. Change my mind, *human*." She spat the last word like it was an insult.

"Five minutes," I reminded her.

If I could figure out how to dream walk in five minutes, I would have more time to change her mind. I would have endless hours. A dream could feel like a lifetime, despite only spanning a few moments.

She crossed her arms over her chest. The copies watched. Night watched. Finian tried to sit up, but his arms couldn't support his weight. I pressed my hands on her face.

She flinched. "I didn't say you could touch me." Burke slapped my hands away, but Night never needed to touch me to put me back in a dream. I had already grazed her skin, so that should be enough.

I pressed my eyes shut. Sadness flowed out of her, spreading across the field. It was her magic, her influence. She polluted everything with her hollowness, creating a self-fulfilling prophecy. Burke was afraid of being alone, of people not wanting to be around her, of losing everything she had worked for.

And yet, by being as sad and empty as she was, she drove people away. No one could stand being near her for longer than they needed to be. Whenever she left and her magic went with her, there was relief. Shoulders lifting, backs straightening, as she removed herself from them.

She would never feel love because she couldn't stand to love herself.

"What are you doing other than wasting my time?"

I popped an eye open. "It is *my* time to waste. You granted me five minutes."

"Well, you have four left."

I breathed out. "Then shut up and let me show you."

Burke sighed, running her hands through her orange hair. "I don't think you understand, princess. I am going to destroy everything. There is nothing you can do about it to change my mind. Five minutes is a joke. I should have agreed to three."

"But you didn't."

Burke smirked. "Three."

I pressed my eyes closed again, refusing to listen as she prattled on. I found the thread of her sorrow, and I followed it. Tracing it back up her arm—

"I am *waiting*. Two minutes."

I winced, focusing again on the thread. It trailed up her arm, around her neck. It flowed into her veins, into her brain, down into her cells.

"One minute. I am going to enjoy keeping you as a pet."

And each of her cells contained multitudes. Everything in her brain was on fire—endless opportunity and feelings. They toppled over one another, each vying for existence inside the darkness of her soul. I reached out again, pressing my hands on either side of her face.

And this time, she couldn't do anything to stop me.

Thirty-Six

FINIAN RASKOS

My body was slow to stitch itself back together. I felt like a newborn fire pauldrin—pink, squirmy, and useless. I was broken in more ways than one. Watching Jules cross into the sea of Burkes after taking a deal with her made me want to vomit. If I lost her now, the only thing I would have left would be rage.

But somehow, Jules found her. She sought her out, not based on luck, but with her power. She was figuring it out. I leaned up finally, coughing so much that blood leaked out of my lungs. Burke had hit something vital when she had pounded into me. My body wanted to shut down, but as long as I stayed alive, I could heal from this.

With my pride gone, there was little left to lose. I crawled over to where Night landed. "Feed on me."

"What? Raskos, fuck that."

"You're at death's door, and I can take it. Give me your worst."

311

I latched my hands onto his wrist. "Besides, one of us needs to defend her if this goes awry." I met his blue gaze. He could barely sit up. His skin had blackened, practically turning to ash in front of me. He had a better chance of helping her at this point than I did. It would take me much longer to heal, but he could heal with one good meal. It was a sacrifice I would always be willing to make. "Please?"

His hard eyes softened, and his lids pressed shut. I stumbled into the perfect nightmare to end this day—because it *was* this day, except Burke stole Jules away from us, taking her back to her court and still demanding the mountain of debt be paid. And when Night and I tried to rescue her, both of us ended up skewed outside of her court with our hearts cut out.

"Fucking morbid, Finian." Night sat up, eyes swirling silver. It settled me to watch his skin return to its normal color. "I thought out of the both of us, you were the optimist."

"That's always been you—or rather, you're a do whatever you want and hope for the best kind of guy, right?" I gave him a weak grin.

Night's eyes flickered to Burke and Jules.

Burke's eyes had stopped swirling. They were a hazy brown underneath her magic, and it had been years since I had seen them that way. Her jaw was slack. Her eyes looked blissed out.

Jules's hands were on either side of her face, eyes glowing a bright yellow.

"What the hell is happening?"

"She figured it out."

"What?"

"She's feeding." Night leaned back on his palms, nudging me with his shoulder. "Sit back and watch, Finian. Our girl's about to save your entire court with nothing more than her mind." He let out a long breath. "And how fucking sexy of a mind it is."

A watery film trailed over Burke's eyes.

"Shouldn't we be ready to—" I struggled to stand, but Night pulled me back down. I groaned from the impact, bones rattling.

"Watch." His word was a command that etched straight into my soul. I listened to him, my curiosity getting the better of me. How could she possibly save us by wrapping someone up in a beautiful dream?

Burke blinked, stumbling backward a step. Her eyes narrowed. "Your time is up."

"Yes," Jules said, holding out her hands in a gesture of surrender. My heart stopped. "And I meant what I said. I think we could have an interesting time together, Burke." A smile broke across her face, and my heart stuttered in my chest.

Lady Burke licked her lips, eyes darting to us sitting on the ground. Her lip curled at the corner. Turning her attention back to Jules, she said, "I don't see how this changed anything."

"Okay." Jules nodded. "I understand."

Burke blinked, scowling. Her throat moved as she swallowed. Her voice came out so small, I almost missed the words. "But could it... really change?"

"It could. It's what you want, isn't it? Friendship is more obtainable than you think, but you need to *listen*."

Burke worried her lower lip with her teeth. She let out a long, low whistle and clapped her hands together. Her magic cascaded around her, and just as soon as she had descended on my court, her followers scrambled backward. "Finian, you and I have some matters to discuss."

"You aren't taking my wife." I stood up, dusting off my trousers. Pain rocketed through my core, but I kept my eyes steady, putting on the lackadaisical attitude of a Lord. To my surprise, my legs held despite my injuries.

"Mother, no. As much as I would love to have someone with her assets in my court, I think this one belongs to you." Burke shook her head. "I think we had some debts to discuss, some payment plan options, and we have the matter of my... accounting error." Her gaze slid back to Jules.

"An accounting error?"

"Yes, it seems I might have miscalculated the cost of some of my wares. It should be an easy enough thing to discuss. If you have a moment."

I eyed her, not sure how to attribute this change of personality so quickly.

Night leaned close. "If I were to have found her, Lady Burke would be a puddle of mush or pissing herself. Be grateful Jules seems to have the power to bring out hope instead." His words licked the shell of my ear. "And don't look a gift horse in the mouth."

"You can send the new documents to me. I have nine thousand coin for right now."

She nodded. "I will take seven. We can settle the rest once we've discussed the new terms of our trade routes."

My brows lifted. "I thought I owed—"

Burke held up her hand, eyes darting to Jules. "I will send you the new invoices by scytheseer. Please expect them in a few days once we've had the time to travel back to my court. I expect you will give some of my higher officers a free drink whenever they visit in the future?"

I already owed Evander more than his share of drinks, so what the hell was adding a few more? "Yeah, sure, as long as we come to a reasonable price of imports."

Burke chuckled, her smile slithering up her lips. "That won't be a problem. Plus, I might owe you a few additional kegs for the chaos I've created today." Disgust curled her lips up and scrunched her nose. "I will leave some of my healers behind, too. They'll assist with the clean up as a gesture of good faith. But Finian, you really need to do something about... this." She gestured widely to my streets—the rubble, the chaos, which was now coated with blood.

Fae were already healing the fallen, slowly righting the wrongs of the battle. Burke's light-hearted way of viewing this like it could be fixed so easily made me angry. She had created another scar on my court.

Still, I wouldn't press my luck. Night placed a hand on my shoulder, preventing me from doing something I would regret.

Strange how he was providing the voice of reason.

"Thanks for the visit, Burke. Always a pleasure," he said dismissively.

Burke tossed me and Night a kiss. Then she looked at Jules. The Lady threw her arms around her and squeezed her so tightly both of us took a step forward. Jules looked sheepish with a blush rising to her cheeks when Burke pulled away.

"Ta-ta, boys." She gave us a wave with her fingers. "Let's hope next time I have a hot date to bring with me." Burke whistled again, and her crew surrounded her. They were broken and bleeding, much like members of my court, but they staggered out toward the boundary of the wilds.

I let out a breath as Jules bounced over to us. I threaded my fingers through hers, not wanting to be away from her for a second longer. Those brief moments where we'd be separated forever had made my heart stop.

"You terrified me."

She gave me a weak smile. "I terrified myself."

"What did you show her?"

A smile lit up her face. "I showed her what would happen if she started talking to people—having honest and real conversations with them."

"And?"

"And she finally felt it—the connection she's been missing. It filled the hollowness she's carried inside her soul and showed her there was another possibility out there for her. That type of dream is inspiring. It changed her life, and it changed ours." She pressed a kiss to my cheek, squeezing my fingers.

"We're an interesting pair, Jules. I show people their inner demons, and you allow them to see past them."

I blinked, because I hadn't seen it before, but it was as if the Mother had gifted my court a second chance. "I have an idea. And it's okay if you hate it, but in case Lady Burke was lying about her... change of mind, I might know how we can become more independently wealthy."

"How, Finian? Want me to torture people?" Night smirked.

"Actually, yes."

Night's eyes flashed a brighter silver. "I was kidding, but now I'm intrigued."

"Torture isn't the correct word. But you make people confront their worst fears, and you—" I stared at Jules like the Mother had sent her. She had already fixed everything in my life, but did I dare ask her for one more thing? It would be up to her; I would never push her for this. "—you could make people move past those fears."

Jules shifted her gaze to Night. "We'd be like therapists."

"They go to Night for exposure therapy—" I offered.

"And they come to me to heal," Jules said, face brightening.

"You both get to feed, and we'd make money off it. Night

doesn't have to slink in the shadows anymore."

"I like shadow walking, Finian." Night crossed his arms over his chest, but the teasing way his smile crawled up his face let me know I had him.

He wanted a place to belong—he always had.

"Jules won't have to hide who she is, either. There are so many humans and Fae with histories they cannot overcome, and—" My mind whirled from the possibilities.

I thought about Scarlet the Fae Slayer. Meeting her had been terrifying, and seeing her the second time hadn't been much better. She was haunted—I could tell by the look in her eyes. Perhaps if Voss came for me, I could offer something better than my head on a platter.

Because ultimately, I knew how Devoss felt about his toys, and there was no way we'd get away with what we did to her. As soon as he had fixed the kingdom, he'd come for us. Our history would catch up to us.

But if we helped heal Scarlet? If the rumors were to be believed, she had a traumatic past that needed healing. If Jules had fixed Burke, perhaps she could do something similar for the Fae Slayer.

Jules could help a lot of people.

"I could provide closure." She looked at me with wide eyes, her honey-hue coming through. "I'm not sure if I can do what I did every day, though. I'm still figuring it out, and I got there today because I needed to keep both of you safe."

I shrugged. "We could offer it for free when you want to try it again. That way, if it doesn't go as planned, they haven't paid for anything. Test the waters, see if you want to pursue it. And no pressure."

"I will try." She smiled and placed a kiss on the side of my lips.

My gaze shifted to Night. "You, though—"

Night didn't let me finish, cutting me off with a kiss. His tongue tangled with mine, so desperate his teeth mashed against my own. His fingers weaved through my hair as he pressed us closer together. "Any time people want me to help them confront their fears, I am yours."

"Are the three of you going to keep making out, or are you going to help us clean up this mess?" A Fae woman had her hands on her hips as Night pulled away from me.

I laughed. "Let's organize the healers, get everyone fixed up who needs it." Turning toward the destruction, I sent out a wave of my power. It wasn't much, but my court turned their attention to me. "Thank you, everyone who showed up today. This court holds a lot more heart than anyone gave us credit for. The first round of drinks is on me."

"When you only have moonshine left, that's easy to commit to," the Fae grumbled.

"And none for you."

She rolled her eyes but gave me a smile. "You heard the Lord! Healers, get your asses in gear."

I wrapped my arms around Jules and Night, pulling both of them in for another hug. "Duty calls. See you both in a few hours?"

"I'd like to stay and help." Jules brushed her lips against my cheek.

"And I'll prepare the club for the next shipment."

"Thank you," I said. I never thought I would feel this amount of gratitude toward a Dream Walker, and now I had two to be thankful for.

Thirty-Seven

NIGHTMARE

Finian's head was in my lap, and Jules was curled into my side. We were stretched out on the living room couch. Jules had jumped several times during the movie, but once the credits rolled, I scoffed. There had been nothing *scary* about this horror film.

"I still don't understand what the humans are afraid of."

"Clowns are terrifying," Jules says.

I frowned. "But it isn't about a clown. It's about a Dream Walker."

They looked at me. I sighed and counted off the facts. "One, they pass it off as some kind of alien, but it's clearly a Dream Walker shown in a really poor form. As a *clown*, of all things." I was livid. "Two, he feeds off nightmares and fear. He gets stronger the more fear he feels. Three, he's a fucking Dream Walker."

Jules inched away from me, staring at me with wide eyes. "Maybe that's where he got inspiration for the story. Maybe he met

319

a Dream Walker."

"Unlikely. There is no way someone met a Dream Walker and decided to depict them as a clown." I folded my arms over my chest. "Seriously, I fucking hate clowns. They are boring and mundane. It's an insult." My voice rose so much the sofa shook.

Actually, the sofa shook because Finian was chuckling. He stared at me with wicked mirth in his eyes.

"Oh, you think you're so funny." I slammed a brief nightmare into his mind of the clown eating his foot.

He yelped and jumped up from the couch, glaring at me. His green eyes swirled, as if his shields could save him from me. "You promised not to give me nightmares."

"And *you* promised I would finally understand why humans are afraid of clowns. You broke yours first, as far as I'm concerned."

Jules laughed, and the sound melted my heart. She placed her hand in front of her mouth, and her warm eyes gazed at us. "Their fear stems from the unknown. Anyone could be behind the painted make up. Any monster could mask themselves from the rest of the world. A murderer could dress up in… well, clown clothes. *That* is what makes people afraid of clowns."

"See? She makes sense." I pointed my thumb at Jules, giving Finian a hard stare. "And we didn't have to watch a long, stupid movie for that explanation."

A week had passed since Lady Burke tried to take over Ceilidh, and a few days since we started offering therapeutic Dream Walker services. They had been slow to start, but yesterday, we had a fully booked day. Coin flowed into Finian's court for the first time since leaving Faerie. Fae and humans looked at me warily, but already I had helped someone through their fear of heights.

It would be a longer road for other people to heal, and it was strange to think I now had a place in that process.

Today, Finian held a lightness to him, and I felt decent enough to indulge him by watching one of his favorite movies. But since the movie was terrible, I was left wondering why I liked this Fae so much. If this was his favorite movie, we were going to have problems.

"If it makes you feel any better, Night, you are much more attractive than the clown," he said.

I glared at Finian.

"Enough for me to beg for your forgiveness."

I arched an eyebrow. Okay, *that* was why I loved the male. "Maybe later. We need to watch something better to remove the astronomical amount of garbage that movie put into my brain." Shadow stepping to his collection, I pulled several off the shelf and placed them onto the coffee table. "Any of these."

Finian made a face. "These are all romances."

I licked my lips. "Of course they are. I feel like rewarding my wife."

She snickered. "Rewarding me and punishing Finian?"

"I'm not sure why he has the movies if he doesn't secretly love them," I accused.

"Because some of my guests liked them." Finian sighed. "Do I have to explain this again?"

"Yes." I leaned over him, grabbing his chin with my hand. "I want you to explain it in extreme detail."

"Finian wanted to make panties wet," Jules giggled.

"And did it work?" I kept my eyes on him.

"Of course it does." Jules reached forward and snatched one movie. "At least, it does for me. This one."

Finian groaned.

"You'll be happy when we're able to slide our fingers into her without any resistance." I turned his head, so he was looking at our wife. "Or… do we not need the movie?"

Jules blushed. Whenever red crept over her cheeks, I wanted to capture her lips in between mine and *bite*. I was never going to let this woman go. "Maybe we don't."

"I can work with that." I pressed my thumb down on her lower lip and pushed the best version of her worst nightmare into her head. Finian smiled as she rubbed her legs together, squirming under my touch.

She gasped when I pulled her out of the dream, eyes fueled with liquid heat. "Can we show Finian?"

I slid my gaze over to Finian. "I don't know. What if he's not into it?"

He practically salivated from the challenge. Eyes soft and green, taking us in as Jules groaned. "Show me what?"

I smirked. "I thought you'd never ask."

Don't miss the Blood Hunted Series

SUGGESTED READING ORDER:

Blood Hunted
Blood Trail
Mister Nightmare
Blood Queen

The Playlist

Usually, my characters have their own playlist, but there was something about this playlist that worked for the entirety of the story.

Silver Screen by Jonny T, Foreign Figures
Redlight by Creative Differences
C'est la vie by Weathers
Killing Time by Jordan Fiction
Sim City by Halo Boy
So Beautiful by Creative Differences
Rhinestone Eyes by James Supercave
Breaking My Bones by Friday Pilots Club

Acknowledgments

When I started writing this book, I thought, "I am going to make this cute little novella with my favorite nightmare creator and Finian." Then it became a monster of a book and ended up being only a few thousand words shorter than the books in the main series. Oops. If we're being honest, I am happy with the way it turned out.

I want to thank my betas for giving me early feedback on the book and giving me ideas on where I could improve my writing—Jackie, Mary Lou, and Victoria. Thank you from the bottom of my heart.

Thank you to my husband for listening to endless amounts of ideas and copious notes. I appreciate the tireless way you listen to my rants and ravings, especially when it comes to books.

And to you, readers, for giving a chance to an independent author. Thank you for your time. I appreciate you, and I wouldn't be doing this if you weren't here.

To my family who have decided to come with me on this

journey, I really hope you skipped this one. But if you are here for some strange reason, thank you for continuing to support me.

Subscribe to the publisher's newsletter on https://www.spacefoxbooks.com for regular updates or apply to become a Cadet Fox and join the street team!

Follow the publisher on Instagram, TikTok, or Facebook @spacefoxbooks

Thank you for reading.

About the Author

Ariel Rae was raised in a small New Hampshire town, but left it behind to attend Emerson College in Boston. After graduating with a degree in Writing, Literature, and Publishing, she moved to southern California.

Working as a barista, she somehow turned her life into a cliché and met her husband while serving him coffee. They fell in love, got married, adopted a bunch of cats, moved to the rainy side of Oregon, and eventually moved back to New England.

When she's not writing, she plays video games, drinks tea, reads way too much (though, she wonders if there is such a thing as too much reading), and snowboards.

She also writes YA literature under R. A. Desilets.

Find her online @arielraeauthor

spacefoxbooks.com/ariel-rae-links

Other Work

Remember to sign up to the newsletters to be kept up to date with the latest releases: https://www.spacefoxbooks.com/newsletter

Drag Her Down duet by Ariel Rae
Spicy Dark Demon/Horror Romance

Society has rules. All it takes is one night in a deadly house party to break them all. Survive the night to claim your demon.

Haden

Being attached to an incorruptible man is my personal fires. The demon inside me desires chaos and craves ruination. When Zoe breezes into my life, she might become my chance at salvation.

Throwing a cursed house party might not be the easiest approach, but how else will I convince an innocent soul to tap into her feminine rage and kill for me?

Zoe

Being at this house party is my personal fires, but everything changes with him. Haden ignites something in me, threatening to unleash the rage I never knew I had.

When the deadly curse begins, everyone pales at the bloodshed. What does it say about me that this is the first time I feel free? Finally, I have somewhere to direct my anger and a chance at revenge against those who wronged me.

Carter Ortese is Trouble by R. A. Desilets
YA Contemporary Romance

Everyone knows Carter Ortese is trouble, so it's a shock when band geek Emma asks him out as a dare. When he says yes, she refuses to back down. But no one knows why she asks him on a second date. Or a third.

A contemporary young adult romance you don't want to miss.

Other Young Adult titles by R. A. Desilets
Break Free
Start Small
Girl Nevermore
In a Blue Moon (Blue Moon #1)
Hipstopia (The Uprising #1)
The Collapse (The Uprising #2)
My Summer Vacation by Terrance Wade

Free Short Stories with Young Adult Newsletter Sign Up
Zero
The Body in the Basement
Blame it on the Rain